PENGUIN  CLASSI

THE VOYAGE OF ARGO

ADVISORY EDITOR: BETTY RADICE

Little is known of the life of APOLLONIUS OF RHODES. Despite his surname he was a citizen of Alexandria in the time of the Ptolemies. His fame rests solely on the *Argonautica*, a poem which was from the first unfairly compared with Homer's *Odyssey*, but which Virgil was not ashamed to borrow from. Unlike his life-long rival Callimachus, Apollonius developed the classical traditions of the Homeric epic, expanding them to include a flair for romance and psychological insight which were entirely his own. He published his first version of the *Argonautica* sometime in the middle of the third century B.C. He was met with derision both from the public and the influential Callimachus, and Apollonius prepared a second and probably shorter version. This was so well received by the Rhodians that he was honoured with their franchise and for some years lived on that island. Later he returned to Alexandria to find his work now held in high esteem. At the end of his life he was Director of the famous library of Alexandria, which was the principal storehouse of all pagan literature and learning.

E. V. RIEU, editor of the Penguin Classics from 1944 to 1964, was a scholar of St Paul's School and of Balliol College, Oxford. He joined Methuen in 1923 and was Managing Director from 1933 to 1936, and then Academic and Literary Adviser. He was President of the Virgil Society in 1951 and Vice-President of the Royal Society of Literature in 1958. He was awarded an honorary D.Litt. by Leeds University in 1949 and the C.B.E. in 1953. Among his publications are *The Flattered Flying Fish and other poems*, and translations of the *Odyssey*, the *Iliad*, Virgil's *Pastoral Poems*, *The Voyage of the Argo* by Apollonius of Rhodes and *The Four Gospels* in the Penguin Classics. He died in 1972.

Apollonius of Rhodes

THE VOYAGE OF ARGO
The Argonautica

TRANSLATED WITH AN INTRODUCTION

BY

E. V. RIEU

PENGUIN BOOKS

PENGUIN BOOKS

Published by the Penguin Group
Penguin Books Ltd, 27 Wrights Lane, London W8 5TZ, England
Penguin Putnam Inc., 375 Hudson Street, New York, New York 10014, USA
Penguin Books Australia Ltd, Ringwood, Victoria, Australia
Penguin Books Canada Ltd, 10 Alcorn Avenue, Toronto, Ontario, Canada M4V 3B2
Penguin Books (NZ) Ltd, Private Bag 102902, NSMC, Auckland, New Zealand

Penguin Books Ltd, Registered Offices: Harmondsworth, Middlesex, England

This translation first published 1959
Second edition 1971
21 23 25 27 29 30 28 26 24 22

Copyright © E. V. Rieu, 1959, 1971
All rights reserved

Printed in England by Clays Ltd, St Ives plc
Set in Monotype Bembo

CONTENTS

INTRODUCTION

In the *Argonautica* of Apollonius of Rhodes, we have the only full account that has come down to us of Jason's voyage in quest of the Golden Fleece, a tale which seems to have stood, in the estimation of the Greeks, second only to the great cycle of legend which centred in the Trojan War. Apollonius' poem is thus unique. Yet it has on the whole been neglected, or even dismissed as second-rate, not so much on the Continent as by our own scholars. When I was at school our Greek masters, instead of recommending us to read it, if only in translation, found it a convenient source of passages to give us as 'unseens', knowing well that we would never have come across them. And even had they wished to take the then unusual step of suggesting an English version for our pleasure, there was none that they could honestly commend. The *Argonautica* had been admirably translated into French by H. de la Ville de Mirmont, but unlike the *Odyssey* it had never found its Butcher and Lang.*

Of the life of its author we know little for certain except that in spite of his surname he was a citizen of Alexandria and produced his poem in that city at a date not far from the middle of the third century before Christ. Ancient biographies appended to the manuscripts do more to whet than satisfy our curiosity. But I think it worth while to quote them here, for they do at least tell us how Apollonius came to be called 'the Rhodian', and if we read between the lines, throw some light on the bitter quarrel between him and a rival poet, Callimachus, which reached its climax with the publication of the first version of the *Argonautica*. Here then is a summary of what they say:

'Apollonius lived at Alexandria in the time of the Ptolemies.

* R. C. Seaton's *Loeb* translation was not published till 1912.

9

He was a pupil of the scholar Callimachus and at first adhered to his master, but later took to writing poetry. He was still quite young when he produced the *Argonautica*. It met with derision both from the public and the other poets. This so disheartened him that he retired to Rhodes, where he settled and taught rhetoric. After polishing his poem, he reissued it with such success that the Rhodians honoured him with their franchise. Later he returned to Alexandria, where his work was now esteemed so highly as to win him the directorate of the great Library and burial beside the remains of Callimachus himself.'

Recent research has thrown some doubts on the authenticity of this account. It seems that the two poets were of much the same age, not that that would make it quite impossible for Apollonius to have been a pupil of Callimachus. It appears, further, that though Apollonius was indeed Director of the Library, Callimachus never occupied the chief post. If that is true, we might have to abandon the pleasing fancy suggested by the notes that the two men, friends at first and later bitter enemies, were reunited in the grave. This would be a pity. But what I myself regret still more is the failure of these ancient annotators to dilate a little on the 'polishing' that Apollonius gave to the *Argonautica* before he issued the second version, the only one we have. For they possessed, or at least knew something of, the first. They quote a few lines from it, but tell us of no major alterations, leaving us to guess to what extent, if any, Apollonius took note of the strictures of Callimachus, that hater of the long book, and abridged his poem.*

* Paul Händel, in his *Beobachtungen zur Epischen Technik des Apollonios Rhodios* (Munich, 1954), shows that in making his *Argonautica* far shorter than the *Iliad* and *Odyssey* Apollonius was acting in conformity with the general tendencies of Hellenistic poetry. Nevertheless it is not unlikely that the second version was even shorter than the first. The abrupt approach of *Argo* to the Clashing Rocks (II, 549) and her sudden transference from Eridanus to Rhone (IV, 627) both suggest that passages have been omitted. Again, the absurdity of Here's claim to have helped her through the Wandering Rocks (IV, 786) may well be due to abridgement or maladjustment of material.

A comparison of the first with the second edition, if we had both, might explain the change of taste in literary circles which enabled Apollonius to conquer the city that had once rejected him. As it is, we are left to assume that in the interval the influence of Callimachus had waned.

This poet, abandoning the forms of the golden age of Greek poetry and setting his face against long and ambitious works, had produced, besides some excellent epigrams, a number of short poems exquisitely modelled in melodious verse, imbued with scholarship, and somewhat precious in quality.* His rival, Apollonius, had been more daring. He did not break with tradition, but built upon it. He went straight back to Homer and used the manner and matter of epic to write a tale of high romance and incredible adventure, and he gave reality to this fantastic story, not only by handling his characters with a psychological insight as novel as that of any of his contemporaries, but by the equally non-epic device of writing it from a personal point of view and standing by in every scene as a critical observer. Such was the crime for which he suffered literary banishment. It is not surprising that 'the other poets', faced by the sudden appearance of a long work recounting an oft-told tale and superficially at least written in the style of Homer, should have failed to see what a new spirit he had infused into the old bones of epic. What is surprising is that any of us, detached as we are from the controversies of their day, should have echoed their criticisms and added others.

Coming now to the *Argonautica* itself, I shall attempt to meet the opposition by putting together some of the impressions I have received during my study of the work, and I shall not hesitate to quote the adverse findings of modern scholars as I go along.

* For the nature and extent of the Alexandrian poets' break with the past, see an article on *The Future of Studies in the Field of Hellenistic Poetry* by R. Pfeiffer, in the *Journal of Hellenic Studies*, Vol. LXXV, 1955.

In his introduction to the *Loeb* edition of the poem, R. C Seaton says that Apollonius 'seems to have written the *Argonautica* out of bravado, to show that he *could* write an epic poem.' This, if it could be substantiated, would be a damning criticism. But since Apollonius is dead and cannot tell us why he wrote, all we can do is to put our questions about his motives and his personality to the poem itself. And I find no bravado there. On the contrary I see a young poet, full of zest and conscious of his talent, but at the same time diffident of his reception, constantly appealing to the Muses for help at awkward moments, and even putting the blame on them when he is going to tell a really tall story such as the portage of *Argo*; turning to his audience with naïve asides to excuse himself for a digression that may have bored them; pausing to make personal comments on his characters; apologizing to the Physician of the gods when he seems to underestimate his powers; and in the end committing his work to the world in the trembling hope that 'as the years go by, people may find it a sweeter and yet sweeter song to sing.'

In all this a sympathetic character begins to emerge, and we also see what pains the poet took to distinguish the tone of his work from that of the great master of epic.* He knew as well as we do Homer's impersonal manner and Olympian reserve.

In criticisms of the structure of the poem, it is the word 'episodic' that most often lifts its questionable head, with 'lack of unity', a comparable term, as runner-up. Objection is taken, not to the magnificent Third Book, which has received some rather grudging praise, but to the poet's handling of the outward and homeward voyages. One is tempted to ask what the critics themselves would have done with a story that committed them to take their hero half-way across the known world before he reached the scene of his

---

* Besides a change of tone, there are many factual differences. For example, in the *Iliad* dead heroes are cremated; in the *Argonautica* they are buried.

ordeal. Would it have been more artistic to give *Argo* a non-stop run from Pagasae to Colchis and back again, neglecting the numerous exploits on land and sea with which her crew were credited by tradition? Again, are not the adventures of another unwilling traveller episodically told in the *Odyssey*; and in the *Iliad* is not a battle held up so that Glaucus may give Diomedes the life-story of his grandfather Bellerophon? One can only conclude that what is found unsatisfying is the *manner* in which Apollonius enlivens the long journeys. And here I must quote some remarks made by a modern editor on one of the episodes, the quarrel between Idas and Idmon, which Apollonius inserts at an early moment in order to bring out the characters of four of the leading Argonauts, and perhaps to show that a company of heroes are as likely to get on each other's nerves as any other ship's crew. This quarrel is described by Dr M. M. Gillies as a vulgar brawl used as an unworthy means of drawing attention to the magic powers of Orpheus' music; and he goes on to say, 'It is little wonder that many who have set out conscientiously to read the *Argonautica* have at this point closed the volume in disgust for ever.' In spite of this, I hope I may induce a few less conscientious people to proceed a little further in their reading of the poem.

The first point I wish to make concerning Apollonius' treatment of the two journeys is that he himself has lent it unity, in the only way a poet could, by displaying throughout exactly those qualities which have made the Third Book famous – his deep understanding of human nature, his unerring eye for a dramatic moment, and his quiet sense of humour.* All the time we feel that we are in the hands of one man, whatever the picture he may be presenting – Lemnian Hypsipyle praying in tears for the lover she is losing; Queen

---

* Resisting the temptation to give a list of humorous remarks, I refer the reader only to the last sentence of the central paragraph on p. 187 – 'They also took the sheep.'

Arete giving Alcinous a curtain-lecture (the first in literature and perhaps the most effective); young Hylas with the full moon shining for the last time on his beauty; or, most memorable of all, the unforgiving and indomitable Fury taking quick note, with eyes askance, of the murder of Apsyrtus.

But this is not the only unity that Apollonius imposes on his work. Its very title suggests that we shall find a unifying personality in the good ship *Argo* herself. He wisely leaves the boring details of her infancy to other poets; but from the moment when, reaching maturity, she slips into the sea and has to be restrained with hawsers from travelling farther on her own account, she dominates the tale. The divine ship even has a human voice and loudly expresses her anxiety to start. Once on the way nothing can daunt her, not even the loss of her 'tail-feathers' to the Clashing Rocks. She is for ever pressing on, running as sweetly when her highborn crew are tugging at the oars as when she speeds over the sea with all her canvas spread 'like a high-flying hawk that has set its pinions to the breeze, and flapping them no more glides swiftly on with wings at rest.' Before her thrusting prow, the mighty River Phasis rolls in foam to either bank. And having conquered this oriental stream, she turns her thoughts to European rivers, sails up the Danube and down its non-existent branch, explores the Eridanus to its source, crosses the uncharted country of the Celts, samples the Rhine, extracts herself from the wilds of southern Germany, and sails triumphantly down the Rhone into the Mediterranean Sea. But before she reaches her home port and the huge circle is closed, Sea-nymphs have yet to toss her hull from hand to hand at the Wandering Rocks, her own crew to carry her across the desert dunes of Libya, and a Sea-god to lead her by the nose and thrust her forth on her last trip. And so to Pagasae where she was born. I am quite sure that the poet means us to keep an eye on this gallant ship, even when her crew are disporting themselves on land, even when he himself leaves them to sail on, and steps ashore to count the branches of the River Thermodon or tell us how the Mossynoeci misconduct themselves in public.*

This brings me to the heart of the tale, the crisis in Aea, where all the powers that the poet has lavished on the so-called episodes are put to their severest test. It has often been claimed that here we have the finest psychological study of love that the Greeks have left us. Granting that, I go a little further. I find in Apollonius' handling of Medea's passion something more than a sympathetic insight into human suffering, a marriage of romance and realism which seems to me as fresh and arresting, in spite of the intervening centuries and all the novels written since, as it must have seemed to his kindly audience in Rhodes. I spoke advisedly of novels, for I think that if we wish to appreciate what Apollonius has done, it is as a novelist that we must read him and analyse the characters he has created.

Let us take Jason first. If he is to be the hero of an epic poem, that is his place. But long before he reaches Colchis, we begin to wonder what kind of a hero we have here, a leader who not only takes a back seat when action is called for, but does not scruple to infect his men with his own innate despondency. The term that Apollonius most often applies to him is *amechanos*, 'without resource' – in other words, Jason had no self-starter. Why this very human failing, which is the last defect we find in Achilles, Odysseus, Diomedes, and all the other heroes of Greek epic? Was it impossible to make Jason outshine his own distinguished company, the pick of all Achaea? It is true that he had on board several heroes whom we might describe as specialists.

* My friend, the late Dr M. Cary, in his *History of the Greek World, 323–146 B.C.* (Methuen, 1951), wrote, 'The good ship *Argo* meant little to Apollonius.' Why then did the poet content himself with bringing *Argo* back to Pagasae? There is surely significance in the fact that he tells us nothing further of the Golden Fleece or of Jason and Medea's married life.

When Amycus challenged the Argonauts to put up a champion able to box him and ready to be killed, why should Jason sacrifice himself, seeing that Polydeuces, the father of the boxing art, was standing at his side? Or when it came to chasing Harpies through the boundless air, how could he, with no wings on his feet, compete with Zetes and Calaïs, the Flying Children of the North Wind? Again, with a helmsman like Tiphys, who had come to him with credentials from Athene, why should he take it on himself to manipulate the steering-oar of *Argo*? But the strange thing is that even after Tiphys' death, Jason neither takes the vacant place, nor in his despair makes any move to find him a successor. In other words, he does not *lead*; and it is only with Medea's magic aid that he attains heroic stature, conquers the mighty bulls and reaps the deadly harvest of the earthborn men.

The truth, as I see it, is that Apollonius sets out to portray, not an epic hero, but an ordinary man; and so at every crisis he puts himself in Jason's place, asking, for instance, what *he* would have felt when he found that it was part of his assignment to drive a ship between the Clashing Rocks. But in spite of all misgivings Jason does go on; and we begin to see that he possesses after all some of the qualities that make a leader – brains, abundant charm, and above all a most persuasive tongue. He is a man who gets things done for him. Even the shipwrecked and reluctant Argus rallies to his side. And if his eloquence is momentarily stanched by Aeetes, who but a demigod could have quelled that angry and black-hearted king? In any case, the real test has yet to come. He has to meet and win Medea. And in their very first encounter, Apollonius subtly employs the qualities he has given Jason to bring him both victory and defeat. To have cited once the exploits of the beautiful young Ariadne as a stimulus for Medea was a happy thought; but to bring them up again when they had served their purpose was the error of a man whose eloquence outruns his tact. Medea reacts with passion, and for Jason the issue is decided. The golden fleece is his; but so is Medea. And Medea proved no easy character to handle, either for Jason or Apollonius.

How did the poet deal with the fascinating witch? For whatever else he made of her, she had to be a witch. The story demanded it, and he does not shrink from the challenge. We may even suspect him of an overstatement when he tells us that she was able, with a little supernatural help, 'to arrest a star and check the movement of the sacred moon'. But Medea also had to be a beautiful young woman capable of winning Jason's heart, not by the witchcraft she had learnt from Hecate, but by her own unconscious witchery.* To have brought this dual personality to life was Apollonius' greatest achievement. But he was by nature well equipped: romance was in his blood. His very similes betray him. The man who shows us Jason rejoicing in the fiery glow of the golden fleece 'glad as a girl who catches on her silken gown the lovely light of the full moon as it looks into her attic room' – this was the man to fall in love with his own creation and make Medea live. But when I suggest that he fell in love with her I am far from saying that he lost his head. On the contrary, he maintains a perfect balance between realism and his duty to the tale. From the moment when Eros has shot his fatal arrow at Medea, Olympian causation is rightly set aside, and the poet himself creeps into the heart of the unhappy girl and feels with her the overwhelming impact of a first and fatal love. Yet all the while, to check himself and us, reminders that she is a sorceress are quietly slipped in. And in case these fail to prepare us for what is to follow, her vehemence with Jason at the end of their first talk comes as an early warning that this golden-haired maiden has it in her to become a murderess. In due course we witness the appalling deed. Yet even after this, if I read the poet's mind

* It seems that ancient and medieval witches alike were bereft of their formidable powers when they themselves stood most in need of them.

aright, all sympathy is not to be withdrawn. Circe, the aunt both of Medea and the murdered man, feels some pity for her weeping niece when she comes to her for absolution. And Apollonius enters into the mind of Zeus himself to tell us how the god of suppliants abhors the killing of a man and yet befriends the killer. Such is the Medea of Apollonius. He cannot make her happy; but he does contrive to lift her from the dusty pages of mythology and make her a living woman. And he gives her so much of his heart that he makes us love her too.

Equal care, if not quite the same affection, is devoted to the minor characters of the tale – Mopsus, the prophet who can see a joke against himself; Orpheus, the divine musician who finds in jazz a non-Homeric way of getting past the Sirens; Idas, the irritable braggart who does not scruple, in his cups, to underestimate the power of Zeus. Even people who play no part in the action of the tale, receive the tribute of a sigh or smile – Cleite, that peerless but unhappy bride who was unable to face life alone, with her husband in the grave; Dipsacus, the unassuming hero who preferred a pastoral to a public life; and virginal Sinope, whose intellectual agility saved her even from the arms of Zeus. Of course in cases such as these consistency is not required; but if we watch the more important figures, such as Peleus and Telamon, we see how carefully the poet keeps them in character throughout the book. And for these two he does more. He gives them each the qualities we might expect in the fathers of men who fought and died before the walls of Troy. Peleus has all the daring and initiative of his great son Achilles – indeed at times he leads the expedition; while Telamon, for all his prowess, twice comes near to wrecking it through that ungovernable temper that brought his son Aias to a lament-able end. It is only in his treatment of Heracles that Apollonius seems to be a little inconsistent, though perhaps no more so than the average Greek. To us, at all events, it is surprising to find that this magnanimous hero whose bulk is dwelt on with affectionate humour, is credited, as the tale proceeds, with a series of ruthless murders, including that of his own children, and at his final appearance is described by his inno-cent victims, the Hesperides, as an ill-conditioned bully with the table manners of a beast. We can only conclude that the Greeks were so much amused by his enormous size and fascinated by his strength that they condoned its uninhibited misuse – they were quarrelsome themselves. But in the end common sense stands baffled before this enigmatic figure. And after all, Apollonius had behind him the authority of Homer, who roundly condemns the brutal cruelty of Heracles in killing Iphiclus, his host, and gives us a horrifying vision of his wraith in Hades, yet is careful to point out that 'he himself banquets at ease with the immortal gods and has for consort Hebe of the slim ankles, the Daughter of Almighty Zeus and golden-sandalled Here.'

The great Olympians are treated by Apollonius with as much levity as Homer allowed himself; indeed, in the visit which Here and Athene pay to Aphrodite, I detect a little more. There is no break with tradition. At the same time there is no question of direct imitation. Apollonius gives us his own picture of the three goddesses, and in Here's case it is a masterly study of a self-important, pompous, and vindictive woman, whose interest in Jason is inspired far more by her desire to bring King Pelias to book than by the slight service that Jason had rendered her one day when she was mas-querading in the haunts of men. Her brusque response to the gentle persiflage of Aphrodite; her patronizing attitude to that afflicted mother of a problem child; her parting shot, 'do not argue with your child when he annoys you' – all this calls to my mind visions of Victorian matrons visiting the poor. And she is much the same when asking Thetis for a favour. A long list of benefits conferred is followed up by unsolicited advice on the way to mend a broken marriage.

The portrait is so life-like as to leave one wondering what Alexandrian lady Apollonius had in mind.*

Those who have followed Odysseus under the guidance of the incomparable Athene may ask why Jason's fortunes are committed to a far less prepossessing deity. Why should the goddess who built *Argo* and saw her through the Clashing Rocks yield the command to Here throughout the rest of the adventure? The obvious reason is that Apollonius was bound by a convention as old as Homer which made Here the patroness of Jason. But there is also a subtler and more amusing reason which he discloses through the mouth of Athene herself. How could a goddess who had sprung in full armour from her Father's head and had never 'felt the arrows of the Boy' take the leading part in a conspiracy to make a young girl fall in love with a complete stranger and run away with him from a comfortable home? Athene *had* to take the second place. Yet even so, Apollonius makes her honourable amends. When the two goddesses in a fever of anxiety are watching Argo's passage through the Wandering Rocks, it is Here, not Athene, who breaks down and throws her arms around the other.

There is no reason to suppose that Apollonius, because he treated the Olympian family in a light-hearted manner, was an irreligious man. On the contrary, when he is not dwelling with amusement on the infidelities of Zeus, he writes of the King of gods and men in a way that bespeaks in him not only a genuine faith but a deep insight into the problems of religion. I have already referred to his mention of Zeus as the god of forgiveness. Elsewhere he puts into the mouth of the blind seer, Phineus, who was punished by Zeus for disclosing the god's intentions in full, a remark that carries in it a warning for all those who look for mathematical precision in the fulfilment of Biblical, or any other prophecies.

* Readers of the *Aeneid* have sometimes been astonished by the virulence of Virgil's Juno. There is little doubt that Apollonius' Here was her prototype.

'Zeus himself,' says the seer, 'intends a prophet's revelations to be incomplete, so that humanity may miss some part of Heaven's design.' Such passages as these are by no means inconsistent with, but rather reinforce, the strong impression we receive from others that Apollonius, like many of his time, had sought in the Mysteries something more satisfying than the ritual of the state religion. His awe-struck silences are as eloquent as words.

It may at first seem strange that so philosophical a poet should throw no light on the meaning of the chief myths embedded in the tale, but write in factual terms of Phrixus flying on his Golden Ram, Jason's mysterious quest, the sowing of the serpent's teeth, and the slaughter of the earthborn men, an exercise which King Aeetes apparently indulges in for fun. Later writers offered 'rational' explanations, most of them absurd;* and I think we should be grateful to Apollonius for having approached the legend in the spirit of a novelist and added no such speculations.

There remain the animals; they clamour for attention. I am not thinking so much of the lions and small fry of the similes, attractive though they are, as of the Great Snakes. Some people dislike snakes. I do not think that Apollonius did so. Even the minor snake that caused the death of Mopsus is treated by him with characteristic fairness – it would not bite except in self-defence. And when Heracles resorts to poisoned weapons to destroy the Guardian of the Golden Apples, it is quite clear where the poet's sympathy lies. But of the three large serpents who figure in the tale, it is only the Warden of the Fleece of whom we get a full-

* Strabo (I, 2, 39; and XI, 2, 19) mentions the gold of the Caucasus as a reasonable motive for Jason's expedition, pointing out that the natives collected gold dust from the rivers on fleecy skins. Diodorus Siculus (IV, 47) accounts for Phrixus and his ram in an even more amusing way – he sailed in a ship with a ram's head on the prow, and his sister Helle, a very bad sailor, tumbled overboard. Tacitus (*Ann.* VI, 34) seems to agree with him as far as the ram's head is concerned.

length portrait. And the noble beast deserves it. It is true
that in the discharge of his duties he emits a hiss that travels
to the confines of the Colchian land and frightens babies
sleeping in their mothers' arms, but none the less, when he
succumbs to the magic of Medea and lets his head sink to
the ground, we are left with a feeling of relief – life is not
over for him though he has lost his job.* Valerius Flaccus, a
Roman poet of Domitian's time, goes even further, in his
unfinished *Argonautica*, to evoke our sympathy for this
delightful snake. He is Medea's pet; every night she brings
him supper (he is very fond of honey); and when the magic
deed is done and his unsleeping eyes are closed, she throws
her arms around him and laments her treachery. Following
the fascinating creature down the centuries, we meet him
once again in Caxton, who portrays him thus in his *History
of Jason*: 'He was as grete as an hors and was thretty foot
long, the whiche incontinent assone as he was out of the
temple he began to ryse his neck, sette up his eeris, stracche
him self, opende his throte and cast out brennyng flawme
and smoke by a mervaillous voyding which departed out of
his stomach.' And there I leave him, but with a caution. I
accuse Caxton of a taxonomic error: he has made a dragon †
of a snake. Dragons, as every schoolboy knows, have legs;
the Keeper of the Golden Fleece had none. He was a true
serpent.‡

But I must not linger too long with the snakes, nor dwell
on the picture Apollonius gives us of the slaughter of the

* The strength of the hiss is confirmed in the *Orphic Argonautica*, a shorter
and much later version than that of Apollonius, in which Orpheus relates the
adventure in the first person, and spoils this scene by stepping in before Medea
and himself putting the snake to sleep.

† Who presently *runs* into the temple. Perhaps we ought to blame the
Frenchman, Raoul Le Fevre, from whom Caxton was translating.

‡ In his *Life and Death of Jason*, William Morris, who ought to have known
better, also makes the creature run, and still worse, asks us to believe that

'Hideous he was, where all things else were fair;
Dull-skinned, foul-spotted, with lank rusty hair.'

earthborn men, which is equally instructive. In both cases he has set before us fabulous monsters whom we not only *see*, but view with sympathy. Living in an age when there was no complete divorce between poetry and science, he could look with the eyes both of a poet and a scientist at phenomena he had himself created.

He was certainly abreast of all the scientific movements of his day, and probably ahead of some of them, as for instance in the field of what we now call abnormal psychology. Consider the passage in Book IV (1650 ff.) where Medea undertakes to dispose of the brazen giant Talos. She begins with prayers and incantations. This was normal procedure; she had used it on the Snake, who 'was enchanted by her song'. But Talos is clearly a far tougher proposition. So next she resorts to mesmerism – the Greeks knew much about the powers of the human eye. And finally 'in an ecstasy of rage she plies him with images of death'. Here, if I have not mistranslated (and I do not think I have, though 'annihilating images' would be more literal), we have the first clear description of direct action on the subconscious mind – with this amazing sequel. Talos does not at once fall dead. Medea's suggestion takes time to work. But in the end it robs him of his normal caution, and he wounds himself at the one point where his bronze frame is vulnerable. And Apollonius, as though he did not understand the whole affair, modestly appeals to Father Zeus and asks him whether a man can actually be killed by telepathic means.

There is another most impressive passage. The Argonauts, on reaching a desert island, are granted a vision of Apollo. The whole scene and the god himself are beautifully described. But I saw nothing more in it than that till I looked again and noted how Apollonius had emphasized the fact that the men were exhausted when they landed – 'all through the day and through the night they had laboured at the indefatigable oar.' Our own men in the retreat from Mons had laboured even harder. And each party had its own appropriate vision: Angels for the British troops; Apollo for the Greeks.

The poet constantly shows a peculiar interest in time, a keen awareness of the aeons stretching back behind him. Hence his addiction to archaeology and myth, which is evinced throughout the poem.* If, on occasion, he is a little wild, as when he speaks of the Arcadians as having lived 'before the moon itself was there,' in other places he seems to anticipate notions of geological time which we ourselves did not conceive till the nineteenth century. He writes, for example, of 'a smooth ledge of rock which in the past had been scoured by winter seas but now stood high and dry'; and after describing the nondescript monsters whom Circe's sorcery produced, he remarks that in the end, 'Time, combining this with that, brought the animal creation into order.' I may add that to the best of my knowledge he is the first writer to mention an iron ship. It would be too fanciful to cite this as a forecast in the field of applied science. But I cannot help recording my own pleasure when, in the course of translation, I encountered the appalling fog which the Argonauts ran into on their homeward voyage, and reading on, in great anxiety, was relieved to find that Phoebus had sped down from heaven, taken his stand on a convenient rock, and pierced the circumambient gloom with the beams of his golden bow. This took me straight to my reference books, where I found that the dates fitted – Apollonius might well have been inspired by the great Pharos of Alexandria, the most famous lighthouse of the ancient world.

* Some of his excursions into the by-ways of mythology explain themselves. Others do not: he wrote for an audience who could fill in the gaps. In such cases reference may be made to H. J. Rose, *Handbook of Greek Mythology* (Methuen, 1955), or R. R. Graves, *The Greek Myths* (Penguin Books, 1955). But the only story which it is necessary to know when reading the *Argonautica* (since it crops up throughout the book) is that of Phrixus and his Golden Ram. I have given an account of this under *Phrixus* in the Glossary.

If so, no poet has ever put the science of mechanics to more delightful use. It is also interesting to note that though the bronze giant Talos had appeared in myth before Apollonius wrote, the Colossus of Rhodes, a gigantic statue of the Sun-god sheathed in bronze, was still standing when he visited the island.

The stars and other heavenly bodies fascinated Apollonius, who frequently employs his knowledge of their habits for romantic purposes. He is particularly fond of those that rise above the roof-tops (he was a city-dweller) to shine into the bedrooms of maidens in distress, and on one occasion he extorts from the Lady Moon herself the admission that she is not as passionless as she appears. Modern astronomers, with other moons to watch, may question the accuracy of his observations. But at one point at least I feel moved to defend him against previous translators. He is not guilty of causing the Great Bear to *set* in the latitude of Colchis.* Even if he had been uncertain, he had only to look up his Homer to find that 'the Great Bear never bathes in Ocean Stream'; or, failing that, to walk over to the Library and have his doubts resolved by his contemporary, the great Eratosthenes, who was the first man to measure the circumference of the earth.

His geography is quite another matter. Even the Romans scoffed at it. But we must remember that he did not set out to write a text-book, but a fresh version of an ancient myth. And if, in examining his conduct of *Argo*, we bear in mind that happy blend of actuality and fiction by which he brought to life the legendary figure of Medea, I think we shall find

* I refer to III, 1196, where the word used of the Great Bear's movement does not mean 'set' but 'sloped down' or 'declined'. It is similarly used of the sun, *before* he sets, in I, 452. In the latitude of Colchis (44° N) the Bear never sank below the horizon in Apollonius' time. The same is true if we regard him as having written from the latitude of Alexandria (roughly 31° N). The fact that the Bear sets there at the present day (though not in Colchis) is due to the precession of the equinoxes. In Homer's time a man would have had to travel a long way south of the Nile delta to lose sight of the Bear.

that as a poet he knew very well what he was doing, and perhaps that he knew more than he reveals.

Little fault, if any, can be found with his description of the outward voyage.* He was taking *Argo* along sea-ways known to his contemporaries, and he makes it obvious when he lapses into myth. For instance, he is careful to tell us that the Clashing Rocks were induced to abandon their objectionable habits, once *Argo* had passed safely through them. What is not so obvious is why, in bringing her down the west coast of Italy, he begins by being quite precise and correctly placing Elba, but becomes completely vague when he reaches southern Italy, Sicily, and the Ionian Islands, which had been colonized by Greeks centuries before his time. I think it was because he was entering Homer's seas. Homer's nebulous geography was sacrosanct, and Apollonius does little to clear it up, even though he places Circe's home somewhere on the coast of Italy and ventures to identify Corcyra (under a different name) with the Phaeacia of the *Odyssey*. In order to maintain the legendary atmosphere of the tale, he has concealed his own knowledge.

In taking *Argo* across central Europe through regions unfamiliar to the Greeks, it was even more the poet's duty, as well as his pleasure, to give his readers fairy-tale geography. Yet even here there are signs that, while apparently endorsing the popular belief that the great rivers had managed to unite their waters for the convenience of travellers, he was not so ignorant as he pretends. He evidently knew what Switzerland is like, and his mention of the name 'Hercynian', often used by Roman historians when writing about Germany, supports me in suggesting this. Yet he certainly gives *Argo* an outrageous route – from the Po (if that is his Eridanus) to the Rhone; from the Rhone into the storm-swept lakes of Switzerland; from there, apparently into the Rhine; and from the

* R. C. Seaton, in the *Loeb* volume, goes so far as to pay it a back-handed compliment. He calls it a 'metrical guide-book'.

Rhine once more into the Rhone. Now I know that one tributary of the Po rises not so very far from the sources of the Rhine and Rhone, which are close together. But having seen these rivers in their newborn state and observed the mountains that lie in between them, I am convinced that Apollonius was wise at this point not to fall back on portages, but to waft *Argo* from river to river by a few strokes of his powerful pen. A single portage, the one in Libya, was quite enough. And even in describing that, he asks us to believe the Muses' tale, not him.*

In this study of the poet's mind, one of my aims has been to establish his originality without, I hope, suggesting that he wrote the *Argonautica* out of his own head and invented all its incidental decorations. To deal with these first, it is impossible for us to trace all his sources, but anyone who has read the *Anabasis* will realize what he owes to Xenophon, especially in his amusing description of the Mossynoeci. Again, the account which Argus gives in Book IV of the amazing exploits of a certain Egyptian king is clearly based on Herodotus.† But where we are able to catch Apollonius out in

---

* We know that the Vikings crossed Russia from north to south, probably by the Volga or the Don, dragging their longboats from one river to another; also that neolithic immigrants from the East came up the Danube valley into that of the Rhine. With these facts in mind we can work out a *possible* itinerary for *Argo*: up the Danube to Donaueschingen; a six-mile portage to the Wutach, which flows into the Rhine; up the Aar to the Lakes of Bienne and Neuchatel; thence by portage to the Lake of Geneva, and so into the Rhone. The fact that Apollonius causes *Argo* to take a wrong turning out of the Celtic lakes and sail down the Rhine, but turn round and reach the Rhone, certainly suggests that he knew something of this portion of the route. But if so, he does not exploit his knowledge in our version of the *Argonautica*, though he may have done so in the first. As for the earlier portion, he causes *Argo* to leave the Danube long before it approaches the Rhine, and sail down into the Adriatic, thus committing himself to the task of getting *Argo* from the Po into the Rhone, which is impossible.

† *Histories*, II. Herodotus calls this king Sesostris; Apollonius does not name him. But we have good reasons for identifying him with Ramses II, and also for regarding him as a far less energetic and successful conqueror than both Herodotus and Apollonius depict.

borrowing, we can at least say that he makes the borrowed stuff his own. Sometimes we can give him even greater credit. In Book II he tells us that Persephone sent up to the Argonauts 'the mourning ghost of Sthenelus, who craved to see some men of his own kind, if only for a moment.' Here, one of the scholiasts tells us that Apollonius had derived his information concerning the death and burial of Sthenelus from a writer called Promathidas, but adds that the poet himself had invented 'everything about the ghost'. For me, these few words, scribbled in the margin of a manuscript by some obscure grammarian, throw more light on the methods and imaginative powers of Apollonius than any learned commentary that I have read. They also suggest that we must be careful not to underestimate the originality of the poet in handling his main theme.

I spoke of this earlier as an oft-told tale, and must now expand that phrase. The Argonautic legend had passed through many hands before it reached Apollonius. Homer himself (*Odyssey* XII, 69–72) speaks of 'the celebrated *Argo*', but though the epithet suggests that he knew all about her and may himself have sung her praises in an earlier work, he tells us nothing here except that with Here's help Jason brought her through the Wandering Rocks when 'homeward bound from Aeetes' coast'. Such is *Argo*'s first and unobtrusive appearance in the written word. Hesiod adds a little, telling us that Jason, after accomplishing the many tasks set him by King Pelias (not King Aeetes), returned to Iolcus on his swift ship with 'the bright-eyed damsel whom he made his loving wife'. The following centuries add further details; Pindar in his Fourth Pythian Ode gives a brief account of Jason's expedition; Aeschylus, Sophocles, and Euripides each select and dramatize some incident or other; and so the story grows. But the more it grows, up to the time of Apollonius and after, the more it varies. Pindar says that the Argonauts came home by way of Ocean Stream, the Red Sea, and the

Isle of Lemnos, and he gives Zetes and Calaïs wings on their backs, while Apollonius very firmly puts them on their ankles. Pherecydes states that Orpheus did not sail in *Argo*; that Heracles, on account of his weight, was put on shore at the first stop; and that Jason killed the Snake. Diodorus Siculus rashly permits the beautiful Atalanta to join the expedition: Jason, in Apollonius' account, is not so silly. Again, although we learn from Apollonius that Theseus was unhappily detained in Hades when the rest were rallying to Jason's aid, Statius, writing later, brushes this alibi aside and makes an Argonaut of Theseus. Still later, the author of the *Orphic Argonautica*, omitting Theseus from the crew, brings the heroes home by an Atlantic route, sighting Ireland on the way. We can conclude that the tale was never standardized. In fact, like the Arthurian legend, it was anybody's playground. Agreement was never reached even on the list of those who sailed in *Argo*, and one could bring her home from Colchis either by the way she went or by one or other of at least three longer routes, with variations and incidental episodes introduced at will.*

It follows from all this that in estimating Apollonius' contribution to the tale we are faced by the same sort of questions that arise when we discover that Shakespeare was not the first man to write a play about the Prince of Denmark. It is of less importance to find out, where we can, the poet's source for this or that than to ask ourselves whether he has so handled and embellished the diverse material at his disposal as to leave the imprint of his own genius on every portion of the work. In the case of *Hamlet*, others have found the answer to this question: in that of the *Argonautica*, I have already done my best to answer it myself.

If the ancients had indeed regarded borrowing as a literary

---

* Miss J. R. Bacon, in her valuable work, *The Voyage of the Argonauts* (Methuen, 1925), discusses all these routes and their possible connexion with the ancient 'amber' routes from the Baltic Sea.

crime, which they did not, we might well claim that Apollonius was more sinned against than sinning. Quite apart from Valerius Flaccus who, in his charming poem, often follows Apollonius step by step, Virgil's less considerable, but not less genuine indebtedness to the *Argonautica* is often pointed out by scholars. And rightly so. Doubts of their impartiality arise in me only when I read judgements such as these, which I quote from the introduction to the *Loeb* edition of Apollonius – 'Some of his finest passages have been appropriated and improved by Virgil by the divine right of superior genius'; and later, 'The Medea of Apollonius is the direct precursor of the Dido of Virgil, and it is the pathos and passion of the fourth book of the *Aeneid* that keep alive many a passage of Apollonius.' This is going much too far. In appreciating Virgil's success need we imply that Apollonius failed in a similar attempt? He did nothing of the kind – he saw in his Medea neither an epic nor a tragic heroine. And incidentally, is there not something lacking in this suggestion that Medea was the literary ancestress of Dido? Virgil may well have been thinking of Medea's passion for Jason when he wrote the Fourth Book, but when he caused Aeneas to leave Dido at the behest of Heaven, his thoughts must surely have turned to that equally pathetic and far more patient lady, Hypsipyle of Lemnos, deserted by Jason on a comparable excuse.

So far, this essay has been devoted to a just appraisal of Apollonius' merits and to rebutting his detractors. Now, I must in all honesty add a few criticisms of my own. Unlike Homer, whose epic Greek he reproduces, though with many Alexandrian innovations, he is not a uniformly admirable stylist. He often sets before us with startling clarity exactly what he sees – for instance, the monstrous eagle of Prometheus flying over *Argo* with the long quill-feathers of each wing rising and falling 'like a bank of polished oars'. At other times either his diction or his syntax fails him. For example, his elaborate attempt (Book II, 541 ff.) to convey to us by a simile the speed of Athene's descent from the sky, has baffled all translators, including myself. And in case it is argued that on such occasions all that is required of us is literal translation, I quote the following passage from the *Loeb* version (IV, 435 ff.): 'And when she had worked upon the heralds to induce her brother to come, as soon as she reached the temple of the goddess, according to the agreement, and the darkness of night surrounded them, that so she might devise with him a cunning plan for her to take the mighty fleece of gold and return to the home of Aeetes, for, she said . . .' and all our early hopes of meeting a main verb are dashed.

Apollonius is also accused of exaggeration. It is pointed out that whereas Homer (*Iliad* v, 303), to give us an idea of a really large lump of rock, says that 'even to lift it was a feat beyond the strength of any two men bred today', Apollonius (III, 1367) doubles the number of the strong men whose powers would have proved inadequate. The size of rock which Amphion and Zethus found convenient when laying the foundations of Thebes is also indicated in hyperbolic terms (II, 735). But here the poet no doubt had authority for his statements, possibly a vase-painting.* And I for one am prepared to condone his wildest departures from exactitude – he makes them with such zest and obvious enjoyment. He has, however, one mannerism which cannot be dismissed so lightly, and that is redundancy. When he has told us (III, 1240 ff.) that Aeetes, Lord of the Colchians, driving off to see Jason tussle with the bulls, looked like Poseidon setting out in his chariot to attend the Isthmian Games, we feel that the picture is complete and gains nothing by the addition of seven alternative destinations that the god might have had in mind.

* One is often inclined to conjecture such sources for scenes in the *Argonautica*. The picture of Eros and Ganymede playing with knucklebones (III, 117 ff.) may well have been suggested to Apollonius by a group which the elder Pliny describes as standing in the palace of Titus and attributes to the famous sculptor Polycleitus (*N.H.*, XXXIV, 55).

But it seems that the Alexandrians liked this sort of thing. What I deplore is its appearance in that delightful passage where 'Medea's heart fluttered within her, restless as a patch of sunlight dancing up and down on a wall as the swirling water poured into (a cauldron or) a pail reflects it,' (III, 755). Virgil, in adopting this simile (*Aeneid* VIII, 22), wisely spares us a choice of vessels for the agitated water; and I have ventured to follow his example.

The ancient critic Longinus, in a famous essay, denies Homer's sublimity to Apollonius, but says he is a faultless poet. This is an unexpected epithet, and I wonder whether the excellent Longinus, who was a Greek, would have used it if he had had to translate the *Argonautica*. I myself have often found it undesirable, if not impossible, to keep as close to the idiom of the text as I did in the case of Homer. At the same time I have striven throughout to convey to English readers the exact meaning and spirit of Apollonius. If I have failed at all in this attempt, I hope to be forgiven from the Elysian Fields by a great story-teller and most lovable, if not quite flawless, poet.

E. V. R.

Highgate, 1958

ACKNOWLEDGEMENTS

I HAVE to thank my friend, Mr W. F. Jackson Knight, of Exeter University, for the scholarly help and kind encouragement he has given me at various stages of my task; Sir Gavin de Beer for showing me how *Argo* might have found her way from the Rhine into the Rhone; and Dr T. C. S. Morrison-Scott for a precise account of the changing habits of the Great Bear.

The map of the voyage of the Argonauts and the bibliography have been supplied by Juliet S. M. Maguinness.

THE VOYAGE OF ARGO

BOOK ONE

PREPARATION AND DEPARTURE

Moved by the god of song, I set out to commemorate the heroes of old who sailed the good ship Argo *up the Straits into the Black Sea and between the Cyanean Rocks in quest of the Golden Fleece.*

IT was King Pelias who sent them out. He had heard an oracle which warned him of a dreadful fate – death through the machinations of the man whom he should see coming from the town with one foot bare. The prophecy was soon confirmed. Jason, fording the Anaurus in a winter spate, lost one of his sandals, which stuck in the bed of the flooded river, but saved the other from the mud and shortly after appeared before the king. He had come for a banquet that Pelias was giving in honour of his father Poseidon and all the other gods, except Pelasgian Here to whom he paid no homage. And no sooner did the king see him than he thought of the oracle and decided to send him on a perilous adventure overseas. He hoped that things might so fall out, either at sea or in out-landish parts, that Jason would never see his home again.

The ship was built by Argus, under Athene's eye. But as poets before me have told that tale, I will content myself by recounting the names and lineage of her noble crew, their long sea voyages, and all they achieved in their wanderings. Muses, inspire my lay.

The name which I put first is that of Orpheus, borne, so the story goes, by Calliope herself to her Thracian lover Oeagrus near the heights of Pimplea. They say that with the music of his voice he enchanted stubborn mountain rocks and rushing streams. And testifying still to the magic of his song, there are wild oaks growing at Zone on the coast of Thrace, which he lured down from Pieria with his lyre, rank upon rank of them, like soldiers on the march. Such was Orpheus, lord of Bistonian Pieria, when Jason son of Aeson, acting on a word from Cheiron, enrolled him as a partner in his venture.

Asterion was quick to join them. Born to Cometes beside the eddying waters of Apidanus, he lived at Peiresiae near Mount Phylleium, where great Apidanus and noble Enipeus meet each other and mingle their far-travelled streams.

Next to them came Polyphemus son of Eilatus from his home in Larissa. In his younger days he had fought in the ranks of the mighty Lapithae when they were at war with the Centaurs. But by now his limbs were heavy with age, though he had not lost the fighting spirit of his youth.

Iphiclus next. He was not left behind in Phylace; for he was Jason's uncle. His sister Alcimede, daughter of Phylacus, was Aeson's wife. The bonds of kinship compelled him to enlist.

Then came Admetus, King of Pherae, rich in sheep. He was not going to linger in his town below Chalcodon's peak.

Erytus and Echion, sons of Hermes and endowed with all his guile, were quick to leave Alope and their many corn-fields. Their kinsman Aethalides came also, adding a third to the pair as they set out. He was borne near the waters of Amphrysus by a daughter of Myrmidon, Eupolemeia of Phthia; but the other two were sons of Antianeira daughter of Menetes.

From wealthy Gyrton came Coronus, Caeneus' son, a man of valour, but no better than his father. For Caeneus, so the bards relate, was destroyed by the Centaurs yet remained alive. Unaided by his noble friends he had routed the enemy, and even when they rallied against him they could not bend his back or kill him. Unbroken and unbowed he sank below the earth, overwhelmed by the massive pines with which they beat him down.

Then came Titaresian Mopsus, whom Leto's son, Apollo,

had trained to excel all others in the art of augury from birds. Also Eurydamas son of Ctimenus, who lived in Dolopian Ctimene near the lake of Xynia.

Menoetius too was sent from Opus by his father, Actor, to join the chieftains in their voyage.

Eurytion and the valiant Eribotes followed, one the son of Teleon, and one of Irus son of Actor. Illustrious Eribotes was Teleon's son; Eurytion was the son of Irus. And with them was a third, Oïleus, the bravest of the brave and a great man for dashing after the enemy when their ranks were giving way.

From Euboea, Canthus came. Canethus son of Abas sent him – not that he hesitated to enlist. Yet there was to be no home-coming for him, no return to Cerinthus. Fate had decided that he and the great seer Mopsus should wander to the ends of Libya to be destroyed. Which shows that Death can overtake us, however far we go: these two were buried in Libya, which is as far from Colchis as the sun travels in a day.

The next to join were Clytius and Iphitus, Wardens of Oechalia and sons of the cruel Eurytus, to whom the Archer-King Apollo gave his bow, though the gift did him little good when he challenged the great giver to a match.

Next came Telamon and Peleus. sons of Aeacus; but not together and not from the same place. In a mad moment they had killed their brother Phocus, and they had to put a long way between Aegina and themselves. Telamon settled in the island of Salamis, but Peleus parted from him and made himself a home in Phthia.

After them, from Attica, came battle-loving Butes son of the excellent Teleon, and Phalerus of the good ashen spear, whom his father Alcon had allowed to go. Alcon had no other sons to look after him when he was old, yet he despatched that only son of his declining years to make his mark among these men of valour. Meanwhile Theseus, finest of the Attic

37

line, who had gone with Peirithous into the underworld, was kept a prisoner in unseen bonds below the earth at Taenarum. Had this pair been with them, the Argonauts would indeed have had a lighter task.

Next, from the Thespian town of Siphae, came Tiphys son of Hagnias, an expert mariner, who could sense the coming of a swell across the open sea, and learn from sun and star when storms were brewing or a ship might sail. Athene herself, the Lady of Trito, had urged him to join the band of chieftains, who had hoped for this accession to their strength and welcomed his arrival. It was a fitting thing that he should be sent them by the very goddess who had built their ship, which she did with Argus son of Arestor working under her direction. No wonder that *Argo* proved the finest of all ships that ever braved the sea with oars.

After them came Phlias, from Araethyrea, where he lived in affluence through the good will of his father Dionysus in his home by the springs of Asopus.

From Argos came Talaus and Areius sons of Bias, and also the powerful Leodocus, all of whom Pero daughter of Neleus bore. It was on her account that the Aeolid Melampus suffered great hardships in the farmstead of Iphiclus.

And nobody can say that the mighty and stout-hearted Heracles neglected Jason's call. A rumour of the chieftains' gathering came to his ears when he was on a journey and had just arrived from Arcadia in Lyrceian Argos. It was that time he carried on his back, alive, the boar which fed in the thickets of Lampeia near the great Erymanthian swamp. And no sooner did he hear the news than he dropped the boar, tied up as it was, from his broad shoulders at the entrance to the market at Mycenae, and promptly set out—he did not even ask permission of Eurystheus. Hylas, his noble squire, in the first bloom of youth, went with him to carry his arrows and serve as keeper of the bow.

After him came Nauplius, whose lineage we can trace to

King Danaus himself. For his father was Clytoneus son of Naubolus; Naubolus was the son of Lernus; and we know that Lernus was the son of Proetus, himself the son of an earlier Nauplius, who proved to be the finest sailor of his time, offspring as he was of one of Danaus' daughters, the lady Amymone, and her lover the Sea-god.

Of all that lived in Argos, Idmon was the last to come, last because his own bird-lore had told him he would die. And yet he came: he was afraid for his good name at home. This Idmon was not really Abas' son, but one whom Apollo had fathered to take his place among the illustrious Aeolids. The god himself had taught him the prophetic art, how birds should be observed, and how to find omens in burnt-offerings.

And now, from Sparta, Aetolian Lede sent the mighty Polydeuces and Castor, that famous master of the racing horse. She had borne these two in Tyndareus' palace at a single birth. She loved them dearly, but she did not try to keep them back: hers was a spirit worthy of the love of Zeus.

From Arene came the sons of Aphareus, Lynceus and the insolent Idas. Both had the courage that great strength inspires. And in addition Lynceus enjoyed the keenest eye-sight in the world, if we may credit the report that it came easy to the man even to see things underground.

Periclymenus son of Neleus set forth also. He was the eldest of the sons King Neleus had in Pylos, and Poseidon had endowed him with enormous strength, together with the power when fighting to assume whatever form he might desire in the stress of battle.

Next, from Arcadia came Amphidamas and Cepheus, two sons of Aleus, who possessed the town of Tegea and the estate of Apheidas. Ancaeus followed them and made a third. He was encouraged to go by his father Lycurgus, an elder brother of the pair, who remained at home himself to look after the ageing Aleus, but parted with this son of his to please his brothers. Ancaeus set out clad in a bearskin from Maenalus and brandishing a huge two-edged axe in his right hand; for his grandfather Aleus had hidden his equipment in a corner of the barn, hoping to the very last to find some way of stopping him.

Augeias also came, whose father was believed to be the Sun. Lord of the Eleans, he enjoyed great wealth. And he wished for nothing better than to see the land of Colchis and Aeetes himself, the king of the Colchians.

Asterius and Amphion, sons of Hyperasius, came from Achaean Pellene, a city founded by their grandfather Pelles on the cliffs of Aegialus.

After them, from Taenarum, came Euphemus, the fastest runner in the world, whom Europa daughter of the mighty Tityos bore to Poseidon. This man could run across the rolling waters of the grey sea without wetting his swift feet. His toes alone sank in as he sped along his watery path.

And there were two more of Poseidon's sons who came. One was Erginus, hailing from the city of illustrious Miletus; and the other, proud Ancaeus, who came from Samos, the seat of Imbrasian Here. Each of these two could boast his skill in seamanship and war.

Next, bidding farewell to Calydon, came the valiant Meleager son of Oeneus, and Laocoon, a brother of Oeneus, though not by the same mother – his mother was a servant-girl. Oeneus had sent Laocoon, who was no longer young, as guardian of his son; and so it was that Meleager found himself among these bold adventurers when he had scarcely ceased to be a boy. Yet I feel that only one more year of training in his Aetolian home might well have made him the best recruit they had, excepting Heracles. Moreover, he was accompanied on his journey by his maternal uncle, Iphiclus son of Thestius, a good fighter both with the javelin and hand to hand.

At the same time came Palaemonius, who was the son, or rather the reputed son, of Olenian Lernus, his real father having been Hephaestus. This accounted for his being lame. Yet no one could have made light of his manhood and his manly form. Indeed, they won him his place in that noble company and he did Jason credit.

From Phocis came Iphitus, the son of Naubolus, himself the son of Ornytus. This man had once been Jason's host, when Jason went to Pytho to consult the oracle about his voyage. He had entertained him there in his own house.

Next came Zetes and Calaïs, children of the North Wind, whom Oreithyia daughter of Erechtheus had borne to Boreas in the wintry borderland of Thrace. It was from Attica that Thracian Boreas had brought her there. She was whirling in the dance on the banks of Ilissus when he snatched her up and carried her far away to a spot called Sarpedon's Rock, near the flowing waters of Erginus, where he wrapped her in a dark cloud and overcame her. And now, these sons of hers could soar into the sky. Astounding spectacle! As they flapped the wings on either side of their ankles, a glint of gold shone through from spangles on the dusky feathers; and their black locks streaming from head and neck along their backs were tossed by the wind to this side and that.

Last, not even Acastus, son of the great King Pelias himself, had any wish to stay behind in his father's palace. Nor had Argus, who had built the ship under Athene's orders. They too were planning to enlist.

Such and so many were the noblemen who rallied to the aid of Aeson's son. The people of the place called them all Minyae, since most of them and all the best could claim descent from the daughters of Minyas. Thus, Jason himself was the son of Alcimede, whose mother was Clymene, one of Minyas' daughters.

Everything was ready. *Argo* had been equipped by the serfs with all that goes into a well-found ship when business takes people overseas. And now her crew made their way through the city to where she lay on the shore called Magnesian Pagasae. A throng of eager townsfolk gathered round them. But they themselves stood out like bright stars in a cloudy sky; and as the people watched them hurrying along in their armour, one man voiced the thoughts of all.

'Lord Zeus!' he cried. 'What is Pelias doing? Into what exile from Achaea is he banishing this crowd of noblemen? If Aeetes won't give them the fleece of his own free will, they could send his palace up in flames on the very day they land. But they must get there first; and the going will be hard.'

Such was the general feeling in the town. Meanwhile the women kept lifting up their hands to heaven in prayer to the immortals for the happy return that all desired. One of them burst into tears and in her sorrow said to her neighbour: 'Poor Alcimede, tasting calamity at last, so late in life, with no hope now of an unclouded end! And what an evil stroke for Aeson too! Better for him if he had long since been lying in the grave, wrapped in his shroud, in happy ignorance of this ill-starred expedition. How I wish that the dark waves in which the lady Helle perished had closed over Phrixus and his ram as well.* Instead, the wicked monster actually spoke to him. Hence all this misery and heartache for Alcimede.' Such were the lamentations of the women at the Argonauts' departure.

In Jason's home, his many servants, men and women, had by now assembled. His mother too was there, clinging round his neck. The women were all overcome with grief; and his age-stricken father lying wrapped in bed, like a figure cut in stone, added his moans to theirs. But Jason soothed them in their sorrow with comfortable words, then, turning to his

* For the story of Phrixus and the Ram, see under *Phrixus* in the Glossary.

pages, told them to pick up his equipment; and they obeyed
him in silence, with their eyes on the ground. But his mother
held her son as fast as ever in her arms, weeping without
restraint, like a girl who in her loneliness falls into the arms
of her old nurse, her one remaining friend, to ease her heart,
fresh from the blows and insults of the stepmother who
makes her life a misery. She weeps, and in such black despair
that the sobs come welling up too fast for utterance. Thus
Alcimede wept as she held her son in her arms, and in her
anxious love she cried:

'Alas! I wish I could have died, forgetting all my cares, on
the very day when I heard King Pelias make his evil pro-
clamation, so that you, my child, might have buried me with
your own dear hands. That was the only service I hoped you
still might render me; apart from that, you have long since
repaid me for all a mother's care. But as it is, I that have stood
as high as any woman in Achaea shall be left like a servant in
an empty house, pining in misery for love of you, my pride
and glory in days gone by, my first and last, my only son,
seeing that the goddess has begrudged me the many children
she bestows on others. How blind I was! Never once, not
even in a dream, did I imagine that the flight of Phrixus could
bring calamity to me.'

She wept and moaned, and the waiting-women round her
joined in her lamentations. But Jason gently urged her to
take heart.

'Mother,' he said, 'I beg you not to dwell so bitterly on
your distress. No tears of yours will save me from mis-
fortune; you will only be piling trouble upon trouble. We
mortals cannot see what blows the gods may have in store for
us; and you, for all your heartache, must endure your share
with fortitude. Take courage from Athene's friendliness and
the omens we have had from Heaven – the oracles of Phoebus
could hardly have been more propitious. Remember too by
what a noble company I am supported. Stay here, then,

quietly in the house with your waiting-women, and do not
be a bird of ill omen to my ship. I am going down to her now,
together with my servants and retainers.'

With that he set out from the house, looking as he made
his way through the crowd like Apollo when he issues from
some fragrant shrine in holy Delos or Claros, or maybe at
Pytho or in the broad realm of Lycia where Xanthus flows.
The people, shouting as one man, saluted him; and Iphias, the
aged priestess of Artemis, their city's Guardian, came forward
and kissed his right hand, but was unable for all her eagerness
to say a word to him as the crowd swept on. She was left there
by the roadside, as the old are left by the young. Jason had
passed and soon was out of sight.

When he had put the well-made city streets behind him,
he came down to the beach of Pagasae, and his friends, await-
ing him in a body by the ship, waved their hands in welcome.
Jason paused before approaching, and they, who were all
looking in his direction, were amazed to see Acastus and
Argus speeding down from the city in defiance of the king's
orders. Argus had thrown round his shoulders a black bull's
hide which reached his feet, while Acastus wore a fine double
cloak, a present from his sister Pelopeia. Jason refrained from
asking them the many questions that occurred to him, and
told the whole company to take their places for a conference.
They all sat down in rows on the furled sail and the mast,
which was lying there; and Aeson's son addressed them in a
friendly spirit.

'*Argo*,' he said, 'has been fitted out as a ship should be. All
is in order and ready for the voyage. So far as that is concerned,
we could start at once, given only a favourable wind. But
there is still one thing for you to do, my friends. We are all
partners in this voyage to Colchis; partners too in the return
to Hellas that we hope for. So now it is for you to choose the
best man here to be our leader. And choose him in no partial
spirit. Everything will rest with him. When we meet

foreigners, it will be he who must decide whether to deal with them as enemies or friends.'

As he finished, the young men's eyes sought out the dauntless Heracles where he sat in the centre, and with one voice they called on him to take command. But he, without moving from his seat, raised his right hand and said: 'You must not offer me this honour. I will not accept it for myself, nor will I let another man stand up. The one who assembled this force must be its leader too.'

The magnanimity that Heracles had shown won their applause and they accepted his decision. Warlike Jason was delighted. He rose to his feet and addressed his eager friends.

'If you do indeed entrust me with this honourable charge, let nothing further keep us back – there have been enough delays already. The time has come for us to offer a pleasing sacrifice to Phoebus; we will prepare the feast at once. But while we are waiting for my overseers, who have been told to pick out some oxen from the herd and drive them here, let us drag the ship down into the water. Then you must get all the tackle on board and cast lots for your places on the rowing-benches. Also, we must build an altar on the beach for Apollo, the god of embarkation, who promised me through his oracles that he would be my counsellor and guide in our sea faring if I offered him a sacrifice as I set forth on my mission for the king.'

He was the first to turn to the business in hand. The rest leapt to their feet and followed his example, piling their clothes on a smooth ledge of rock which in the past had been scoured by winter seas but now stood high and dry. First of all, at a word from Argus, they strengthened the ship by girding her with stout rope, which they drew taut on either side, so that her planks should not spring from their bolts but stand any pounding that the seas might give them. Next they quickly hollowed out a runway wide enough to take her beam, extending it into the sea as far as the prow would reach when they launched her, and as the trench advanced, digging deeper and deeper below the level of her stem. Then they laid smooth rollers on the bottom. This done, they tipped her down on to the first rollers, on top of which she was to glide along. Next, high up on both sides of the ship, they swung the oars inboard and fastened each handle to its thole-pin so that a foot and a half projected. They themselves took their stance on either side, one behind the other, breasting the oars and pressing with their hands. And now Tiphys leapt on board to tell the young men when to push. He gave the order with a mighty shout and they put their backs into it at once. At the first heave they shifted her from where she lay; then strained forward with their feet to keep her on the move. And move she did. Between the two files of hustling, shouting men, Pelian *Argo* ran swiftly down. The rollers, chafed by the sturdy keel, groaned and reacted to the weight by putting up a pall of smoke. Thus she slid into the sea, and would have run still farther, had they not stood by and checked her with hawsers.

They fitted the oars to the tholes, and got the mast, the well-made sail, and the stores on board. Then, after satisfying themselves that all was shipshape, they cast lots for the benches, which held two oarsmen each. But the midships seat they gave to Heracles, selecting as his mate Ancaeus, the man from Tegea, and leaving this bench to the pair for their sole use, with no formalities and no recourse to chance. Also they all agreed that Tiphys should be the helmsman of their gallant ship.

Next, piling up shingle on the beach, they made a seaside altar for Apollo as god of shores and embarkation, and on the top they quickly laid down some dry logs of olive-wood. Meanwhile Jason's herdsmen had arrived, driving before them two oxen from their herd. The younger members of the party dragged the animals to the altar, the others came forward with the lustral water and barley-corns, and Jason, calling on Apollo, the god of his fathers, prayed in these words:

'Hear me, Lord, you that dwell in Pagasae and the city of Aesonis, which bears my father's name; you that promised me, when I sought an oracle in Pytho, to be my guide throughout my journey to its goal. You were the cause of my adventure: I look to you to bring my ship to Colchis and back to Hellas with my comrades safe and sound. Then we will once more glorify your altar, with a bull for each man that gets safely home; and I will bring you countless other gifts, some in Pytho, some in Ortygia. Come then, Archer-King, and accept the sacrifice we lay before you by way of payment for our passage on this ship – the very first that we have made for *Argo*. Lord, may your good will bring me luck as I cast off her cable; and may there be fair weather and a gentle breeze to carry us across the sea.'

As he prayed he sprinkled the barley-corns. And now Heracles and the powerful Ancaeus girt themselves for their task with the oxen. Heracles struck one of them full on the forehead with his club, and the steer, collapsing where it stood, sank to the ground. Ancaeus, with a bronze axe, smote the other on the nape of the neck, severing the mighty sinews, and it pitched forward on to both its horns. Their comrades promptly slit the animals' throats, then flayed them, chopped them up, and carved the flesh. They cut out the sacred pieces from the thighs, heaped them together, and after wrapping them in fat burnt them on faggots. Jason poured out libations of unmixed wine; and Idmon, watching intently, was glad to see bright flames all round the offering, and the smoke going up from them in dark spirals, exactly as it should. He spoke at once, telling them all that Apollo had in mind.

'For you,' he said, 'it is decreed by Heaven and Destiny that you should return to this place, bringing the fleece, though countless trials await you on the voyage out and

47

back. I, on the other hand, am doomed by a god's malignant will to die in some remote spot on the Asian continent. From evil omens I have long since learnt my fate. Nevertheless, I left my country to embark, so that at home they might think well of me as one who sailed in *Argo*.'

This was all. The young men listening to the prophecy rejoiced to know that they would see their homes again, but were filled with grief for Idmon and his doom.

The time of day had come when the sun, after his midday rest, begins to throw the shadows of the rocks across the fields as he declines towards the evening dusk. So now they strewed the sand with a thick covering of leaves and lay down in rows above the grey line of the surf. They had beside them plentiful supplies of appetizing food and mellow wine which the stewards had drawn off in jugs; and presently they began to tell each other stories, as young men often do at a banquet to amuse themselves, when all goes pleasantly and nobody is in a mood to pick an ugly quarrel. But Jason, his resolution failing, retired within himself to brood on all his troubles. He looked like a man in despair, and Idas, noticing this, took him to task in a loud voice.

'Jason!' he cried. 'What are these deep thoughts that you are keeping to yourself? Tell us all what is the matter with you. Has panic got you in its grip? It often leaves a coward dumb. Then hear me swear. By my keen spear, with which I win the foremost honours in the wars, the spear that helps me more than Zeus himself, I swear that no disaster shall be fatal, no venture fail, with Idas at your back, even if a god comes up against us. That is the kind of ally you have got in me, the man from Arene.'

As he finished, he lifted a full beaker with both hands and drank the sweet unwatered wine till his lips and his dark beard were drenched with it. There was an outcry from them all; but it was Idmon who stood up and spoke his mind.

'Sir!' he said. 'Your words are deadly, and you will be the first to suffer for them. You are a bold man; but it seems that this strong wine has made you overbold, blinding your judgement when it led you to insult the gods. Surely there are other ways of putting fresh heart into a friend. Your whole effusion was outrageous. Have you not heard that long ago Aloeus' sons blasphemed, as you have done, against the happy gods? Those two were by no means your inferiors in courage; yet for all their prowess they were struck down by the swift arrows of Leto's Son.'

This brought a loud laugh from Aphareian Idas. Then, with an evil look at Idmon, he made an insolent reply:

'Come now, employ your second sight and tell me whether I too shall be brought by the gods to some such end as your Father provided for Aloeus' sons. Ask yourself too how you are going to get away from me alive, should you be caught out in an idle prophecy.'

He spoke in anger with the will to wound; and the quarrel would have gone still further, had not their comrades checked the contending pair with loud remonstrances. Jason himself intervened. And so did Orpheus. Raising his lyre in his left hand, he leapt to his feet and began a song.

He sang of that past age when earth and sky and sea were knit together in a single mould; how they were sundered after deadly strife; how the stars, the moon, and the travelling sun keep faithfully to their stations in the heavens; how mountains rose, and how, together with their Nymphs, the murmuring streams and all four-legged creatures came to be. How, in the beginning, Ophion and Eurynome, daughter of Ocean, governed the world from snow-clad Olympus; how they were forcibly supplanted, Ophion by Cronos, Eurynome by Rhea; of their fall into the waters of Ocean; and how their successors ruled the happy Titan gods when Zeus in his Dictaean cave was still a child, with childish thoughts, before the earthborn Cyclopes had given him the bolt, the thunder

49

and lightning that form his glorious armament today.

The song was finished. His lyre and his celestial voice had ceased together. Yet even so there was no change in the company; the heads of all were still bent forward, their ears intent on the enchanting melody. Such was his charm – the music lingered in their hearts. But presently they mixed the libations that pious ritual prescribes for Zeus, poured them out on the burning tongues, and then in the dark betook themselves to sleep.

When radiant Dawn with her bright eyes beheld the towering crags of Pelion, and the headlands washed by wind-driven seas stood sharp and clear, Tiphys awoke and quickly roused his comrades to embark and fix the oars. At the same moment there came an awe-inspiring call from the harbour of Pagasae; and Pelian *Argo* herself, who was chafing to be off, cried out, for she carried a sacred beam from the Dodonian oak* which Athene had fitted in the middle of her stem. So they followed one another to the rowing-benches and, taking their allotted places, sat down in proper order with their equipment by them. Ancaeus sat amidships beside the mighty bulk of Heracles, who laid his club near by and made the ship's keel underfoot sink deep into the water. And now the hawsers were hauled in and they poured libations on the sea.

Jason wept as he turned his eyes away from the land of his birth. But the rest struck the rough sea with their oars in time with Orpheus' lyre, like young men bringing down their quick feet on the earth in unison with one another and the lyre, as they dance for Apollo round his altar at Pytho, or in Ortygia, or by the waters of Ismenus. Their blades were swallowed by the waves, and on either side the dark salt water broke into foam, seething angrily in answer to the strong men's strokes. The armour on the moving ship glittered in the sunshine like fire; and all the time she was

* See Glossary, p. 204

50

followed by a long white wake which stood out like a path across a green plain.

All the gods looked down from heaven that day, observing *Argo* and the spirit shown by her heroic crew, the noblest seamen of their time; and from the mountain heights the Nymphs of Pelion admired Athene's work and the gallant Argonauts themselves, tugging at the oars. Cheiron son of Philyra came down from the high ground to the sea and wading out into the grey surf waved his great hand again and again and wished the travellers a happy home-coming. His wife came too. She was carrying Peleus' little boy Achilles on her arm, and she held him up for his dear father to see.

Till they had left the harbour and its curving shores behind them, the ship was in the expert hands of Tiphys, wise son of Hagnias, who used the polished steering-oar to keep her on her course. But now they stept the tall mast in its box and fixed it with forestays drawn taut on either bow; then hauled the sail up to the masthead and unfurled it. The shrill wind filled it out; and after making the halyards fast on deck, each round its wooden pin, they sailed on at their ease past the long Tisaean headland, while Orpheus played his lyre and sang them a sweet song of highborn Artemis, Saver of ships and Guardian of those peaks that here confront the sea, and of the land of Iolcus. Fish large and small came darting out over the salt sea depths and gambolled in their watery wake, led by the music like a great flock of sheep that have had their fill of grass and follow their shepherd home to the gay sound of some rustic melody from his high-piping reed. And the wind, freshening as the day wore on, carried *Argo* on her way.

Already dim, the rich Pelasgian land was quickly out of view; and pressing on they passed the rocky flanks of Pelion. Cape Sepias disappeared, and sea-girt Sciathus hove in sight. Then far away they saw Peiresiae and under a clear sky the mainland coastline of Magnesia and the tomb of Dolops. Here, as the wind had veered against them, they beached their ship at nightfall, and in the dark, while the sea ran high, they made a sacrifice of sheep in the hero's honour. For two days they lingered on this coast, but on the third they hoisted their broad canvas and put out to sea. The beach is still called *Argo*'s Aphetae because she took off there.

Forging ahead they ran past Meliboea, leaving its stormy beaches on their lee. And in the morning they saw Homole sloping down to the sea quite close to them. They skirted it, and had not long to wait before they passed the mouth of the River Amyrus, and presently could see Eurymenae and the scarred ravines of Ossa and Olympus. Then, running all night before the wind, they made Pallene, where the hills rise up from Cape Canastra. And as they sailed on in the dawn, Mount Athos rose before them, Athos in Thrace, the peak of which, though as far from Lemnos as a well-found merchantman can travel by evening, throws its shadow over the island right up to Myrine. For the Argonauts there was a stiff breeze all that day and through the night; *Argo*'s sail was stretched. But with the sun's first rays there came a calm, and it was by rowing that they reached the rugged isle of Lemnos, where once the Sintians lived.

Here, in the previous year, the women had run riot and slaughtered every male inhabitant. The married men, seized with loathing for their lawful wives, had cast them off, conceiving an unruly passion for the captured girls they brought across the sea from raids in Thrace. The Lemnian wives had for long neglected the homage due to Aphrodite, and this was the angry Cyprian's punishment. Unhappy women! Their soul-destroying and insensate jealousy drove them to kill not only their husbands and the girls who had usurped their beds, but every male as well in order that they might not have to pay the price one day for this atrocious massacre. The only woman to forbear was Hypsipyle. She spared her aged father Thoas, who was king of Lemnos, and sent him drifting over the sea inside a chest, in the hope that he might yet escape. And so he did. Some fishermen dragged him ashore at the island then called Oenoe, but later renamed Sicinus after the son whom the nymph Oenoe bore to Thoas.

The Lemnian women found it an easier thing to look after cattle, don a suit of bronze, and plough the earth for corn than to devote themselves, as they had done before, to the tasks of which Athene is the patroness. Nevertheless they lived in dire dread of the Thracians; and they cast many a glance across the intervening sea in case they might be coming. So when they saw *Argo* rowing up to the island, they at once equipped themselves for war and poured out in wild haste from the gates of Myrine, like ravening Thyiads, thinking that the Thracians had come. Hypsipyle joined them, dressed in her father Thoas' armour. It was a panic-stricken rabble, speechless and impotent with fear, that streamed down to the beach.

Meanwhile the Argonauts despatched Aethalides from their ship. He was the swift herald to whom they entrusted their messages and the wand of his own father, Hermes, who had endowed him with an all-embracing memory that never failed. He has long since been lost in the inexorable waters of Acheron, yet even so, Lethe has not overwhelmed his soul, whose destiny it is to be for ever changing its home, now staying with the dead men down below, now with the living under the beams of the sun. But why should I enlarge on the story of Aethalides? What he did now was to persuade Hypsipyle, as the day was spent, to let the travellers stay there for the night. But even when morning came, bringing a breeze from the north, they did not cast their hawsers off.

The Lemnian women made their way through the town to take their seats in the meeting-place. Hypsipyle herself had summoned them, and when the great assembly was complete, she rose to give them her advice.

'My friends,' she said, 'we must conciliate these people by

our generosity. Let us supply them with food, good wine, and all that they may want to have with them on board, so as to make sure that they shall never come inside our walls, or get to know us well, as they would do if they were driven by their needs to mingle with us freely. The evil news of what we did would travel everywhere. It was a great crime that we committed, and one by no means likely to endear us to these men, if they came to know it, or indeed to others. Well, you have heard what I propose. If any woman among you has a better plan, let her stand up. It was for that purpose that I brought you here.'

After Hypsipyle had finished and sat down on her father's marble throne, the next to rise was her dear nurse Polyxo, an aged woman tottering on withered feet and leaning on a staff, but none the less determined to be heard. Four young girls were sitting by her, their virginal appearance contrasting with Polyxo's crown of white hair. She made her way to the centre of the meeting-place, raised her bowed head with a painful effort and began:

'Hypsipyle is right. We must accommodate these strangers: it is better to give than to be robbed. But that alone will not ensure your future happiness. What if the Thracians attack us, or some other enemy appears? Such things happen. And they happen unannounced – you saw how these men came. But even if Heaven spares us that calamity, there are many troubles worse than war that you will have to meet as time goes on. When the older ones among us have died off, how are you younger women, without children, going to face the miseries of age? Will the oxen yoke themselves? Will they go out into the fields and drag the ploughshare through the stubborn fallow? Will they watch the changing seasons and reap at the right time? As for myself, though Death still shudders at the sight of me, I have the feeling that the coming year will see me in the grave, duly and solemnly buried before the bad times come. But I do advise you younger ones to think. Salvation lies before you at your very feet, if only you will entrust your homes, your livestock, and your splendid city to these visitors.'

Polyxo's speech was greeted with applause from every side. They liked her plan; and Hypsipyle immediately stood up again and said, 'Since you are all agreed, I will send a messenger to the ship at once.' And turning to Iphinoe, who was at her side, 'Go, Iphinoe, and ask the captain of this expedition, whoever he may be, to come to my house and hear what the people have decided – it will please him. And tell his men that they may land, if they wish to do so, without fear and come into our town as friends.' With that, she dismissed the meeting and set out for home.

Iphinoe meanwhile presented herself to the Minyae, and when they asked what had brought her, she poured out her tale: 'The lady Hypsipyle, daughter of Thoas, sent me here to invite the captain of your ship, whoever he may be, to come and hear from her what the people have decided – she said it would please him. Also I am to tell the rest of you that you may land at once, if you wish to do so, and come into the town as friends.'

This struck them all as a very fit and proper welcome. They thought that Thoas must be dead and Hypsipyle, his only daughter, queen. So they urged Jason to set out at once and themselves prepared to go.

Jason fastened round his shoulders a purple cloak of double width which Pallas Athene, the Lady of Trito, had made and given him when she was laying down the props for *Argo*'s keel and showing him how to measure timber for the cross-beams with a rule. The brilliance of this mantle outdid the rising sun. It was of crimson cloth surrounded by a purple border and embroidered at each end with a number of distinct and curious designs.

Here were the Cyclopes sitting at work on an imperishable thunderbolt for Zeus the King. One ray was lacking to complete its splendour, and this lay spurting flame as they beat it out with their iron hammers.

And here were shown Antiope's two sons, Amphion and Zethus, with the town of Thebes, as yet unfortified. They were busy laying its foundations. Zethus was shouldering a mountain peak – he seemed to find it heavy work. Amphion walked behind, singing to a golden lyre; and a boulder twice as large as that of Zethus came trundling after him.

Next, Aphrodite of the long locks, wielding Ares' formidable shield. On the left side her tunic had slipped down from her shoulder to her forearm. It hung below her breast, and all was mirrored to perfection in the bronze shield that she held in front of her.

Elsewhere a woodland pasturage was shown with oxen grazing. For these a battle was afoot. Electryon's sons had been attacked by a band of Taphian raiders, who wished to walk off with their cattle. The dewy grass was drenched with their blood. But the herdsmen were too few, and the larger force had got the upper hand.

Next came a race between two chariots. In the leading car was Pelops, shaking the reins, with Hippodameia beside him. And close behind came Oenomaus, with Myrtilus driving the horses. Oenomaus was trying to catch Pelops with a spearcast in the back. But just as he had poised his spear, the axle of his chariot twisted and broke in the hub; and out he fell.

And here was Phoebus Apollo, pictured as a sturdy youth shooting an arrow at the gigantic Tityos, who was boldly dragging off his mother Leto by her veil. Tityos was the lady Elare's son; but he was nursed and borne again by Mother Earth.

Phrixus the Minyan was also shown together with his ram. So vividly were they portrayed, the ram speaking and Phrixus listening, that as you looked you would have kept quiet in the fond hope of hearing some wise words from their lips. And still you would have gazed and still have hoped.

Such was the cloak that Athene, Lady of Trito, had made for Jason. In his right hand he held another gift, a light spear that Atalanta had given him, when she welcomed him in Maenalus, in token of her friendship and her strong desire to join him in the quest. But he had dissuaded her, fearing the bitter quarrels that a lovely girl would cause.

Jason set out on his way to the city, looking like that bright star whose beautiful red beams, piercing the darkness as he rises over the roof-tops, delight a girl shut up in her new bridal-bower and longing for the youth for whom her parents destine her, still far away in foreign lands. Thus Jason looked as he approached the city, and no sooner was he through the gates than the women of the town came flocking after him, charmed by their visitor's appearance. But Jason kept his eyes on the ground and walked resolutely on till he reached Hypsipyle's royal palace. There the double doors with their closely fitted panels were thrown open for him by the maids; and Iphinoe led him quickly through the noble hall and brought him to a polished chair, in which he sat down facing her mistress.

Hypsipyle turned her eyes aside and blushed as maidens do. Yet for all her modesty, her speech was calculated to deceive.

'Stranger,' she said, 'why have you stayed so long outside our city – a city that has lost its men? They have migrated to the mainland to plough the fields of Thrace. But let me tell you the whole sorry tale; I wish you all to know the truth. When my father Thoas was king our men-folk used to sail across from here to the mainland opposite and raid the Thracian farmsteads from their ships. They brought home plenty of booty, and they brought women too. But that malignant goddess Aphrodite had for some time had her eye on them. And now she struck, depriving them of all sense of right and wrong. As a result they conceived a loathing for their wedded wives; they turned them out of doors; and then the brutes indulged their passion by sleeping with the captives

57

of their spears. For a long time we put up with this. We hoped there might be a change of heart before it was too late. But the evil grew; and it had a double consequence. In every household, the lawful children were neglected, while a bastard generation was growing up. Meanwhile unmarried girls, besides the mothers who had lost their homes, were left to wander in the streets. No father took the slightest notice of his daughter; for all he cared, a cruel step-mother could kill her in his sight. No son was ready now to protect his mother from outrage. No brother loved his sisters as he should. Whether at home or dining out, dancing or talking politics, the men could think of nothing but the captured girls. But at last some god inspired us with a desperate resolve. We had the courage, when the men returned one day from Thrace, to shut the city-gates against them, in the hope that they might come to their senses, or take themselves elsewhere, trollops and all. In the end they begged us for all the male children left in the town, and so went back to Thrace. And there they are now, making a living from its snowy fields.

'So I invite you all to stay here and settle with us. If you yourself accept and the prospect pleases you, my royal father's sceptre shall certainly be yours. And I have no fear that you may think poorly of our land. It has the richest soil of any isle in the Aegaean Sea. But first go to your ship and tell your comrades what I say. And pray do not avoid the city any more.'

Thus she glossed over the massacre and what had really happened to the men.

'Hypsipyle,' Jason replied, 'we need your help, and all you may give us will indeed be welcome. I shall come back to the city when I have told my people everything. But I must leave this island and its sovereignty to you. I refuse, not through indifference, but because a hazardous adventure calls me on.'

As he finished, he touched her right hand; then quickly turned and went. Countless young girls ran up from every

58

side and danced round him in their joy, till he had passed through the city-gates. Then, when he had reported to his friends all that Hypsipyle had summoned him to hear, the girls drove down to the beach in smooth-running wagons laden with gifts. And they did not find it difficult to make the Argonauts come home with them for entertainment. Cypris, the goddess of desire, had done her sweet work in their hearts. She wished to please Hephaestus, the great Artificer, and save his isle of Lemnos from ever lacking men again.

Jason himself set out for Hypsipyle's royal home, and the rest scattered as chance took them – all but Heracles, who chose to stay by the ship with a few select companions. Soon the whole city was alive with dance and banquet. The scent of burnt-offerings filled the air; and of all the immortals, it was Here's glorious son Hephaestus and Cypris herself whom their songs and sacrifices were designed to please. Day followed day, and still they did not sail. Indeed there is no knowing when they would have left if Heracles had not summoned a meeting, from which the women were excluded, and sharply admonished his friends.

'My good sirs,' he began, not without irony. 'Are we exiled for manslaughter? Cast out for killing relatives at home? Or have we come here for brides, not fancying our own women there? Are we really content to stay and cultivate the soil of Lemnos? We shall get no credit, I assure you, by shutting ourselves up with a set of foreign women all this time. And it is no good praying for a miracle. Fleeces do not come to people of their own accord. We might as well go home, leaving this captain of ours to spend all day in Hypsipyle's arms till he has won the admiration of the world by repopulating Lemnos.'

Such was the force of his rebuke that not a man could look him in the eye or answer him. With no more said, the meeting broke up and they hurried off to make ready for departure. But when the women got wind of their intention, they came running down and swarmed round them, moaning for grief, as bees come pouring out from their rocky hive when the meadows are gay with dew, and buzz about the lilies, flitting to and fro to take their sweet toll from the flowers. There was a loving hand and a kind word for every man, with many a prayer to the happy gods for his safe return. Hypsipyle took Jason's hands in hers and prayed in tears for the lover she was losing.

'Go,' she said, 'and may the gods bring you and all your comrades home with the golden fleece for the king, since that is what you have set your heart on. This island and my father's sceptre will be waiting for you if you ever choose to come again when you are back in Hellas. You could easily collect a host of emigrants from other towns. But that is not what you will wish; something tells me that it will not happen. Nevertheless, remember Hypsipyle when you are far away and when you are at home. But tell me what I am to do if the gods allow me to become a mother; and I will gladly do it.'

Jason was moved. 'Hypsipyle,' he said, 'may the happy gods grant all the prayers you made on my behalf. But I hope that you will not think ill of me if I elect, with Pelias' permission, to live in my own country. Release from toil is all I ask of Heaven. But if I am not destined to return to Hellas from my travels, and you bear me a son, send him when he is old enough to Pelasgian Iolcus. I should like him to console my father and mother in their grief if he finds them still alive, and to care for them at their own fireside at home with no interference from the king.'

With that, Jason led the way on board. The other chieftains followed him, went to their seats and manned the oars; Argus loosed the stern-cable from its sea-beaten rock; and they struck the water lustily with their long blades of pine.

In the evening, at the suggestion of Orpheus, they beached

the ship at Samothrace, the island of Electra daughter of Atlas. He wished them, by a holy initiation, to learn something of the secret rites, and so sail on with greater confidence across the formidable sea. Of the rites I say no more, pausing only to salute the isle itself and the Powers that dwell in it, to whom belong the mysteries of which we must not sing.

From Samothrace they rowed on eagerly over the deep gulf of Melas, with the land of the Thracians on the left, and Imbros northward on the right. And just as the sun was setting they reached the foreland of the Chersonese. There they met a strong wind from the south, set their sail to it and entered the swift current of the Hellespont, which takes its name from Athamas's daughter. By dawn they had left the northern sea; by nightfall they were coasting the Rhoetean shore, inside the straits, with the land of Ida on their right. Leaving Dardania behind, they set course for Abydos, and after that they passed in turn Percote, Abarnis with its sandy beach, and sacred Pityeia. Before dawn, *Argo* by dint of sail and oar was through the darkly swirling Hellespont.

In the Propontis there is an island sloping steeply to the sea, close to the rich mainland of Phrygia, and parted from it only by a low isthmus barely raised above the waves. The isthmus, with its two shores, lies east of the River Aesepus; and the place itself is called Bear Mountain by the people round about. It is inhabited by a fierce and lawless tribe of aborigines, who present an astounding spectacle to their neighbours. Each of these earthborn monsters is equipped with six great arms, two springing from his shoulders, and four below from his prodigious flanks. But the isthmus and the plain belonged to the Doliones, who had for king the noble Cyzicus, son of Aeneus and Aenete, daughter of the godlike Eusorus. These people were never troubled by the fearsome aborigines: Poseidon, from whom they were descended, saw to that.

Argo, pressing on with a stiff breeze from Thrace behind

her, reached this coast and ran into a harbour called Fairhaven.
Here, on the advice of Tiphys, they discarded their small
anchor-stone and left it at the spring of Artacie, replacing it
with a heavier and more suitable rock. Later, at the prompting
of Apollo, the original stone was transferred by the Ionian
followers of Neleus to the temple of Jasonian Athene, where
it was rightly treated as a sacred relic.

The Doliones and Cyzicus their king received the Argonauts
in a friendly spirit, and when told who they were and the
object of the expedition, offered them hospitality, inviting
them to row farther in and moor in the town harbour. Here
they built an altar on the beach for Apollo, god of happy
landings, and made him a sacrifice. The king himself supplied
them with the good wine they lacked and also with sheep –
he had been warned by an oracle that when some such
dedicated band of noblemen arrived he must receive them with
civility and no display of arms. This man, with the soft down
on his cheeks, somewhat resembled Jason. He too had no
children to delight him in his home, where his wife, the gentle
lady Cleite, daughter of Percosian Merops, had not as yet
experienced the pangs of childbirth. Indeed he had but lately
brought her from the mainland opposite, paying a princely
dowry to her father. Nevertheless he left his young wife in
their bridal chamber and joined his visitors at dinner with no
misgivings. And they questioned one another. Cyzicus asked
about their destination and the task that Pelias had set them;
and in answer to their own inquiries he told them about the
neighbouring towns and the whole broad Propontic Gulf.
But farther than that his knowledge did not go, much as they
wished to learn what lay beyond.

In the morning some of the Argonauts climbed towards
the top of Dindymum in the hope of seeing for themselves
the waters they would have to cross – the way they took is still
called Jason's path. Another party brought the ship from her
former anchorage to the harbour of Chytus.

But now the earthborn savages, coming from the other side, dashed down the mountain and blocked the mouth of the ample harbour of Chytus with boulders, in an attempt to pen them like wild beasts in a trap. However, Heracles had been left there with the younger men. He quickly bent his recurved bow and brought a number of the monsters down. The rest retaliated by pelting him with jagged rocks. And I cannot but surmise that these redoubtable beasts were bred by Here, Wife of Zeus, as an extra labour for Heracles. But just at this moment, the rest of the Argonauts, who had turned back before reaching the summit, appeared on the scene to take their part in the slaughter. The monsters charged with fury more than once, but the young warriors were ready for them with their spears and arrows and in the end they killed them all.

When the long timbers for a ship have been hewn by the woodman's axe they are laid in rows on a beach and there they lie and soak till they are ready to receive the bolts. That is how these fallen monsters looked, stretched out in a row on the grey beach by the harbour mouth. Some were sprawling in a mass with their limbs on shore and their heads and breasts in the sea. Some lay the other way about; their heads were resting on the sands and their feet were deep in the water. But in either case they were carrion for birds and fish. The day was won and the Argonauts had no more to fear.

They loosed the hawsers of their ship, caught the breeze, and forged ahead through a choppy sea. They sailed all day, but the wind began to fail at dusk. Then it veered against them, freshened to a gale, and sent them scudding back towards their hospitable friends the Doliones. And that same night they went ashore. The rock round which they cast the ship's hawsers in their haste is still called the Sacred Rock.

But no one had the sense to note that they were landing on the very island they had left; and in the darkness the Doliones themselves failed to realize that the Argonauts were back. They thought that some Pelasgian raiders had landed, Macrians perhaps. So they donned their armour and attacked. And now there was a clash of shields and ashen spears as the two parties met, with the impact of a forest fire when it pounces on dry brushwood and leaps into the sky. The Doliones were plunged into all the horrors and turmoil of a war.

Their king himself was not allowed to cheat the Fates and come home from the battle to his young wife in her bridal bed. Jason, as the king swung round to face him, leapt in and struck him full in the breast, shattering the bone with his spear. Cyzicus sank down on the sands; he had had his span of life, and more than that no mortal can command – we are like birds trapped in the wide net of Destiny. And so this man was caught: he thought he had escaped the worst that the Argonauts might do to him, but that very night he fought them and died. And he was not their only champion to fall. Heracles killed Telecles and Megabrontes; Acastus killed Sphodris; Zelys and stalwart Gephyrus fell to Peleus. Telamon with his great ashen spear killed Basileus; Idas killed Promeus; and Clytius, Hyacinthus; while Castor and Polydeuces despatched Megalossaces and Phlogius. Meleager added two to these, the dauntless Itymoneus, and Artaces, a dashing leader. Their countrymen still honour all the slain as heroes.

The rest gave way and fled in panic, like a flock of doves with a swift hawk after them. There was a wild rush for the gates, and the city was soon loud with lamentation for the catastrophe. Then came the dawn and taught both sides their grievous and irreparable error. The Minyae were overcome with sorrow when they saw Cyzicus lying in the dust and blood; and for three whole days they and the Doliones wailed for him and tore their hair. Then they marched three times round the dead king in their bronze equipment, laid him in his tomb, and held the customary games out on the grassy plain, where the barrow they raised for him can still be seen by people of a later age.

Cleite the king's bride was unable to face life alone, with her husband in the grave. Capping the evil she had suffered with a worse one of her own devising, she took a rope and hanged herself by the neck. Her death was bewailed even by the woodland nymphs, who caused the many tears they shed to unite in a spring, which the people call Cleite in memory of a peerless but unhappy bride. It was a day of horror for the Doliones, the worst that Zeus had ever sent their women or their men. Not one of them could even bear to eat, and such was their grief that for a long time they let their hand-mills stand idle and lived on uncooked food. To this very day the Ionians of Cyzicus, when they make their yearly libations, grind the meal for the cakes at the public mill.

For twelve days after this there was foul weather day and night, and the Argonauts were unable to put out. But towards the end of the next night, while Acastus and Mopsus watched over their comrades, who had long been fast asleep, a halcyon hovered over the golden head of Aeson's son and in its piping voice announced the end of the gales. Mopsus heard it and understood the happy omen. So when the sea-bird, still directed by a god, flew off and perched on the mascot of the ship, he went to Jason, who lay comfortably wrapped in fleeces, woke him quickly with a touch and said:

'My lord, you must climb this holy peak to propitiate Rhea, Mother of all the happy gods, whose lovely throne is Dindymum itself – and then the gales will cease. I learnt this from a halcyon just now: the sea-bird flew above you as you slept and told me all. Rhea's dominion covers the winds, the sea, the whole earth, and the gods' home on snow-capped Olympus. Zeus himself, the Son of Cronos, gives place to her when she leaves her mountain haunts and rises into the broad sky. So too do the other blessed ones; all pay the same deference to that dread goddess.'

This was welcome news to Jason, who leapt up from his bed rejoicing. He hastily woke the rest and told them how

Mopsus had interpreted the signs. They set to work at once. The younger men took some oxen from the stalls and began to drive them up the steep path to the top of Dindymum. The others loosed the hawsers from the sacred rock and rowed *Argo* to the Thracian anchorage. Then, leaving a few of their comrades in the ship, they too climbed the mountain. From the summit they could see the Macrian heights and the whole length of the opposite Thracian coast – it almost seemed that they could touch it. And far away on the one side they saw the misty entrance to the Bosporus and the Mysian hills, and on the other the flowing waters of Aesepus and the city and Nepeian plain of Adresteia.

Standing in the woods, there was an ancient vine with a massive trunk withered to the roots. They cut this down to make a sacred image of the mountain goddess; and when Argus had skilfully shaped it, they set it up on a rocky eminence under the shelter of some tall oaks, the highest trees that grow, and made an altar of small stones near by. Then, crowned with oak-leaves, they began the sacrificial rites, invoking the Dindymian Mother, most worshipful, who dwells in Phrygia; and with her, Titias and Cyllenus. For these two are singled out as dispensers of doom and assessors to the Idaean Mother from the many Idaean Dactyls of Crete. They were borne in the Dictaean cave by the Nymph Anchiale as she clutched the earth of Oaxus with both her hands.

Jason, pouring libations on the blazing sacrifice, earnestly besought the goddess to send the stormy winds elsewhere. At the same time, by command of Orpheus, the young men in full armour moved round in a high-stepping dance, beating their shields with their swords to drown the ill-omened cries that came up from the city, where the people were still wailing for their king. This is why the Phrygians to this day propitiate Rhea with the tambourine and drum.

The goddess they invoked must have observed the flawless sacrifice with pleasure, for her own appropriate signs appeared.

The trees shed abundant fruit; the earth at their feet adorned itself with tender grass; beasts left their lairs and thickets and came to them with wagging tails. And these were not her only miracles. Until that day there had been no running water on Dindymum. But now, with no digging on their part, a stream gushed out for them from the thirsty peak. And it did not cease to flow; the natives of the place still drink from it. They call it Jason's Spring.

As a finish to the rites, they held a feast on Bear Mountain in honour of Rhea and sang the praises of the venerable goddess. By dawn the wind had dropped and they rowed off from the island in a spirit of rivalry, each trying to outlast the others at the oars. The windless air had smoothed the waves on every side and put the sea to sleep. So they took advantage of the calm to drive the ship forward by their own power; and as she sped through the salt water, not even Poseidon's team, the horses of the whirlwind feet, could have overtaken her. Later, however, when the sea was roughened by the strong winds that blow down rivers in the afternoon, they wearied and relaxed. It was left to Heracles to bring the whole exhausted crew along with him, pulling his hardest with his great arms and sending shudders through the framework of the ship. They were anxious to reach the Mysian coast. But as they passed within sight of the mouth of the Rhyndacus and the great barrow of Aegaeon, not far from Phrygia, Heracles, ploughing furrows in the choppy sea, broke his oar in half and fell sideways off the bench with one end in his hands while the other was swept away by the receding waves. He sat up, speechless and glaring. He was not used to idle hands.

They made their landfall at the time of day when the vine-dresser or ploughman, filled with thoughts of supper, reaches home at last and, pausing at the door, begrimed with dust, bends a weary knee and looks at his worn hands with a curse for the belly that commands such toil. They had struck the Cianian coast near Mount Arganthon and the estuary of Cius. And coming as they did with no hostile intent, they were kindly received by the Mysian inhabitants, who supplied their needs with sheep and wine in plenty. Some of the Argonauts went to fetch dry wood; some collected leaves from the fields and brought them in for bedding; others twirled firesticks; and others again mixed wine in the bowls for the feast that was to follow a sacrifice at nightfall to Apollo, god of happy landings.

But Heracles son of Zeus, leaving his friends to prepare the banquet, set out for the woods, anxious before all else to make himself a handy oar. Wandering about he found a pine that was not burdened with many branches nor had reached its full stature, but was like a slender young poplar in height and girth. He promptly laid his bow and quiver down, took off his lion-skin and began by loosening the pine's hold in the ground with blows of his bronze-studded club. Then he trusted to his own strength. With his legs wide apart and one broad shoulder pressed against the tree, he seized it low down with both hands and gripping hard he tore it out. Deep-rooted though it was, it came up clods and all like a ship's mast torn from its stays, together with the wedges, by a sudden squall in the stormy days when Orion sets in anger. Thus Heracles tore out the pine; then he picked it up, with his bow and arrows, lion-skin and club, and started to go back.

Meanwhile Hylas had gone off by himself with a bronze ewer in search of some hallowed spring where he could draw water for the evening meal and be in time to get everything ready, like a good servant, for his master's return. Heracles himself had trained him in these ways ever since he had taken him as a child from the house of his royal father, Theiodamas, whom he had ruthlessly killed at the head of his Dryopians after a quarrel about a ploughing ox. The doomed man was ploughing up a piece of fallow when Heracles, anxious to find a pretext for attacking the Dryopians, a lawless tribe, asked him for the ox and was refused. But the whole tale would take me too far from my present theme.

Hylas soon found a spring, which the people of the neighbourhood call Pegae. He reached it when the nymphs were about to hold their dances – it was the custom of all those who haunt that beautiful headland to sing the praise of Artemis by night. The nymphs of the mountain peaks and caverns were all posted some way off to patrol the woods; but one, the naiad of the spring, was just emerging from the limpid water as Hylas drew near. And there, with the full moon shining on him from a clear sky, she saw him in all his radiant beauty and alluring grace. Her heart was flooded by desire; she had a struggle to regain her scattered wits. But Hylas now leant over to one side to dip his ewer in; and as soon as the water was gurgling loudly round the ringing bronze she threw her left arm round his neck in her eagerness to kiss his gentle lips. Then with her right hand she drew his elbow down and plunged him in midstream.

The lord Polyphemus son of Eilatus, who had gone some way along the path in the hope of meeting the gigantic Heracles, was the only member of the company to hear the boy's cry. Led by the sound he rushed off towards Pegae, like a wild animal who hears the bleating of a distant flock and in his hunger dashes after them, only to find that the shepherds have forestalled him, the sheep are in the pen, and he is left to roar in protest till he tires. Thus Polyphemus groaned in his distress and shouted as he prowled about the place. But there was no answering voice. So he drew his great sword and began to extend the search, fearing that Hylas might have fallen to a wild beast or been ambushed by some men, who would have found the lonely boy an easy prey. Then, as he ran along the path brandishing his naked sword, he met Heracles himself hastening back to the ship through the darkness. Polyphemus knew him at once and blurted out his lamentable tale, gasping for breath:

'My lord! It falls to me to give you dreadful news. Hylas went out for water. He has not come back. Some brigands must have got him. Or beasts are tearing him to pieces. I heard him cry.'

When Heracles heard this, the sweat poured from his forehead and the dark blood boiled within him. In his fury he threw down the pine and rushed off, little caring where his feet were carrying him. Picture a bull stampeded from the water-meadows by a gadfly's sting. He takes to his heels. The herd and herdsmen are nothing to him now; and off he goes, sometimes pressing on without a stop, sometimes pausing to lift his mighty neck and bellow in his pain. Thus Heracles in his frenzy ran at top speed for a while without a break, then paused in his exertions to fill the distance with a ringing cry.

But now the morning star rose above the topmost peaks, and with it came a breeze. Tiphys urged his comrades to embark at once and take advantage of the wind. They went on board in eager haste, pulled up the anchor-stones and hauled the ropes astern. Struck full by the wind, the sail bellied out, and soon they rejoiced to find themselves far out at sea, passing Poseidon's Cape.

But presently, at the hour when bright-eyed Dawn comes up to light the eastern sky, and all the paths stand out and the fields glisten with dew, they realized that they had heedlessly left two of their number behind. Tumult and fierce recriminations followed: they had sailed without the bravest Argonaut of all. But Jason, paralysed by a sense of utter helplessness, added no word to either side in this dispute. He sat and ate his heart out, crushed by the calamity.

Telamon was enraged. 'You may well sit there at your ease,' he cried, 'since nothing suits you better than to abandon Heracles. You planned the whole affair yourself so that his fame in Hellas should not eclipse your own, if we have the good fortune to return. But why waste my breath? I am determined to go back, and that without consulting those friends of yours who abetted you in this plot.'

As he finished he made a rush at Tiphys, his eyes ablaze with angry fire. And they would soon have been on their way back to Mysia, forcing *Argo* through the sea against a stiff and steady breeze, if the two sons of the North Wind, Zetes and Calaïs, had not checked Telamon with a stinging rebuke. Unhappy pair! A dreadful punishment was coming to them at the hands of Heracles for having thus cut short the search for him. He killed them in sea-girt Tenos on their way home from the games at Pelias' funeral, made a barrow over them and on top set a couple of pillars, one of which amazes all beholders by swaying to the breath of the roaring North Wind. But all this was yet to come. Now, they suddenly saw Glaucus, the sage spokesman of the sea-god Nereus, emerge from the salt depths. Raising his shaggy head and front, as far down as the waist, he laid his sturdy hand on the side of the ship and cried to the contending Argonauts:

'Why do you propose, in defiance of almighty Zeus, to bring the dauntless Heracles to Colchis? Argos is his place. There he is fated to serve his cruel master, Eurystheus; to accomplish twelve tasks; and if he succeeds in the few that yet remain, to join the immortals in their home. So let there be no regrets for him. Nor for Polyphemus, who is destined to found a famous city among the Mysians where Cius flows into the sea, and to meet his end in the broad land of the Chalybes. As for Hylas, who caused these two to go astray and so be left behind, a Nymph has lost her heart to him and made him her husband.'

With that, he plunged and was swallowed by the restless waves. The dark water swirled round him, broke into foam, and dashed against the hollow ship as she moved on.

The Argonauts were filled with joy, and Telamon went straight up to Jason. He gripped his hand, kissed him, and said, 'My lord, do not be angry with me if in a foolish moment I was blinded. An intolerable affront was forced from me in my distress. May the winds blow away the offence, and let us two, who always have been friends, be friends again.'

The son of Aeson answered him with wise forbearance. 'My good sir,' he said, 'you did indeed insult me grievously when you accused me, before all these, of having wronged a loyal friend. I was cut to the quick, but I am not going to nurse a grudge. For you were not quarrelling with me about a flock of sheep or worldly goods, but about a man, a comrade of your own. And I like to think that if the occasion arose you would stand up for me against others as boldly as you did for him.'

This was enough. They both sat down, united as they had been before, and Zeus concerned himself with the other pair. He destined Polyphemus to build in Mysia a city which should bear the river's name, and Heracles to resume his labours for Eurystheus. But before he left Mysia, Heracles threatened to lay waste the land if the people failed to find out for him what had become of Hylas, living or dead. The Mysians then gave him some of their best young men as hostages and solemnly swore that they would never abandon the search. For which reason the people of Cius enquire after Hylas son of Theiodamas to this very day, and take a friendly interest in the well-built city of Trachis, where Heracles settled the youthful hostages they had let him take from Cius.

All that day and through the following night a stiff breeze carried *Argo* on; but at daybreak there was not a breath of air. However, they saw land ahead. There was a beach that showed up from a bay, and it seemed to be a wide one. So they rowed the ship towards it and ran her ashore as the sun rose.

BOOK TWO

ONWARD TO COLCHIS

THIS was where Amycus, the arrogant king of the Bebryces, had his farm and cattle-yards. Borne to Poseidon by the Bithynian nymph Melie, he was the world's greatest bully. It was his barbarous custom to allow no one, not even a foreign visitor, to leave his country before trying conclusions with him in a boxing-match. He had already killed a number of his neighbours. And now he came down to the ship, planted himself among the Argonauts and not even troubling to ask who they were or what had brought them overseas, had the effrontery to say:

'Listen, sailormen, to something you should know. No foreigner calling here is allowed to continue his journey without putting up his fists to mine. So pick out your best man and match him against me on the spot. Otherwise you will find to your sorrow that if you defy my laws you will be brought by main force to obey them.'

His high-handed manner roused them to fury, and Poly-deuces, who took his threat as a personal affront, stepped forward at once to champion his friends.

'Enough!' he said. 'Whoever you may be, let us have no more of this parade of violence. You have stated your rules and we accept them. Here I am, ready to meet you of my own free will.'

He spoke bluntly, and Amycus glared at him with rolling eyes, like a lion who is hit by a javelin when they hunt him in the mountains, and caring nothing for the crowd that hems him in, picks out the man who wounded him, and keeps his eyes on him alone.

Polydeuces was wearing a light and closely-woven cloak,

73

the parting gift of some Lemnian girl. This he now laid aside. The other threw down his dark double mantle with its clasps, and the knotty staff of mountain olive that he carried. Then they looked round, chose a satisfactory spot near by, and told their friends to sit down in separate groups on the sands.

In build and stature the two men showed a complete contrast. Amycus made one think of some monstrous offspring of the ogre Typhoeus or of Earth herself, the kind she used to bear in the old days of her quarrel with Zeus. But Polydeuces was like a star of heaven shining in all its beauty out of the western night. Such was the son of Zeus, with the bloom of the first down still on his cheeks and the twinkle still in his eyes, though in strength and spirit he was hardening like a wild beast.

He began by feinting with his arms to see whether they were still supple and not benumbed by all the hard work and rowing he had done. Amycus did not follow his example, but stood off in silence, eyeing his opponent and all agog at the thought of drawing blood from his breast. And now Amycus' steward Lycoreus placed between them, at the feet of each, a pair of raw-hide gloves thoroughly dried and toughened, and the king addressed the other in his domineering style:

'We will cast no lots for these, but to avoid recriminations later, I make you a present of whichever pair you fancy. So bind them on your hands. And when you have found out you can tell your friends how good I am at cutting dried ox-hide and staining a man's cheeks with blood.'

Polydeuces indulged in no answering taunt. With a quiet smile and no parley he took the pair that lay at his feet. Castor and the great Talaus came up and quickly bound his gauntlets on, with a flow of encouraging words, while Aretus and Ornytus did the same for their king, little knowing that, as ill luck decreed, it was for the last time.

74

They stood apart while this was being done, but when all was ready they put up their heavy fists in front of their faces and went for each other with a will. In a rough sea a great wave will curl up over a ship, but just as it seems ready to pour in across the bulwarks the steersman's skill saves her by a hair's breadth and away she slips. In much the same way, though the king attacked, always following up and never giving him a moment's rest, Polydeuces had the craft to avoid his rushes and remain unscathed. But there were weak points as well as strong in his opponent's savage style, and once he had taken his measure, he stood up to him and gave him punch for punch. The mingled din that came from cheek and jaw as they resounded to the blows and from the dreadful grinding of their teeth was like the incessant hammering in a shipyard where planks are being joined and driven home on the reluctant bolts. And they did not cease to punish one another till they were beaten by sheer lack of breath, and drawing a little apart wiped the streams of sweat from their foreheads, gasping in exhaustion. Then they fell upon each other once more, like two bulls tussling in grim rivalry for a fattened heifer. And now Amycus, rising tiptoe like a man felling an ox, stretched up to his full height and brought his heavy fist down on the other. But Polydeuces dodged the blow by a turn of his head, taking the forearm on the edge of his shoulder. Then, closing warily, he landed him a lightning blow above the ear and smashed the bones inside. Amycus collapsed on his knees in agony; the Minyan lords raised a shout of triumph; and in a moment the man was dead.

But the Bebryces did not desert their king; they all picked up their spears and hardened clubs, and charged at Polydeuces. His comrades, however, stood in front of him with their keen swords unsheathed, and Castor drew first blood, smiting the head of a man who rushed at him, with such force that the severed halves fell down on his shoulders right

75

and left. Polydeuces himself dealt with the huge Itymoneus and Mimas. He took a running jump at Itymoneus, kicked him in the wind, and felled him in the dust. Then, as Mimas came in, he struck him with his right hand above the left eyebrow and tore away his eyelid, leaving the eyeball bare. Meanwhile, Oreides, an ill-conditioned bully who had served the king as squire, wounded Talaus in the side, but failed to kill him: the bronze spear passed under his belt but only cut the skin and did not penetrate. So too, Aretus gave Iphitus, staunch son of Eurytus, a shrewd blow with his hardened club. But Iphitus was not yet doomed to die; it was Aretus who was soon to fall, to Clytius' sword. And now Ancaeus, Lycurgus' valiant son, seized his enormous axe, and holding a black bearskin as a shield on his left arm, hurled himself with fury on the massed foe. Telamon and Peleus dashed in with him and warlike Jason joined the charge.

Picture a great flock of sheep thrown into panic on a winter's day when the grey wolves have fallen on the folds, eluding shepherds and keen-scented dogs alike. There stand the wolves, inspecting their assembled prey and wondering which to pounce on first and carry off, while all that the sheep can do is to huddle in a mass and trample on each other's backs. Such was the terror that the Argonauts inspired in their presumptuous enemies.

These could no longer stand their ground. They scattered like a great swarm of bees when shepherds or bee-keepers smoke them in their rocky hive. For a while there is tumult in the home and an angry buzzing from the crowded bees; then, when the black smoke has done its work, they dart out from the rock and scatter far and wide. So did the Bebryces, fleeing inland and spreading the news of Amycus' death. Meanwhile another unforeseen disaster was upon them. The poor fools did not know that at this very time their vineyards and villages, deserted by their king, were being ravaged by the hostile arms of Lycus and his Mariandyni, a tribe who had fought them time and again for the possession of the iron-bearing land. And the Argonauts were pillaging their cattle-yards and folds, and rounding up large flocks of sheep.

The victors began to wonder what greater cowardice the Bebryces could have displayed if fortune had permitted Heracles himself to meet them. 'Had he been here,' said one young lord, 'there would certainly have been no sparring. The great club would soon have made the king forget his pride and all the rules he came up to proclaim. And that is the man whom we marooned! Now that we have lost him, we shall soon learn one and all what blind fools we have been.' But what he did not know was that the pattern of all these events had been designed by Zeus.

They stayed there through the night, tended their wounded and with an offering to the immortal gods prepared a mighty feast. Nobody fell asleep by the wine-bowl and the blazing sacrifice. They crowned their golden heads with bay from the tree on the shore round which they had cast their hawsers, and in harmony with Orpheus' lyre they sang a song in praise of Polydeuces, Therapnaean son of Zeus. Their music charmed the windless shore.

When the sun came back from the world's end to light the dewy hills and wake the shepherds, they loosed their hawsers from the trunk of the bay-tree, and after stowing in the ship all of their booty that might be of use, they sailed up the swirling Bosporus before the wind. But here there loomed ahead of them a great wave mountain-high, which over-topped the clouds and threatened to engulf them. Full of menace it hung in the sky above the very centre of the ship – they seemed to be inevitably doomed. Yet even so it came to nothing: all that was needed was a good hand at the helm. And so, through the skill of Tiphys, they came away unhurt, though badly frightened; and the next day they brought their ship to rest on the coast that faces the Bithynian land.

Here by the sea was the home of Phineus son of Agenor.

Phoebus had once endowed this man with prophetic powers, but the gift had brought on him the most appalling tribulations. For he showed no reverence even for Zeus, whose sacred purposes he did not scruple to disclose in full to all. Zeus punished him for this by giving him a lingering old age, without the boon of sight. He even robbed him of such pleasure as he might have got from the many dainties which neighbours kept bringing to his house when they came there to consult the oracle. On every such occasion the Harpies swooped down through the clouds and snatched the food from his mouth and hands with their beaks, sometimes leaving him not a morsel, sometimes a few scraps, so that he might live and be tormented. They gave a loathsome stench to everything. What bits were left emitted such a smell that no one could have borne to put them in his mouth or even to come near.

But directly Phineus heard the voices and footsteps of the Argonauts he knew that these visitors were the very men at whose arrival Zeus had told him he would once more be permitted to enjoy his food. He rose from his bed, like a phantom in a dream, and with the aid of a staff crept to the door on withered feet, feeling his way along the walls. Weakness and age made his limbs tremble as he walked; his shrivelled flesh was caked with dirt, and his bones were held together only by the skin. When he had come out from the hall, his knees gave way and he sat down on the threshold of the courtyard. And there he swooned. The ground beneath him seemed to reel; and he sank down in a coma without the power to speak or stir.

When the Argonauts saw this, they gathered round him in amazement; and after some time Phineus painfully recovered breath enough to speak and uttered these prophetic words:

'Listen to me, flower of Hellenic chivalry, if you are indeed the crew of *Argo*, led by Jason in quest of the fleece at a cruel king's command. Yes, you are they – knowledge of everything still comes to my prophetic soul, for which I render thanks to you, my Lord Apollo, Leto's Son, crushed though I am beneath a load of suffering. And now, by Zeus the suppliants' god, who is the sternest judge of sinful men, by Phoebus, and by Here too, whose special favour brought you here, I beseech you to help me, to save a luckless man from degradation and not to pass on unconcernedly and leave me as I am. Not only has the Fury quenched my sight, so that I drag myself through my last years in misery, but over and above all this I am the victim of another curse, which plagues me more than all. Harpies who live in some abominable haunt that lies beyond our ken swoop down on me and snatch the food from my lips. There is nothing I can do to stop them. It would be easier for me, when I am hungry, to forget my appetite than it would be to escape from them, so swiftly do they dart down from the sky. And if they leave me any food at all it stinks of putrefaction, the smell is intolerable, and no one could bear to come near it, even for a moment, even if he had an adamantine will. Yet bitter necessity that cannot be gainsaid, not only keeps me there, but forces me to pamper my accursed belly.

'But there is an oracle which says that these Harpies shall be dealt with by the two sons of the North Wind – no unknown foreigner shall drive them off. That is the truth, if I indeed am Phineus, once famous for his wealth and his prophetic skill, Phineus, Agenor's son, who when he ruled in Thrace won Cleopatra, sister of that pair, with his bridal gifts and brought her to his home.'

Phineus had spoken; and the young lords were all stirred to pity, Zetes and Calaïs more than any. Brushing their tears away these two went up to the sorrowful old man, and Zetes took his hand in his.

'Poor man!' he said. 'I cannot think that anyone on earth has more to bear than you. What is the reason for this persecution? Have you been rash enough to offend the gods by

79

some misuse of your prophetic skill? Is that why they are so angry with you? We should be quick to help you, if it were true that we are destined for this honour. Yet the thought fills us with dismay. No one is left in doubt when Heaven is punishing a mortal man. And for all our eagerness we dare not undertake to foil the Harpies when they come, unless you can assure us on oath that by doing so we shall not lose the favour of the gods.'

The old man opened his sightless eyes, and raising them as though to look him in the face, replied to Zetes:

'Say no more, my child. I beg you not to entertain such fears. I swear by Leto's Son, who of his own accord taught me prophetic lore; by my own ill-starred fate; by the dark cloud that veils my eyes; by the Powers below – and may they blast me if I die forsworn – that you will not incur the wrath of Heaven by helping me.'

Reassured by these oaths, the pair were eager to take up his cause. The younger members of the party immediately prepared a meal for the old man – the last pickings that the Harpies were to get from him – while Zetes and Calaïs took their stand beside him ready to smite them with their swords when they attacked. And Phineus had scarcely taken the first morsel up when, with as little warning as a whirlwind or a lightning flash, they dropped from the clouds proclaiming their desire for food with raucous cries. The young lords saw them coming and raised the alarm. Yet they had hardly done so before the Harpies had devoured the whole meal and were on the wing once more, far out at sea. All they left was an intolerable stench.

Raising their swords, the two sons of the North Wind flew off in pursuit. Zeus gave them indefatigable strength; indeed, without his aid, there could have been no chase, for whenever the Harpies came to Phineus' house or left it they outstripped the storm winds from the West. But Zetes and Calaïs very nearly caught them. They even touched them,

though to little purpose, with their finger-tips, like a couple
of keen hounds on a hillside, hot on the track of a horned
goat or a deer, pressing close behind the quarry and snapping
at the empty air. Yet even with Heaven against them, the long
chase would certainly have ended in their tearing the Harpies
to pieces when they overtook them at the Floating Isles, but
for Iris of the Swift Feet, who when she saw them leapt down
from Olympus through the sky and checked them with these
words:

'Sons of Boreas, you may not touch the Harpies with your
swords: they are the hounds of almighty Zeus. But I myself
will undertake on oath that never again shall they come near
to Phineus.' And she went on to swear by the waters of Styx,
the most portentous and inviolable oath that any god can
take, that the Harpies should never visit Phineus' house again,
such being Fate's decree. This oath prevailed upon the noble
brothers, who wheeled round and set their course for safety
and the ship; which is the reason why the Floating Isles have
changed their name and are now called the Islands of Return.
The Harpies and Iris went their different ways. The Harpies
withdrew to a den in Minoan Crete, and Iris soared up to
Olympus, cleaving the air with her unflagging wings.

Meanwhile the other Argonauts, after washing all the filth
from the old man's body, picked out the finest of the sheep
they had recently acquired at Amycus' expense and made a
sacrifice. Then they set out a splendid banquet in the hall
and sat down to enjoy it. Phineus joined them and ate
ravenously; he was as happy as a man in a delightful dream.
They took their fill of meat and drink and stayed awake all
night, waiting for Zetes and Calaïs to return. The old man
sat among them by the hearth, and for their benefit rehearsed
the stages of their future journey to its very end.

'Listen now,' he said. 'You are not entitled to know every
detail, but I will tell you what the gods permit. At one time,
in my folly, I was rash enough to disclose the plans of Zeus

from start to finish. I now realize that he himself intends a prophet's revelations to be incomplete, so that humanity may miss some part of Heaven's design.

'When you leave me, the first thing you see will be the two Cyanean Rocks, at the end of the straits. To the best of my knowledge, no one has ever made his way between them, for not being fixed to the bottom of the sea they frequently collide, flinging up the water in a seething mass which falls on the rocky flanks of the straits with a resounding roar. Now if, as I take it, you are god-fearing travellers and men of sense, you will be advised by me: you will not rashly throw away your lives or rush into danger with the recklessness of youth. Make an experiment first. Send out a dove from *Argo* to explore the way. If she succeeds in flying in between the Rocks and out across the sea, do not hesitate to follow in her path, but get a firm grip on your oars and cleave the water of the straits. For that is the time when salvation will depend, not on your prayers, but on your strength of arm. So think of nothing else, be firm, and spend your energies on what will pay you best. By all means pray to the gods, but choose an earlier moment. And if the dove flies on, but comes to grief midway, turn back. It is always better to submit to Heaven; and you could not possibly escape a dreadful end. The Rocks would crush you, even if *Argo* were an iron ship. Ah, my poor friends, I do implore you not to disregard my counsel from the gods, even if you imagine their hatred of myself to be far more bitter than in fact it is. Do not dare to sail farther in, if the bird's failure warns you to desist.

'Well, all this will happen as it must. But if you come safely through the Clashing Rocks into the Black Sea, sail on with the land of the Bithynians on your right, shunning the coastal surf, till you round the mouth of the swift River Rhebas and the Black Cape and come to harbour in the Isle of Thynias. From that point, sail on a little way and beach your ship on the coast of the Mariandyni, which lies opposite.

Here there is a path that leads down to Hades' realm, and rising high above it, the promontory of Acherusias, where the swirling waters of Acheron gush up from the very bowels of the rock and pour down to the sea by way of a deep ravine. A little farther on, you will skirt the hilly land of the Paphlagonians, where Eneteian Pelops reigned. He was their first king and the people claim descent from him.

'Opposite Helice the Bear there is a foreland called Carambis, steep on every side and presenting to the sea a lofty pinnacle which splits the wind-stream from the North in two. When you have rounded this, the whole length of Aegialus will lie before you. But at the very end of it the coast juts out, and there the waters of Halys come down with a terrific roar. Near by, the smaller River Iris rolls foaming to the sea; and farther east a great and lofty cape is thrust out from the land. Then comes the mouth of the River Thermodon, which, after wandering across the continent, flows into a quiet bay by the cape of Themiscyra. Here is the plain of Doeas, and the three towns of the Amazons near by. The Chalybes come next, a miserable tribe, whose land is rugged and intractable; but they toil away and work the iron that it yields. Near them live the sheep-farming Tibareni, beyond the Genetaean Cape, sacred to Zeus the strangers' god. Next, and marching with them, are the Mossynoeci. These people occupy the forest lands below the mountains. They build their wooden houses in the form of towers, which they call 'mossynes', taking their own name from their well-constructed homes. When you have left these behind, you must beach your ship on a low-lying island, though not before you find some means of driving off the innumerable birds that haunt the lonely shore and pay no deference to man. Here the Queens of the Amazons, Otrere and Antiope, built a marble shrine for Ares when they were going to war. And here I advise you – and you know I am your friend – to stay a little while; for a godsend will come to you out of the bitter brine. But I must not sin again by telling you in detail all that I myself foresee.

'Beyond the island and the mainland opposite, live the Philyres; beyond them the Macrones; and farther still the numerous tribes of the Becheiri. Next to these live the Sapeires; beyond their borders, the Byzeres; and beyond them again the warlike Colchians themselves. But sail on till you come to the farthest corner of the Black Sea. There, in the land of Cytaïs, a broad river, which comes from the distant Amarantian Mountains over the Circaean plain, rolls swiftly to the sea. This is the Phasis. Drive *Argo* into the marshes at its mouth, and you will see the walls of King Aeetes' city and the dark grove of Ares, where the fleece is spread on the top of an oak, watched over by a serpent, a formidable beast who peers all round and never, night or day, allows sweet sleep to conquer his unblinking eyes.'

His recital left the Argonauts dismayed. There was a long silence, which the lord Jason was the first to break. He was unmanned by his misgivings.

'Sir,' he said, 'you have rehearsed the hazards of our voyage and brought us to our destination. You have given us the clue for our passage through the hateful Rocks into the Black Sea. But what I also wish to learn from you is whether, after escaping them, we shall get safely back to Hellas. How shall I manage? How am I to find my way once more across that vast expanse of water? My comrades are as inexperienced as I am; and Colchian Aea lies at the far end of the Black Sea and of the world itself.'

'My son,' the old man replied, 'once you have made the passage of the deadly Rocks, fear nothing, for some Power will lead you back from Aea by a different route, and on the outward journey there will be guides enough. But remember this, my friends. You could have no better ally than that artful goddess, Aphrodite. Indeed the happy issue of your venture hangs on her. But question me no more.'

Phineus had scarcely finished when the two sons of
Thracian Boreas came swooping from the sky and brought
their winged feet to rest on the threshold. The moment
they saw them, the whole company leapt from their seats,
and Zetes, still panting from exertion, told his eager friends
how long the chase had been; how Iris had saved the Harpies'
lives, but with a gracious undertaking for the time to come;
and how the frightened monsters had taken refuge in the
great cavern under the cliff of Dicte. The news delighted
everybody in the hall, their own friends as well as Phineus
himself, and Jason in all kindness wished him joy.

'There was a god then, after all,' he said, 'who cared for
you in your terrible affliction and brought us here from distant lands so that the sons of Boreas might save you. If he
should also give you back your sight, I should be as happy as
I shall be if I reach my home again.'

But the old man bowed his head in sorrow and replied:
'Lord Jason, my sight is past recall. My eyes are ruined and
there is no cure. I pray, instead, for death to take me soon.
When I am dead I shall partake of perfect bliss.'

Thus for a little while the two conversed. They were still
engaged in talk when the first light of dawn appeared. And
now there came to Phineus' house the daily crowd of visitors
with their customary offerings from their own larders. The
old man had always treated rich and poor with equal courtesy,
telling their fortunes and in many cases saving them from evil
by his own foreknowledge. No wonder that they came there
and looked after him.

On this occasion they were joined by his best friend,
Paraebius, who was delighted to find a party of strangers in
the house, since Phineus had once told him that a band of
noblemen on their way from Hellas to Aeetes' city would
come to land on the Thynian coast and with the good will
of Zeus put an end to the Harpies' depredations. So now the
old man, after satisfying his visitors with sage replies to their

enquiries, dismissed them all except Paraebius, whom he invited to stay there with his noble guests. But presently he sent him too away, telling him to come back with the finest of his sheep. And when Paraebius had left the hall he addressed the oarsmen of *Argo* in a gentle voice:

'You see, my friends, that not everyone is graceless or forgetful of benefits received. I am thinking of Paraebius, who came here just now to have his fortune told. There was a time in that man's life when the more he toiled the harder he found it to keep body and soul together. He sank lower day by day, and there was no respite from his labours. He was paying in misery for a sin committed by his father, who had refused to listen to a Hamadryad's prayers when he was felling trees one day, alone in the mountains. She wished him to spare the stump of an oak which was as old as she and had been her only home for many a long year. She wept and pleaded with him piteously. But in the headstrong arrogance of youth he cut it down; and in revenge the nymph laid a curse on him and his children. When Paraebius consulted me, I realized the nature of the sin and told him to build an altar to the Thynian nymph and there make an offering in atonement, with prayers for release from his father's doom. Thus he escaped the wrath of Heaven, and never since that day has he forgotten or neglected me. Indeed, he is so determined to stand by me in my troubles that I find it very hard to make him leave the house.'

He had no sooner finished than Paraebius reappeared, bringing two of his sheep along with him. At a word from Phineus, Jason and the two sons of Boreas bestirred themselves and, as evening fell, made a sacrifice on the hearth with invocations to Apollo, Lord of prophecy. The younger men prepared a sumptuous feast, and when all had enjoyed it they lay down to sleep, some by the ship's hawsers, others in groups in various parts of the house.

But at dawn the Etesian Winds were blowing in full force,

as they do throughout the world by an ordinance from Zeus. This is how it came about. Folk say that once upon a time there was a shepherdess called Cyrene who used to graze her flocks in the water-meadows of Peneus. She was a virgin and she prized her maidenhood. But one day when she was tending her sheep down by the river, Apollo carried her off from Haemonia and set her down among the nymphs of the land in distant Libya near the Myrtosian Mount. There she bore him a son called Aristaeus, who is remembered now in the cornlands of Haemonia as the Hunter and the Shepherd. Cyrene herself was left in Libya by Apollo, who in token of his love made her a nymph and huntress with the gift of a long life. But he took his infant son away to be brought up by Cheiron in his cave. When the child had grown up the divine Muses found him a bride, taught him the arts of healing and prophecy, and made him the shepherd of all their flocks that grazed on the Athamantian plain in Phthia, round Mount Othrys and in the valley of the sacred River Apidanus. There came a time, however, when Aristaeus migrated. The Dog-star Sirius was scorching the Minoan Islands from the sky, and the people could find no permanent cure for the trouble till the Archer-King Apollo put it in their heads to send for Aristaeus. So, at his father's command, Aristaeus assembled the Parrhasian tribe, who are descendants of Lycaon, left Phthia, and settled in Ceos. He raised a great altar to the Rain-god Zeus and made ritual offerings in the hills to the Dog-star and to Zeus himself, the Son of Cronos. In response, Zeus gave his orders – and the Etesian Winds refresh the earth for forty days. The priests of Ceos still make yearly sacrifice before the rising of the Dog.

That is the story of the winds that now detained the Argonauts in Thynia. Every day, to please Phineus, the people sent them generous gifts. In the end the young lords built an altar to the Blessed Twelve on the beach beyond the house and after laying offerings on it, embarked and sat down to the oars. And they did not forget the bird that they must carry with them. Euphemus took the shy dove in his hands and brought her on board, trembling with fright, before they cast their double hawsers off.

Argo's departure did not escape Athene's eye. She promptly took her stand on a cloud which, though light, could bear her formidable weight, and swept down to the sea, filled with concern for the oarsmen in the ship. There comes a moment to the patient traveller (and there are many such that wander far afield) when the road ahead of him is clear and the distance so foreshortened that he has a vision of his home, he sees his way to it over land and sea, and in his fancy travels there and back so quickly that it seems to stand before his eager eyes. Such was Athene's speed as she darted down to set foot on the inhospitable coast of Thynia.

In due course they found themselves entering the narrowest part of the winding straits. Rugged cliffs hemmed them in on either side, and *Argo* as she advanced began to feel a swirling undercurrent. They moved ahead in fear, for now the clash of the colliding Rocks and the thunder of surf on the shores fell ceaselessly on their ears. Euphemus seized the dove and climbed on to the prow, while the oarsmen, at Tiphys' orders, made a special effort, hoping by their own strength of arm to drive *Argo* through the Rocks forthwith. They rounded a bend and saw a thing that no one after them has seen – the Rocks were moving apart. Their hearts sank; but now Euphemus launched the dove on her flight and the eyes of all were raised to watch her as she passed between the Rocks.

Once more the Rocks met face to face with a resounding crash, flinging a great cloud of spray into the air. The sea gave a terrific roar and the broad sky rang again. Caverns underneath the crags bellowed as the sea came surging in. A great wave broke against the cliffs and the white foam swept high above them. *Argo* was spun round as the flood reached her.

But the dove got through, unscathed but for the tips of her tail-feathers, which were nipped off by the Rocks. The oarsmen gave a cry of triumph and Tiphys shouted at them to row with all their might, for the Rocks were opening again. So they rowed on full of dread, till the backwash, overtaking them, thrust *Argo* in between the Rocks. Then the fears of all were turned to panic. Sheer destruction hung above their heads.

They had already reached a point where they could see the vast sea opening out on either side, when they were suddenly faced by a tremendous billow arched like an overhanging rock. They bent their heads down at the sight, for it seemed about to fall and overwhelm the ship. But Tiphys just in time checked her as she plunged forward, and the great wave slid under her keel. Indeed it raised her stern so high in the air that she was carried clear of the Rocks. Euphemus ran along shouting to all his friends to put their backs into their rowing, and with answering shouts they struck the water. Yet for every foot that *Argo* made she lost two, though the oars bent like curved bows as the men put out their strength.

But now another overhanging wave came rushing down on them, and when *Argo* had shot end-on like a rolling-pin through the hollow lap of this terrific sea, she found herself held back by the swirling tide just in the place where the Rocks met. To right and left they shook and rumbled; but *Argo* could not budge.

This was the moment when Athene intervened. Holding on to the hard rock with her left hand, she pushed the ship through with the other; and *Argo* clove the air like a winged arrow, though even so the Rocks, clashing in their accustomed way, sheared off the tip of the mascot on the stern. When the men had thus got through unhurt, Athene soared up to Olympus. But the Rocks were now rooted for ever in one spot close to one another. It had been decided by the happy gods that this should be their fate when a human being had seen them and sailed through. The Argonauts, freed from the cold grip of panic, breathed again when they saw the sky once more and the vast ocean stretching out ahead. They felt that they had come through Hell alive.

Tiphys was the first to speak. 'I think,' he said, 'that we can say all's well. *Argo* is safe and so are we. And for that, to whom are we indebted but Athene, who endowed the ship with supernatural strength when Argus drove the bolts home in her planks? *Argo* shall not be caught; that seems to be a law. And so, Lord Jason, now that Heaven has allowed us to pass safely through the Rocks, I beg you not to dread so much the duty that your king assigned you. Has not Phineus told us that from now on we shall meet no obstacle we cannot easily surmount?'

Tiphys, with that, steered straight across the open sea along the Bithynian coast. But Jason, for his own purposes, took him gently to task. 'Tiphys,' he said, 'why do you try to comfort me in my distress? I was blind and made a fatal error. When Pelias ordered me to undertake this mission, I ought to have refused outright, even though he would have torn me limb from limb without compunction. But as things are, I am obsessed by fears and intolerable anxiety, hating the thought of the cruel sea that we must cross and of what may happen when we land and find the natives hostile, as we are sure to do at every point. Ever since you all rallied to my side these cares have occupied my mind, and when each day is done I spend the night in misery. It is easy for you, Tiphys, to talk in a cheerful vein. You are only concerned for your own life, whereas I care nothing for mine, but *am* concerned for each and all alike, you and the rest of my friends. How can I tell whether I shall bring you safely back to Hellas?'

Jason's speech, which was designed to put his noble comrades to the test, met with acclamation. His heart was warmed by their reassuring cries and he spoke again, this time with greater candour. 'My friends, your courage fills me with fresh confidence. The resolution that you show in face of awful perils makes me feel that I could go through Hell itself and fear nothing. However, now that we have left the Clashing Rocks behind us I have no reason to expect another such ordeal, provided that we keep to the course laid down for us by Phineus.'

This ended the discussion and they now devoted all their energies to rowing. Before long they passed the swift River Rhebas and the peak of Colone, and soon after that the Black Cape, and then the outfall of the River Phyllis. It was here that Phrixus son of Athamas had been entertained by Dipsacus when he was flying with his ram from the city of Orchomenus. This Dipsacus was the son of a meadow-nymph and the River Phyllis. He was an unassuming person who was quite content to live with his mother by his father's stream and graze his flocks beside the sea. The Argonauts could see, as they passed them in turn, his shrine, and the broad banks of the river, and the plain, and the deep stream of Calpe; and all that day and through the windless night they laboured at the indefatigable oar. They worked like oxen ploughing the moist earth. The sweat pours down from flank and neck; their rolling eyes glare out askance from under the yoke; hot blasts of breath come rumbling from their mouths; and all day long they labour, digging their hoofs into the soil. Thus the crew of *Argo* all through the night ploughed the salt water with their oars.

But at that time of day when heavenly light has not yet come, nor is there utter darkness, but the faint glimmer that we call twilight spreads over the night and wakes us, they ran into the harbour of the lonely isle of Thynias and went ashore exhausted by their labours. Here they had a vision of Apollo on his way from Lycia to visit the remote and teeming peoples of the North. The golden locks streamed down his cheeks in clusters as he moved; he had a silver bow in his left hand and a quiver slung on his back; the island quaked beneath his feet and the sea ran high on the shore. They were awe-struck at the sight and no one dared to face the god and meet his lovely eyes. They stood there with bowed heads while he, aloof, passed through the air on his way across the sea.

Orpheus found his voice at last. 'Come now,' he said to the Argonauts, 'let us dedicate this island to Apollo of the Dawn and call it by that name, since it was here that we all saw him pass by in the dawn. We will build an altar on the shore and make such offerings as we have at our command. Later, if he grants us a safe return to Haemonia, we will sacrifice to him the thighs of horned goats. Now, let us propitiate him as best we can, with libations and the scent of burnt-offerings. Lord of the Vision, look kindly upon us.'

They set to work at once. Some built an altar with shingle, while others explored the island in the hope of catching sight of a fawn or a wild goat. Its forest pastures promised well, and with the aid of Leto's son they found their game. Then, with due ritual, they wrapped all the thigh bones in fat, burnt them on the sacred altar with invocations to Apollo of the Dawn and danced in a wide ring round the burning sacrifice singing 'Glory to Phoebus; glory to the Healing God!' The lord Orpheus joined them in their worship. Striking his Bistonian lyre, he told them in song how Apollo long ago, when he was still a beardless youth rejoicing in his locks, slew the monster Delphyne with his bow beneath the rocky brow of Parnassus. 'Be gracious to us, King,' he sang, 'and may thy tresses for ever be unshorn, intact for ever! That is their due, the locks that only Leto strokes with her fond hands.' And he sang to them of the daughters of Pleistus, the Corycian Nymphs, who had encouraged the god by their repeated cry of 'Healer'. 'That,' he told them, 'is the origin of the beautiful refrain with which you have been hymning Phoebus.'

When the Argonauts had worshipped the god with dance

and song, they made holy libations and touching the sacrifice
as they swore took an oath to stand by one another in unity
for ever. A temple of Concord can be seen on the spot to this
very day. They built it themselves in honour of the glorious
goddess.

With dawn on the third day there came a fresh west wind,
and they left the lofty island. Skirting the mainland coast,
they saw in turn the mouth of the River Sangarius, the fertile
lands of the Mariandyni, the River Lycus and the Anthemoei-
sian lagoon. The ship's halyards and all the other tackle
quivered in the wind as they sped along; but during the night
the breeze dropped, and with thankful hearts they made
harbour at dawn by the Cape of Acherusias. This lofty headland, with its sheer cliffs, looks out across the Bithynian Sea.
Beneath it at sea level lies a solid platform of smooth rock on
which the rollers break and roar, while high up on the very
summit plane trees spread out their branches. On the land-
ward side it falls away in a hollow glen. Here is the Cavern
of Hades with its overhanging trees and rocks, from the chill
depths of which an icy breath comes up and each morning
covers everything with sparkling rime that melts under the
midday sun. The frowning headland is never visited by
silence; a murmur from the sounding sea mingles for ever
with the rustling of the leaves as they are shaken by the
winds from Hades' Cave.

Here too is the mouth of the River Acheron, which issues
from the mountain-side and falls, by way of a deep ravine,
into the eastern sea. On a later occasion the Megarians of
Nisaea, when on their way to settle in the land of the Mariandyni, had good reason to call this river the Sailors' Saviour:
the harbour at its mouth saved them and their ships when they
were caught in a violent gale. The Argonauts brought their
ship to the same spot. Shortly after the wind had dropped,
they beached her in the shelter of the Acherusian Cape.

Lycus, the local chieftain, and his Mariandyni soon got

word of their arrival. These were surely the slayers of Amycus
– so much they had already heard. And it was quite enough;
they made a league with them forthwith. As for Polydeuces,
they flocked in from every side to welcome him as a god,
bearing in mind their own long struggles with the insolent
Bebryces. Then they all went up to the city like good friends
and spent the day in feasting and agreeable talk in the palace of
Lycus. Jason gave him the name and lineage of each of his
men, and after explaining his mission went on to tell him
of the welcome they had had from the Lemnian women,
and of their dealings with the Doliones of Cyzicus; how they
reached Mysia and Cius, where much against their will they
had left the noble Heracles; of Glaucus's advice; of the
slaying of Amycus and his men, the afflictions and prophecies
of Phineus, their escape from the Cyanean Rocks, and their
meeting with Apollo on the island. Lycus was enthralled by
the tale, but he grieved for the abandoned Heracles and spoke
of him, addressing all the Argonauts:

'My friends, what a powerful ally you have lost for the
rest of your long journey to Colchis. I say this because I
well remember seeing him in my father Dascylus's palace
when he had come to us overland on foot with the belt of
the fighting Amazon Hippolyte. I was a lad then with the
first down on my cheeks. Some Mysians had killed my
brother Priolas, whom the people still lament with the most
piteous dirges, and at the funeral games Heracles beat the
great boxer Titias, the finest and most powerful of our
youths – he knocked out all his teeth. Then he subdued for
my father, not only the Mysians, but the Phrygians whose
fields march with ours, and also the Bithynian tribes, con-
quering their lands as far as the mouth of the Rhebas and the
peak of Colone. After which, Pelops's Paphlagonians, those
whose land is scoured by the dark waters of Billaeus, gave
in to him without a blow.

'But now that Heracles is far away the Bebryces and their

brutal king have long been preying on me. They have cut off large parcels of my land, thrusting their frontier right up to the meadows watered by the deep River Hypius. However, they have paid the price through you. Indeed I think that Heaven had a hand in things that day when Tyndareus' son killed Amycus and so provoked the Bebryces to fight. And I am most willing to repay you by any means within my power. It is only proper that the weak should recompense the strong when they take steps to help them. So now I shall ask Dascylus, my son, to join you in your enterprise. With him on board you will encounter none but friends on your voyage, up to the mouth of the Thermodon itself. Not only that, but I propose to build high up on the Acherusian Cape a great temple to the sons of Tyndareus for sailors out at sea to mark and reverence; and then I will dedicate to them, as gods, some rich acres of the fertile plain outside the town.'

All that day they feasted and made merry; but at dawn they hurried down to the ship. Lycus himself went with them. He had loaded them with countless gifts and he brought his son from home to sail with them.

But at this moment Fate intervened and Idmon son of Abas met his predestined end. He was a learned soothsayer, but not all his prophetic lore could save him now: he had to die. In the water-meadow by a reedy stream there lay a white-tusked boar cooling his flanks and huge belly in the mud. This evil brute, who was feared even by the meadow-sprites, lived all alone in the wide fen, and no one was the wiser. But now, as Idmon made his way along the dykes of the muddy river, the boar leapt out of some hidden lair in the reeds, charged at him and gashed his thigh, severing the sinews and the bone itself. Idmon fell to the ground with a sharp cry. The others gave their stricken friend an answering shout, and Peleus quickly aimed his javelin at the murderous boar as he beat his retreat into the fen. The beast turned and charged again. But this time Idas wounded him, and with a loud grunt he fell impaled on the well-aimed spear. They left him where he fell, but they carried Idmon, who was at his last gasp, to the ship with heavy hearts; and he died in his friends' arms.

All thoughts of sailing were abandoned; they waited there in sorrow for the funeral of their friend. For three days they mourned him and on the fourth they buried him with signal honours. The people and King Lycus himself took part in the rites, and when they had laid him in the earth they slaughtered many sheep, as is a dead man's due. A barrow too was raised near by in the hero's honour, bearing a monument that may still be seen in these latter days, the trunk of a wild olive big enough to make a roller for a ship. It is still alive and putting out its leaves not far below the Acherusian height. But if the whole story must be told (and here I am guided by the Muse), although Apollo strictly commanded the Boeotians and Nisaeans to revere Idmon as the guardian of their settlement and build their town round the trunk of this old olive, they venerate Agamestor to this very day instead of Idmon the god-fearing Aeolid.

Meanwhile the Argonauts soon had to build a second barrow for another comrade dead: two monuments still mark the place. Who then was the next to die? The story goes that it was Tiphys son of Hagnias whom Destiny allowed to sail no farther. There on the spot, far from his home, a short illness laid him to rest while the company paid funeral honours to the son of Abas. Their grief at this catastrophe was profound, and when they had buried him also, close to the other, they cast themselves down by the sea in despair and lay there wrapped up like figures cut in stone, without a word and with no thought of food or drink. There was no spirit left in them; all hope of finding their way back was gone, and they might have stayed there in their grief still longer, had not the goddess Here filled Ancaeus with the courage that dares all. This man was a son of the Sea-god, borne to him by Astypalaea near the waters of Imbrasus, and steersmanship was his especial skill. He ran up to Peleus and said:

'My lord, what sense is there in giving up the quest and wasting time in this outlandish spot? Jason brought me all the way from Parthenia to help him find the fleece, not because I am a fighter, but because I do know something about ships. So believe me, you need have no fears at all for *Argo*. And I am not the only one; there are others here who know the sea. Not one of them would lead us into trouble if we put him at the helm. I beg you to pass all this on at once and to remind them boldly of their duty.'

Peleus' heart leapt up for joy and he quickly summoned the others. 'My friends,' he said, 'why indulge in this unprofitable grief? When our two comrades died, that must have been their destiny. But we have other steersmen with us, plenty of them. On, then, with our adventure; there is no excuse for loitering. Wake up, I say, and work, casting your sorrows to the winds.'

But Jason took him up; he could see no light ahead. 'My lord Peleus,' he said, 'where are these pilots of yours? The seamen whom we used to count on are even more despondent and unmanned than I am. Indeed, I see nothing for us but a fate as sad as that of our lost friends. For it looks as though we should neither reach the terrible Aeetes' city nor find our way back to Hellas past the Clashing Rocks. No, we are doomed to grow old here, inglorious and obscure, with nothing done.'

In spite of this, Ancaeus, inspired by Heaven, promptly undertook to steer the gallant ship. Erginus too, and Nauplius and Euphemus all stood up, eager to have the task. But their comrades held them back as the greater number voted for Ancaeus.

At dawn on the twelfth day a fresh breeze was blowing from the west. So they went on board, rowed swiftly out from the mouth of the Acheron, and then shook out their sail to the wind and forged ahead through clear weather under a broad spread of canvas. They soon came to the mouths of the River Callichorus, where we are told that Dionysus Son of Zeus, when he had left the Indians and was on his way to Thebes, established revels, with dances in front of a cave, in which he himself passed holy and unsmiling nights. Ever since then, the people of the place have called the stream the River of the Lovely Dance, and the cave the Bedchamber.

Next they saw the tomb of Sthenelus son of Actor, who had joined Heracles in his daring attack on the Amazons, and on the way back had died on the beach from an arrow wound. They paused here, for the goddess Persephone sent up to them the mourning ghost of Actor's son, who craved to see some men of his own kind, if only for a moment. He stood on the edge of his barrow and gazed at the ship, appearing to them in his warlike panoply, with the light flashing from the four plates and purple crest of the fine helmet that he used to wear. Then he sank down again into the great abyss. The Argonauts were awestruck at the sight, and Mopsus, speaking as their seer, told them to land and with libations lay the ghost. So they quickly brailed the sail, cast hawsers on the shore, and paid honour to the tomb of Sthenelus. They made libations to him and sacrificed some sheep as offerings to the dead. Then, in a separate place, they built an altar to Apollo, Saver of Ships, and burnt the thighbones of the sheep. Orpheus made an offering of his own. He dedicated a lyre, in memory of which the place is still called Lyra.

When this was done, as the wind was blowing hard, they re-embarked, let down the sail and drew it taut with both sheets. And *Argo* sped eagerly over the sea, like a high-flying hawk that has set its pinions to the breeze, and flapping them no more glides swiftly on across the sunny sky with wings at rest. They were soon past the spot where the Parthenius

flows out to sea; a gentle river this, in whose delectable
waters Artemis refreshes herself before ascending to heaven
after the chase. Then they pressed on in the night without a
stop, passing Sesamus and the crests of Erythini, Crobialus,
Cromna, and wooded Cytorus. At sunrise they rounded Cape
Carambis, and all that day and on through the night they
rowed *Argo* along the endless shores of Aegialus.

They landed on the Assyrian coast, where Zeus himself
had once given a home to Sinope daughter of Asopus,
granting her the boon of virginity. He was trapped by his
own promise. In his passion for the girl he had solemnly
sworn to fulfil her dearest wish, whatever that might be; and
she very cleverly had said, 'I wish to remain a virgin.' By the
same ruse she outwitted Apollo when he made love to her;
and the River-god Halys as well. Men fared no better than
the gods; this woman never was possessed by any lover.

On the coast here, Deïleon, Autolycus, and Phlogius (sons
of the admirable Deïmachus of Tricca) had been living ever
since they lost touch with Heracles. When they saw the
party land from *Argo* and observed their rank, they approached
them, told them who they were and expressed a wish to
leave the place for good. They were taken on board at once,
as the North-West Wind brooked no delay; and the Argonauts, with these recruits, were carried along by the fresh
breeze, leaving behind them the River Halys, its neighbour
the Iris, and the delta-land of Assyria. On the same day they
rounded the distant headland that guards the harbour of the
Amazons. It was here that Melanippe daughter of Ares,
having sallied out one day, was caught in an ambush by the
great Heracles, though he let her go unharmed when her sister
Hippolyte gave him her own resplendent girdle by way of
ransom. And here in the bay beyond the cape, as the sea was
getting rough, the Argonauts ran ashore at the mouth of the
Thermodon.

There is no river like the Thermodon, none that divides

itself into so many branches – only four short of a hundred, if you care to count them all. Yet the real headwater is a single stream which flows down to the lowlands from mountains called the Amazonian Heights, and then on through hilly country, which causes it to follow tortuous ways. Separate streams, at varying distances, meander here and there, each seeking its own easiest way to lower levels. Many of these are swallowed up and end without a name. But there is no mistaking the parent river when, rejoined by a few of them, it bursts with an arching crest of foam into the Inhospitable Sea.

Had the Argonauts stayed here as they intended and come to grips with the Amazons, the fight would have been a bloody one. For the Amazons of the Doeantian plain were by no means gentle, well-conducted folk; they were brutal and aggressive, and their main concern in life was war. War, indeed, was in their blood, daughters of Ares as they were and of the Nymph Harmonia, who lay with the god in the depths of the Acmonian Wood and bore him girls who fell in love with fighting.

But Zeus once more sent forth the North-West Wind, and with its help the Argonauts stood out from the curving shore where the Amazons of Themiscyra were arming for battle. I must explain that the Amazons did not all live in one city; there were three separate tribes settled in different parts of the country. The party on the beach, whose queen at that time was Hippolyte, were Themiscyreans. The Lycastians lived apart, and so did the Chadesians, who were javelin-throwers.

At nightfall on the following day they reached the land of the Chalybes. These people do not use the ploughing ox. They not only grow no corn, but plant no vines or trees for their delicious fruit and graze no flocks in dewy pastures. Their task is to dig for iron in the stubborn ground and they live by selling the metal they produce. To them no morning ever brings a holiday. In a black atmosphere of soot and smoke they live a life of unremitting toil.

Soon after leaving them behind, the Argonauts rounded the headland of Genetaean Zeus and sailed in safety past the country of the Tibareni. Here, when a woman is in childbirth, it is the husband who takes to his bed. He lies there groaning with his head wrapped up and his wife feeds him with loving care. She even prepares the bath for the event.

Next they passed the Sacred Mountain and the highlands where the Mossynoeci live in the *mossynes* or wooden houses from which they take their name. These people have their own ideas of what is right and proper. What we as a rule do openly in town or market-place they do at home; and what we do in the privacy of our houses they do out of doors in the open street, and nobody thinks the worse of them. Even the sexual act puts no one to the blush in this community. On the contrary, like swine in the fields, they lie down on the ground in promiscuous intercourse and are not at all disconcerted by the presence of others. Then again, their king sits in the loftiest hut of all to dispense justice to his numerous subjects. But if the poor man happens to make a mistake in his findings, they lock him up and give him nothing to eat for the rest of the day.

They left these behind them. And now a day of rowing (since the light wind dropped in the night) had brought them almost abreast of Ares' Isle, when they suddenly beheld one of the War-god's birds, which haunt the island, darting through the air. Flapping its wings over the moving ship it dropped a pointed feather down upon her. The plume struck the left shoulder of the noble Oïleus, who let his oar fall at the sudden blow, while the rest looked in amazement at the winged dart. But Eribotes, whose seat was next to his, pulled the feather out, took off the band on which his scabbard hung, and bound up the wound. Then, as though one bird had not sufficed, they saw another swooping in. But this time the lord Clytius son of Eurytus was ready with his bow bent. He let fly an arrow, struck the bird, and brought it spinning down beside the gallant ship. Whereupon Amphidamas son of Aleus was moved to address his friends.

'We are close,' he said, 'to the island of Ares. You can tell by these birds. But as I see it, arrows will not help us much when we try to disembark. If you mean to land, we must remember Phineus' warning and think of some better plan. Why, Heracles himself, when he came to Arcadia, was unable with bow and arrow to drive away the birds that swam on the Stymphalian Lake. I saw the thing myself. What he did was to take his stand on a height and make a din by shaking a bronze rattle; and the astounded birds flew off into the distance screeching for fear. We must take our cue from him. I myself have had an idea which I should like to put to you. I suggest that you should all set your crested helmets on your heads and take it in turns, one half to row, the others to protect the ship with their polished spears and shields. Then the whole company must raise a most terrific shout, so that the birds may be scared away by a noise that will be new to them, as well as by the nodding crests and above them your uplifted spears. When we reach the island, if we make it, you can raise a tremendous racket by banging on your shields.'

His sensible suggestion pleased them all, and they put their helmets on their heads; the glinting bronze and the purple crests waving on top were enough to frighten anyone. Then half the crew rowed in turn while the others covered up the ship with their spears and shields. Locking the shields together, they roofed her over, as a man roofs his house with firmly fitted overlapping tiles, both to add to its beauty and keep out the rain. And the shout that went up from the ship was like the roar that comes from battling armies when the lines charge and meet. However, they did not see a single bird till they reached the island and banged on their shields. Then the birds in their thousands rose into the air and after fluttering about in panic, discharged a heavy shower of feathery darts at the ship as they beat a hasty retreat over the sea towards the mainland hills. But the Argonauts sat there in comfort, like people in a town on which the Son of Cronos has discharged a hail-storm from the clouds. They hear the hailstones rattle on their roofs, but they do not worry. The stormy season has not caught them unprepared: they have roofed their houses well.

Now you may ask what Phineus had in mind when he advised this princely company to put in at such a place. What could they hope to get by landing there?

On the very day of their arrival it happened that the sons of Phrixus were close by. They had left King Aeetes and were on their way to the city of Orchomenus in a Colchian ship. Their purpose was to recover their father's rich possessions. He himself had told them on his death-bed to undertake the voyage. But Zeus had roused the North Wind to show his might, and signalled by a downpour the rainy advent of Arcturus. All day Boreas blew softly through the topmost branches of the mountain trees and scarcely stirred the leaves. But at nightfall he fell on the sea with tremendous force and raised the billows with his shrieking blasts. A dark mist blotted out the sky; not a star showed through the clouds; on all sides nothing but impenetrable murk. The sons of Phrixus, drenched and quaking for their lives, were carried along at the mercy of the waves. But now the fury of the wind tore away their sail and split the battered hull in two. However, all four men, prompted by the gods, managed to get hold of a huge beam, one of the many firmly-bolted timbers that were scattered when the ship broke up; and wind and waves were driving them towards the island more dead than alive, when a sudden and terrific rain-storm added to their troubles. It lashed the sea, the island, and all of the mainland opposite that was occupied by the savage Mossy-

THE VOYAGE OF ARGO

noeci. But at last, in the murky night, the driving billows flung the sons of Phrixus and their mighty beam on the island beach; and the floods of rain from Zeus ceased as the sun rose.

The two parties soon approached and met each other. Argus son of Phrixus was the first to speak. 'Whoever you may be,' he said to the Argonauts, 'we beseech you by all-seeing Zeus to treat us kindly and help us in our need. A gale at sea has shattered all the timbers of the wretched craft in which we were sailing on a business venture. So now, throwing ourselves on your mercy, we beg you to let us have something to put on, and to look after us out of pity for men of your own age who have met with disaster. Have some regard for suppliants and strangers, for the sake of Zeus who is their god. All suppliants and strangers belong to Zeus. And we ourselves, I have no doubt, are in his watchful care.'

In answer, Jason, who saw here the fulfilment of one of Phineus' prophecies, questioned the man closely. 'We shall be glad,' he said, 'to provide at once for all your needs. But first be so good as to tell me where you come from and what business has brought you overseas. And let me know your noble names and pedigrees.'

Argus, though his sufferings had left him dazed, was able to reply: 'You must surely have heard how an Aeolid called Phrixus came to Aea from Hellas. He reached Aeetes' city on the back of a ram which Hermes had turned into gold – you can still see its fleece, spread on the leafy branches of an oak. Phrixus sacrificed the ram at its own suggestion to Zeus alone, because he is the god of fugitives; and Aeetes made him welcome in his palace and married him in all good will to his daughter Chalciope without exacting the usual gifts. Those two were our parents. Phrixus grew old and died in the palace of Aeetes; and now we are carrying out his wishes by travelling to Orchomenus to take possession of our grandfather Athamas's estate. But you also wished to know our names. This then is Cytissorus; this, Phrontis; and this, Melas. My own name is Argus.'

Such was his story; and while the Argonauts, amazed and delighted at this meeting, attended to the shipwrecked men, Jason took up the tale and brought it to a fit conclusion.

'So now we know!' he said. 'You that are begging us to befriend you in your plight are kinsmen of mine on my father's side. Cretheus and Athamas were brothers; and I am a grandson of Cretheus, travelling like Phrixus from Hellas to Aeetes' city with these companions. But we will go into all this later. First put something on. It must indeed have been the gods who brought you to me in your need.'

With that, he gave them clothing from the ship, and then the whole party made their way to the temple of Ares to sacrifice some sheep, and quickly took their places round the altar. It was made of small stones and stood outside the temple, which had no roof. But inside, a black rock was fixed in the ground. This was sacred, and all the Amazons used at times to pray to it. But it was not their custom, when they came over from the mainland, to make burnt-offerings of sheep or oxen on this altar. Instead, they used the flesh of horses. They kept great herds of them.

When the company had sacrificed, prepared their feast, and eaten, the lord Jason rose and addressed the sons of Phrixus. 'Zeus,' he began, 'is the all-seeing god. Sooner or later we god-fearing men, we that uphold the right, are sure to catch his eye. See first how he rescued your father from a murderous stepmother, making him a rich man besides; and then how he saved you also and brought you unharmed through a terrible storm. And now you have the chance, on board our ship, of travelling east or west, whichever you prefer, either to Aea or to the rich city of divine Orchomenus – a ship, mind you, built with the help of Argus by Athene herself of timber she had felled with her bronze axe on Pelion. In any case, your own ship has been smashed to pieces by the angry sea. She never even reached the Rocks that all day long keep clashing in the straits. That being so, will you not help us in your turn by joining us in our endeavour to bring the golden fleece to Hellas and serving as our pilots on the way? After all, it is my mission to atone for the intended sacrifice of Phrixus, the cause of Zeus's wrath against the Aeolids.'

He spoke persuasively, but they were left aghast. They thought it most unlikely that Aeetes would prove affable when they sought to carry off the ram's fleece. And Argus, who had no desire to be involved in any such adventure, replied:

'My friends, you may rely upon us without fail to help you as best we can in any time of trouble. But I do dread the idea of sailing with you now, for Aeetes has it in his power to be a deadly and relentless enemy. He claims to be a son of Helios; his Colchian tribesmen are innumerable; and his terrifying voice and powerful build might well be envied by the god of war himself. No, it would be no easy thing to take the fleece without permission of Aeetes, guarded as it is from every side by such a serpent, a deathless and unsleeping beast, offspring of Earth herself. She brought him forth on the slopes of Caucasus by the rock of Typhaon. It was there, they say, that Typhaon, when he had offered violence to Zeus and been struck by his thunder-bolt, dropped warm blood from his head, and so made his way to the mountains and plain of Nysa, where he lies to this day, engulfed in the waters of the Serbonian Lake.'

When they heard what an ordeal lay before them, the cheeks of many of his listeners grew pale. But Peleus soon gave Argus a spirited reply.

'My good sir,' he said, 'do not give way to such excessive fears. We are not after all so feeble as to be no match for Aeetes if it comes to a fight. He will be meeting men whom I believe to know as much of war as he does; men too who

are not unrelated to the happy gods. And I am confident that
if he does not give us the golden fleece of his own free will his
Colchian tribes will be of little use to him.'

The two men continued their debate in this fashion till at
last, satisfied with their supper, the company retired to rest.
When they woke at dawn a gentle breeze was blowing.
They raised the sail; it opened to the wind; and soon they had
left the Isle of Ares far behind them.

By nightfall they were passing the Isle of Philyra. This was
where Cronos son of Uranus, deceiving his consort Rhea,
lay with Philyra daughter of Ocean in the days when he
ruled the Titans in Olympus and Zeus was still a child,
tended in the Cretan cave by the Curetes of Ida. But Cronos
and Philyra were surprised in the very act by the goddess
Rhea. Whereupon Cronos leapt out of bed and galloped off
in the form of a long-maned stallion, while Philyra in her
shame left the place, deserting her old haunts, and came to
the long Pelasgian ridges. There she gave birth to the monstrous Cheiron, half horse and half divine, the offspring of a
lover in a questionable shape.

From there they sailed on past the Macrones and the far-
flung lands of the Becheiri, past the truculent Sapeires, past
the Byzeres, forging ahead with all the speed that a light wind
gave them. And now the last recess of the Black Sea opened
up and they caught sight of the high crags of Caucasus, where
Prometheus stood chained by every limb to the hard rock
with fetters of bronze, and fed an eagle on his liver. The bird
kept eagerly returning to its feed. They saw it in the afternoon
flying high above the ship with a strident whirr. It was near
the clouds, yet it made all their canvas quiver to its wings as
it beat by. For its form was not that of an ordinary bird: the
long quill-feathers of each wing rose and fell like a bank of
polished oars. Soon after the eagle had passed, they heard
Prometheus shriek in agony as it pecked at his liver. The air
rang with his screams till at length they saw the flesh-devour-

ing bird fly back from the mountain by the same way as it came.

Night fell, and presently, under the guidance of Argus, they reached the broad estuary of Phasis, where the Black Sea ends. They quickly lowered sail and yard and stowed them in the mast-cage; next they let down the mast itself to lie beside them; and then rowed straight up into the mighty river, which rolled in foam to either bank as it made way for *Argo*'s prow. On their left hand they had the lofty Caucasus and the city of Aea, on their right the plain of Ares and the god's sacred grove, where the snake kept watch and ward over the fleece, spread on the leafy branches of an oak. The lord Jason himself poured into the river from a golden cup libations of pure wine sweet as honey, to Earth, to the gods of the land, and to the spirits of its famous sons. He besought them of their grace to give him friendly help and happy anchorage.

And now Ancaeus said: 'We have reached the land of Colchis and the River Phasis. It is time for us to consider whether to speak Aeetes fair or to find some other way of getting what we want.'

Jason, advised by Argus, told his men to row into the reedy marshes and moor the ship with anchor-stones in a spot where she could ride. They found the place a little farther on, and there they passed the rest of the night, waiting for Dawn, who soon appeared to their expectant eyes.

BOOK THREE

JASON AND MEDEA

*Come, Erato, come lovely Muse, stand by me and take up the tale.
How did Medea's passion help Jason to bring back the fleece to
Iolcus? You that share Aphrodite's powers must surely know; you
that fill virgin hearts with love's inquietude and bear a name that
speaks of love's delights.*

WE left the young lords lying there concealed among the
rushes. But ambushed though they were, Here and Athene
saw them and at once withdrew from Zeus and the rest of
the immortal gods into a private room to talk the matter
over.

Here began by sounding Athene. 'Daughter of Zeus,' she
said, 'let me hear you first. What are we to do? Will you
think of some ruse that might enable them to carry off Aeetes'
golden fleece to Hellas? Or should they speak him fair in the
hope of winning his consent? I know the man is thoroughly
intractable. But all the same, no method of approach should
be neglected.'

'Here,' said Athene quickly, 'you have put to me the very
questions I have been turning over in my mind. But I must
admit that, though I have racked my brains, I have failed so
far to think of any scheme that might commend itself to the
noble lords.'

For a while the two goddesses sat staring at the floor, each
lost in her own perplexities. Here was the first to break the
silence; an idea had struck her. 'Listen,' she said. 'We must
have a word with Aphrodite. Let us go together and ask her
to persuade her boy, if that is possible, to loose an arrow at
Aeetes' daughter, Medea of the many spells, and make her

fall in love with Jason. I am sure that with her help he will succeed in bearing off the fleece to Hellas.'

This solution of their problem pleased Athene, who smilingly replied: 'Sprung as I am from Zeus, I have never felt the arrows of the Boy, and of love-charms I know nothing. However, if you yourself are satisfied with the idea, I will certainly go with you. But when we meet her you must be the one to speak.'

The two goddesses rose at once and made their way to the palace of Aphrodite, which her lame consort Hephaestus had built for her when he took her as his bride from the hands of Zeus. They entered the courtyard and paused below the veranda of the room where the goddess slept with her lord and master. Hephaestus himself had gone early to his forge and anvils in a vast cavern on a floating island, where he used to turn out all kinds of curious metalwork with the aid of fire and bellows; and Cypris, left at home alone, was sitting on an inlaid chair which faced the door. She had let her hair fall down on her white shoulders and was combing it with a golden comb before plaiting the long tresses. But when she saw the goddesses outside she stopped and called them in; and she rose to meet them and settled them in easy chairs before resuming her own seat. Then she bound up the un-combed locks with both hands, gave her visitors a smile, and spoke with mock humility:

'Ladies, you honour me! What brings you here after so long? We have seen little of you in the past. To what then do I owe a visit from the greatest goddesses of all?'

'This levity of yours,' said Here, 'is ill-timed. We two are facing a disaster. At this very moment the lord Jason and his friends are riding at anchor in the River Phasis. They have come to fetch the fleece, and since the time for action is at hand, we are gravely concerned for all of them, particularly Aeson's son. For him, I am prepared to fight with all my might and main, and I will save him, even if he sails to Hell to free Ixion from his brazen chains. For I will not have King Pelias boasting that he has escaped his evil doom, insolent Pelias, who left me out when he made offerings to the gods. Besides which I have been very fond of Jason ever since the time when I was putting human charity on trial and as he came home from the chase he met me at the mouth of the Anaurus. The river was in spate, for all the mountains and their high spurs were under snow and cataracts were roaring down their sides. I was disguised as an old woman and he took pity on me, lifted me up, and carried me across the flood on his shoulders. For that, I will never cease to honour him. But Pelias will not be brought to book for his outrageous conduct unless you yourself make it possible for Jason to return.'

Here had finished; but for a time words failed the Lady of Cyprus. The sight of Here begging her for favours struck her with awe; and her answer when it came was gracious. 'Queen of goddesses,' she said, 'regard me as the meanest creature in the world if I fail you in your need. Whatever I can say or do, whatever strength these feeble hands possess, is at your service. Moreover I expect no recompense.'

Here, choosing her words with care, replied: 'We are not asking you to use your hands: force is not needed. All we require of you is quietly to tell your boy to use his wizardry and make Aeetes' daughter fall in love with Jason. With Medea on his side he should find it easy to carry off the golden fleece and make his way back to Iolcus. She is something of a witch herself.'

'But ladies,' said Cypris, speaking now to both of them, 'he is far more likely to obey you than me. There is no reverence in him, but faced by you he might display some spark of decent feeling. He certainly pays no attention to me: he defies me and always does the opposite of what I say. In fact I am so worn out by his naughtiness that I have half a mind to break his bow and wicked arrows in his very sight, remembering how he threatened me with them in one of his moods. He said, "If you don't keep your hands off me while I can still control my temper, you can blame yourself for the consequences." '

Here and Athene smiled at this and exchanged glances. But Aphrodite was hurt. She said: 'Other people find my troubles amusing. I really should not speak of them to all and sundry; it is enough for me to know them. However, as you have both set your hearts on it, I will try and coax my boy. He will not refuse.'

Here took Aphrodite's slender hand in hers and with a sweet smile replied: 'Very well, Cytherea. Play your part, just as you say; but quickly, please. And do not scold or argue with your child when he annoys you. He will improve by and by.'

With that she rose to go. Athene followed her, and the pair left for home. Cypris too set out, and after searching up and down Olympus for her boy, found him far away in the fruit-laden orchard of Zeus. With him was Ganymede, whose beauty had so captivated Zeus that he took him up to heaven to live with the immortals. The two lads, who had much in common, were playing with golden knuckle-bones. Eros, the greedy boy, was standing there with a whole handful of them clutched to his breast and a happy flush mantling his cheeks. Near by sat Ganymede, hunched up, silent and disconsolate, with only two left. He threw these for what they were worth in quick succession and was furious when Eros laughed. Of course he lost them both immediately – they joined the rest. So he went off in despair with empty hands and did not notice the goddess's approach.

Aphrodite came up to her boy, took his chin in her hand, and said: 'Why this triumphant smile, you rascal? I do believe you won the game unfairly by cheating a beginner. But listen now. Will you be good and do me a favour I am going to ask of you? Then I will give you one of Zeus's lovely toys, the one that his fond nurse Adresteia made for him in the Idaean cave when he was still a child and liked to play. It is a perfect ball; Hephaestus himself could not make you a better toy. It is made of golden hoops laced together all the way round with double stitching; but the seams are hidden by a winding, dark blue band. When you throw it up, it will leave a fiery trail behind it like a meteor in the sky. That is what I'll give you, if you let fly an arrow at Aeetes' girl and make her fall in love with Jason. But you must act at once, or I may not be so generous.'

When he heard this, Eros was delighted. He threw down all his toys, flung his arms round his mother and hung on to her skirt with both hands, imploring her to let him have the ball at once. But she gently refused, and drawing him towards her, held him close and kissed his cheeks. Then with a smile she said, 'By your own dear head and mine, I swear I will not disappoint you. You shall have the gift when you have shot an arrow into Medea's heart.'

Eros gathered up his knuckle-bones, counted them all carefully, and put them in the fold of his mother's shining robe. Fetching his quiver from where it leant against a tree, he slung it on his shoulder with a golden strap, picked up his crooked bow, and made his way through the luxuriant orchard of Zeus's palace. Then he passed through the celestial gates of Olympus, where a pathway for the gods leads down, and twin poles, earth's highest points, soar up in lofty pinnacles that catch the first rays of the risen sun. And as he swept on through the boundless air he saw an ever-changing scene beneath him, here the life-supporting land with its peopled cities and its sacred rivers, here mountain peaks, and here the all-encircling sea.

Meanwhile the Argonauts were sitting in conference on the benches of their ship where it lay hidden in the marshes of the river. Each man had taken his own seat, and Jason, who was speaking, was faced by row upon row of quiet listeners. 'My friends,' he said, 'I am going to tell you what action I myself should like to take, though its success depends on you. Sharing the danger as we do, we share the right of speech; and I warn the man who keeps his mouth shut when he ought to speak his mind that he will be the one to wreck our enterprise.

'I ask you all to stay quietly on board with your arms ready, while I go up to Aeetes' palace with the sons of Phrixus and two other men. When I see him I intend to parley with him first and find out whether he means to treat us as friends and let us have the golden fleece, or dismiss us with contempt, relying on his own power. Warned thus, by the man himself, of any evil thoughts he may be entertaining, we will decide whether to face him in the field or find some way of getting what we want without recourse to arms. We ought not to use force to rob him of his own without so much as seeing what a few words may do; it would be much better to talk to him first and try to win him over. Speech, by smoothing the way, often succeeds where forceful measures might have failed. Remember too that Aeetes welcomed the admirable Phrixus when he fled from a stepmother's treachery and a father who had planned to sacrifice him. Every man on earth, even the greatest rogue, fears Zeus the god of hospitality and keeps his laws.'

With one accord the young men approved the lord Jason's plan, and no one having risen to suggest another, he asked the sons of Phrixus, with Telamon and Augeias, to accompany him and himself took the Wand of Hermes in his hand. Leaving the ship they came to dry land beyond the reeds and water and passed on to the high ground of the plain which bears the name of Circe. Here osiers and willows stand in rows, with corpses dangling on ropes from their highest branches. To this day the Colchians would think it sacrilege to burn the bodies of their men. They never bury them or raise a mound above them, but wrap them in untanned ox-hide and hang them up on trees at a distance from the town. Thus, since it is their custom to bury women, earth and air play equal parts in the disposal of their dead.

While Jason and his friends were on their way, Here had a kindly thought for them. She covered the whole town with mist so that they might reach Aeetes' house unseen by any of the numerous Colchians. But as soon as they had come in from the country and reached the palace she dispersed the mist. At the entrance they paused for a moment to marvel at the king's courtyard with its wide gates, the rows of soaring columns round the palace walls, and high over all the marble cornice resting on triglyphs of bronze. They crossed the threshold of the court unchallenged. Near by, cultivated vines covered with greenery rose high in the air and underneath them four perennial springs gushed up. These were Hephaestus' work. One flowed with milk, and one with wine, the third with fragrant oil, while the fourth was a fountain of water which grew warm when the Pleiades set, but changed at their rising and bubbled up from the hollow rock as cold as ice. Such were the marvels that Hephaestus the great Engineer had contrived for the palace of Cytaean Aeetes. He had also made him bulls with feet of bronze and bronze mouths from which the breath came out in flame, blazing and terrible. And he had forged a plough of indurated steel, all in one piece, as a thank-offering to Helios, who had taken him up in his chariot when he sank exhausted on the battlefield of Phlegra.

There was also an inner court, with many well-made folding doors leading to various rooms, and decorated galleries to right and left. Higher buildings stood at angles to this court on either side. In one of them, the highest, King Aeetes lived with his queen; in another, his son Apsyrtus, whom a Caucasian nymph named Asterodeia had borne to him before he married Eidyia, the youngest daughter of Tethys and Ocean. 'Phaëthon' was the nickname that the young Colchians gave Apsyrtus because he outshone them all.

The other buildings housed the maidservants and Chalciope and Medea, the two daughters of Aeetes. At the moment, Medea was going from room to room to find her sister. The goddess Here had kept her in the house, though as a rule she did not spend her time at home, but was busy all day in the temple of Hecate, of whom she was priestess. When she saw the men she gave a cry; Chalciope heard it, and her maids dropped their yarn and spindles on the floor and all ran out of doors.

When Chalciope saw her sons among the strangers, she lifted up her hands for joy. They greeted her in the same fashion and then in their happiness embraced her. But she had her moan to make. 'So after all,' she said, 'you were not allowed to roam so very far from your neglected mother: Fate turned you back. But how I have suffered! This mad desire of yours for Hellas! This blind obedience to your dying father's wishes! What misery, what heartache, they brought me! Why should you go to the city of Orchomenus, whoever he may be, abandoning your widowed mother for the sake of your grandfather's estate?'

Last of all, Aeetes with his queen, Eidyia, who had heard Chalciope speaking, came out of the house. And at once the whole courtyard was astir. A number of his men busied themselves over the carcass of a large bull; others chopped firewood; others heated water for the baths. Not one of them took a rest: they were working for the king.

Meanwhile Eros, passing through the clear air, had arrived unseen and bent on mischief, like a gadfly setting out to plague the grazing heifers, the fly that cowherds call the breese. In the porch, under the lintel of the door, he quickly strung his bow and from his quiver took a new arrow, fraught with pain. Still unobserved, he ran across the threshold glancing around him sharply. Then he crouched low at Jason's feet, fitted the notch to the middle of the string, and drawing the bow as far as his hands would stretch, shot at Medea. And her heart stood still.

With a happy laugh Eros sped out of the high-roofed hall on his way back, leaving his shaft deep in the girl's breast, hot as fire. Time and again she darted a bright glance at Jason. All else was forgotten. Her heart, brimful of this new agony, throbbed within her and overflowed with the sweetness of the pain.

A working woman, rising before dawn to spin and needing light in her cottage room, piles brushwood on a smouldering log, and the whole heap kindled by the little brand goes up in a mighty blaze. Such was the fire of Love, stealthy but all-consuming, that swept through Medea's heart. In the turmoil of her soul, her soft cheeks turned from rose to white and white to rose.

By now the servants had prepared a banquet for the newcomers, who gladly sat down to it after refreshing themselves in warm baths. When they had enjoyed the food and drink, Aeetes put some questions to his grandsons:

'Sons of my daughter and of Phrixus, the most deserving guest I have ever entertained, how is it that you are back in Aea? Did some misadventure cut your journey short? You refused to listen when I told you what a long way you had to go. But I knew; for I myself was whirled along it in the chariot of my father Helios, when he took my sister Circe to the Western Land and we reached the coast of Tyrrhenia, where she still lives, far, far indeed from Colchis. But enough of that. Tell me plainly what befell you, who your companions are, and where you disembarked.'

To answer these questions, Argus stepped out in front of his brothers, being the eldest of the four. His heart misgave him for Jason and his mission; but he did his best to conciliate the king. 'My lord,' he said, 'that ship of ours soon fell to pieces in a storm. We hung on to one of her planks and were cast ashore on the Island of Ares in the pitch-dark night.

But Providence looked after us: there was not a sign of the War-god's birds, who used to haunt the desert isle. They were driven off by these men, who had landed on the previous day and been detained there by the will of Zeus in pity for ourselves – or was it only chance? In any case, they gave us plenty of food and clothing directly they heard the illustrious name of Phrixus, and your own, my lord, since it was your city they were bound for. As to their purpose, I will be frank with you. A certain king, wishing to banish and dispossess this man because he is the most powerful of the Aeolids, has sent him here on a desperate venture, maintaining that the House of Aeolus will not escape the inexorable wrath of Zeus, the heavy burden of their guilt, and vengeance for the sufferings of Phrixus, till the fleece returns to Hellas. The ship that brought him was built by Pallas Athene on altogether different lines from the Colchian craft, the rottenest of which, as luck would have it, fell to us. For *she* was smashed to pieces by the wind and waves, whereas the bolts of *Argo* hold her together in any gale that blows, and she runs as sweetly when the crew are tugging at the oars as she does before the wind. This ship he manned with the pick of all Achaea, and in her he has come to your city, touching at many ports and crossing formidable seas, in the hope that you will let him have the fleece. But it must be as you wish. He has not come here to force your hand. On the contrary, he is willing to repay you amply for the gift by reducing for you your bitter enemies, the Sauromatae, of whom I told him. But now you may wish to know the names and lineage of your visitors. Let me tell you. Here is the man to whom the others rallied from all parts of Hellas, Jason son of Aeson, Cretheus' son. He must be a kinsman of our own on the father's side, if he is a grandson of Cretheus, for Cretheus and Athamas were both sons of Aeolus, and our father Phrixus was a son of Athamas. Next, and in case you have heard that we have a son of Helios with us, behold the man, Augeias. And this is Telamon, son of the illustrious Aeacus, a son of Zeus himself. Much the same is true of all the rest of Jason's followers. They are all sons or grandsons of immortal gods.'

The king was filled with rage as he listened to Argus. And now, in a towering passion, he gave vent to his displeasure, the brunt of which fell on the sons of Chalciope, whom he held responsible for the presence of the rest. His eyes blazed with fury as he burst into speech:

'You scoundrels! Get out of my sight at once. Get out of my country, you and your knavish tricks, before you meet a Phrixus and a fleece you will not relish. It was no fleece that brought you and your confederates from Hellas, but a plot to seize my sceptre and my royal power. If you had not eaten at my table first, I would tear your tongues out and chop off your hands, both of them, and send you back with nothing but your feet, to teach you to think twice before starting on another expedition. As for all that about the blessed gods, it is nothing but a pack of lies.'

Telamon's gorge rose at this outburst from the angry king, and he was on the point of flinging back defiance, to his own undoing, when he was checked by Jason, who forestalled him with a more politic reply.

'My lord,' he said, 'pray overlook our show of arms. We have not come to your city and palace with any such designs as you suspect. Nor have we predatory aims. Who of his own accord would brave so vast a sea to lay his hands on other people's goods? No; it was Destiny and the cruel orders of a brutal king that sent me here. Be generous to your suppliants, and I will make all Hellas ring with the glory of your name. And by way of more immediate re-compense, we are prepared to take the field in your behalf against the Sauromatae or any other tribe you may wish to subdue.'

Jason's obsequious address had no effect. The king was plunged in sullen cogitation, wondering whether to leap up and kill them on the spot or to put their powers to the proof. He ended by deciding for a test and said to Jason:

'Sir, there is no need for me to hear you out. If you are really children of the gods or have other grounds for approaching me as equals in the course of your piratical adventure, I will let you have the golden fleece – that is, if you still want it when I have put you to the proof. For I am not like your overlord in Hellas, as you describe him; I am not inclined to be ungenerous to men of rank.

'I propose to test your courage and abilities by setting you a task which, though formidable, is not beyond the strength of my two hands. Grazing on the plain of Ares, I have a pair of bronze-footed and fire-breathing bulls. These I yoke and drive over the hard fallow of the plain, quickly ploughing a four-acre field up to the ridge at either end. Then I sow the furrows, not with corn, but with the teeth of a monstrous serpent, which presently come up in the form of armed men, whom I cut down and kill with my spear as they rise up against me on all sides. It is morning when I yoke my team and by evening I have done my harvesting. That is what I do. If you, sir, can do as well, you may carry off the fleece to your king's palace on the very same day. If not, you shall not have it – do not deceive yourself. It would be wrong for a brave man to truckle to a coward.'

Jason listened to this with his eyes fixed on the floor; and when the king had finished, he sat there just as he was, without a word, resourceless in the face of his dilemma. For a long time he turned the matter over in his mind, unable boldly to accept a task so clearly fraught with peril. But at last he gave the king an answer which he thought would serve:

'Your Majesty, right is on your side and you leave me no escape whatever. Therefore I will take up your challenge, in spite of its preposterous terms, and though I may be courting death. Men serve no harsher mistress than Necessity, who drives me now and forced me to come here at another king's behest.'

He spoke in desperation and was little comforted by Aeetes' sinister reply: 'Go now and join your company: you have shown your relish for the task. But if you hesitate to yoke the bulls or shirk the deadly harvesting, I will take the matter up myself in a manner calculated to make others shrink from coming here and pestering their betters.'

He had made his meaning clear, and Jason rose from his chair. Augeias and Telamon followed him at once, and so did Argus, but without his brothers, whom he had warned by a nod to stay there for the time being. As the party went out of the hall, Jason's comeliness and charm singled him out from all the rest; and Medea, plucking her bright veil aside, turned wondering eyes upon him. Her heart smouldered with pain and as he passed from sight her soul crept out of her, as in a dream, and fluttered in his steps.

They left the palace with heavy hearts. Meanwhile Chalciope, to save herself from Aeetes' wrath, had hastily withdrawn to her own room together with her sons. Medea too retired, a prey to all the inquietude that Love awakens. The whole scene was still before her eyes – how Jason looked, the clothes he wore, the things he said, the way he sat, and how he walked to the door. It seemed to her, as she reviewed these images, that there was nobody like Jason. His voice and the honey-sweet words that he had used still rang in her ears. But she feared for him. She was afraid that the bulls or Aeetes with his own hands might kill him; and she mourned him as one already dead. The pity of it overwhelmed her; a round tear ran down her cheek; and weeping quietly she voiced her woes:

'What is the meaning of this grief? Hero or villain (and why should I care which?) the man is going to his death. Well, let him go! And yet I wish he had been spared. Yes, sovran Lady Hecate, this is my prayer. Let him live to reach his home. But if he must be conquered by the bulls, may he first learn that I for one do not rejoice in his cruel fate.'

While Medea thus tormented herself, Jason was listening to some advice from Argus, who had waited to address him till the people and the town were left behind and the party were retracing their steps across the plain.

'My lord,' he said, 'I have a plan to suggest. You will not like it; but in a crisis no expedient should be left untried. You have heard me speak of a young woman who practises witchcraft under the tutelage of the goddess Hecate. If we could win her over, we might banish from our minds all fear of your defeat in the ordeal. I am only afraid that my mother may not support me in this scheme. Nevertheless, since we all stand to lose our lives together, I will go back and sound her.'

'My friend,' said Jason, responding to the good will shown by Argus, 'if you are satisfied, then I have no objections. Go back at once and seek your mother's aid, feeling your way with care. But oh, how bleak the prospect is, with our one hope of seeing home again in women's hands!'

Soon after this they reached the marsh. Their comrades, when they saw them coming up, greeted them with cheerful enquiries, which Jason answered in a gloomy vein. 'Friends,' he said, 'if I were to answer all your questions, we should never finish; but the cruel king has definitely set his face against us. He said he had a couple of bronze-footed and fire-breathing bulls grazing on the plain of Ares, and told me to plough a four-acre field with these. He will give me seed from a serpent's jaws which will produce a crop of earthborn men in panoplies of bronze. And I have got to kill them before the day is done. That is my task. I straightway undertook it, for I had no choice.'

The task, as Jason had described it, seemed so impossible to all of them that for a while they stood there without a sound or word, looking at one another in impotent despair. But at

last Peleus took heart and spoke out to his fellow chieftains:
'The time has come. We must confer and settle what to do.
Not that debate will help us much: I would rather trust to
strength of arm. Jason, my lord, if you fancy the adventure
and mean to yoke Aeetes' bulls you will naturally keep your
promise and prepare. But if you have the slightest fear that
your nerve may fail you, do not force yourself. And you
need not sit there looking round for someone else. I, for one,
am willing. The worst that I shall suffer will be death.'

So said the son of Aeacus. Telamon too was stirred and
eagerly leapt up; next Idas, full of lofty thoughts; then Castor
and Polydeuces; and with them one who was already num-
bered with the men of might though the down was scarcely
showing on his cheeks, Meleager son of Oeneus, his heart
uplifted by the courage that dares all. But the others made no
move, leaving it to these; and Argus addressed the six devoted
men:

'My friends, you certainly provide us with a last resource.
But I have some hopes of timely help that may be coming
from my mother. So I advise you, keen as you are, to do as
you did earlier and wait here in the ship for a little while – it
is always better to think twice before one throws away one's
life for nothing. There is a girl living in Aeetes' palace whom
the goddess Hecate has taught to handle with extraordinary
skill all the magic herbs that grow on dry land or in running
water. With these she can put out a raging fire, she can stop
rivers as they roar in spate, arrest a star, and check the movement of the sacred moon. We thought of her as we made our
way down here from the palace. My mother, her own sister,
might persuade her to be our ally in the hour of trial; and with
your approval I am prepared to go back to Aeetes' palace this
very day and see what I can do. Who knows? Some friendly
Power may come to my assistance.'

So said Argus. And the gods were kind: they sent them a
sign. In her terror, a timid dove, hotly pursued by a great

hawk, dropped straight down into Jason's lap, while the hawk fell impaled on the mascot at the stern. Mopsus at once made the omens clear to all:

'It is for you, my friends, that Heaven has designed this portent. We could construe it in no better way than by approaching the girl with every plea we can devise. And I do not think she will refuse, if Phineus was right when he told us that our safety lay in Aphrodite's care; for this gentle bird whose life was spared belongs to her. May all turn out as I foresee, reading the omens with my inward eye. And so, my friends, let us invoke Cytherea's aid and put ourselves at once in the hands of Argus.'

The young men applauded, remembering what Phineus had told them. But there was one dissentient voice, and that a loud one. Idas leapt up in a towering rage and shouted: 'For shame! Have we come here to trot along with women, calling on Aphrodite to support us, instead of the mighty god of battle? Do you look to doves and hawks to get you out of trouble? Well, please yourselves! Forget that you are fighters. Pay court to girls and turn their silly heads.'

This tirade from Idas was received by many of his comrades with muttered resentment, though no one took the floor to answer him back. He sat down in high dudgeon, and Jason rose immediately to give them his decision and his orders. 'We are all agreed,' he said. 'Argus sets out from the ship. And we ourselves will now make fast with hawsers from the river to the shore, where anyone can see us. We certainly ought not to hide here any longer as though we were afraid of fighting.'

With that, he despatched Argus on his way back to the town; and the crew, taking their orders from Aeson's son, hauled the anchor-stones on board and rowed *Argo* close to dry land, a little way from the marsh.

At the same time Aeetes, meaning to play the Minyae false and do them grievous injury, summoned the Colchians to assemble, not in his palace, but at another spot where meetings had been held before. He declared that as soon as the bulls had destroyed the man who had taken up his formidable challenge, he would strip a forest hill of brushwood and burn the ship with every man on board, to cure them once for all of the intolerable airs they gave themselves, these enterprising buccaneers. It was true that he had welcomed Phrixus to his palace, but whatever the man's plight, he certainly would not have done so, though he had never known a foreigner so gentle and so well-conducted, if Zeus himself had not sent Hermes speeding down from heaven to see that he met with a sympathetic host. Much less should pirates landing in his country be left unpunished, men whose sole concern it was to get their hands on other people's goods, to lie in ambush plotting a sudden stroke, to sally out, cry havoc, and raid the farmers' yards. Moreover, Phrixus' sons should make him suitable amends for coming back in league with a gang of ruffians to hurl him from the throne. The crazy fools! But it all chimed in with an ugly hint he had had long ago from his father Helios, warning him to beware of treasonable plots and evil machinations in his own family. So, to complete their chastisement, he would pack them off to Achaea, just as they and their father had wished; and that was surely far enough. As for his daughters, he had not the slightest fear of treachery from them. Nor from his son Apsyrtus; only Chalciope's sons were involved in the mischief. The angry king ended by informing his people of the drastic measures that he had in mind, and ordering them, with many threats, to watch the ship and the men themselves so that no one should escape his doom.

By now Argus had reached the palace and was urging his mother with every argument at his command to invoke Medea's aid. The same idea had already occurred to Chalciope herself; but she had hesitated. On the one hand, she was afraid of failure: Medea might be so appalled by thoughts of her father's wrath that all entreaties would fall upon deaf ears. On the other, she feared that if her sister yielded to her prayers the whole conspiracy would be laid bare.

Meanwhile the maiden lay on her bed, fast asleep, with all her cares forgotten. But not for long. Dreams assailed her, deceitful dreams, the nightmares of a soul in pain. She dreamt that the stranger had accepted the challenge, not in the hope of winning the ram's fleece – it was not that that had brought him to Aea – but in order that he might carry her off to his own home as his bride. Then it seemed that it was she who was standing up to the bulls; she found it easy to handle them. But when all was done, her parents backed out of the bargain, pointing out that it was Jason, not their daughter, whom they had dared to yoke the bulls. This led to an interminable dispute between her father and the Argonauts, which resulted in their leaving the decision to her – she could do as she pleased. And she, without a moment's thought, turned her back on her parents and chose the stranger. Her parents were cut to the quick; they screamed in their anger; and with their cries she woke.

She sat up, shivering with fright, and peered round the walls of her bedroom. Slowly and painfully she dragged herself back to reality. Then in self-pity she cried out and voiced the terror that her nightmare had engendered:

'These noblemen, their coming here, I fear it spells catastrophe. And how I tremble for their leader! He should pay court to some Achaean girl far away in his own country, leaving me content with spinsterhood and home. Ah no! Away with modesty! I will stand aside no longer; I will go to my sister. She is anxious for her sons and well might ask me for my help in the ordeal. And so my heartache would be eased.'

With that she rose, and in her gown, with nothing on her feet, went to her bedroom door and opened it. She was resolved to go to her sister and she crossed the threshold. But once outside she stayed for a long time where she was, inhibited by shame. Then she turned and went back into the room. Again she came out of it, and again she crept back, borne to and fro on hesitating feet. Whenever she set out shame held her back; and all the time shame held her in the room shameless desire kept urging her to leave it. Three times she tried to go; three times she failed; and at the fourth attempt she threw herself face downward on the bed and writhed in pain.

Her plight was like that of a bride mourning in her bedroom for the young husband chosen for her by her brothers and parents, and lost by some stroke of Fate before the pair had enjoyed each other's love. Too shy and circumspect as yet to mingle freely with the maids and risk an unkind word or tactless jibe, she sits disconsolate in a corner of the room, looks at the empty bed and weeps in silence though her heart is bursting. Thus Medea wept.

But presently one of the servants, her own young maid, came to the room, and seeing her mistress lying there in tears, ran off to tell Chalciope, who was sitting with her sons considering how they might win Medea over. Chalciope did not make light of the girl's story, strange as it seemed. In great alarm she hurried through the house from her own to her sister's room, and there she found her lying in misery on the bed with both cheeks torn and her eyes red with weeping.

'My dear!' she cried. 'What is the meaning of these tears? What has made you so terribly unhappy? Have you suddenly been taken ill? Or has Father told you of some awful fate he has in mind for me and my sons? Oh, how I wish I might never see this city and this home of ours again, and live at the world's end, where nobody has even heard of the Colchians!'

Medea blushed. She was eager to answer, but for a long while was checked by maiden modesty. Time and again the truth was on the tip of her tongue, only to be swallowed back. Time and again it tried to force a passage through her lovely

lips, but no words came. At last, impelled by the bold hand
of Love, she gave her sister a disingenuous reply: 'Chalciope,
I am terrified for your sons. I am afraid that father will destroy
them out of hand, strangers and all. I had a little sleep just now
and in a nightmare that is what I saw. God forfend such evil!
May you never have to suffer so through them!'

Medea was trying to induce her sister to make the first
move and appeal to her to save her sons. And indeed Chalciope
was overwhelmed by horror at her disclosure. She said: 'My
fears have been the same as yours. That is what brought me
here. I hoped that you and I might put our heads together
and find a way of rescuing my sons. But swear by Earth and
Heaven that you will keep what I say to yourself and work in
league with me. I implore you, by the happy gods, by your
own head, and by your parents, not to stand by while they are
mercilessly done to death. If you do so, may I die with my
dear sons and haunt you afterwards from Hades like an
avenging Fury.'

With that she burst into tears, sank down, and throwing
her arms round her sister's knees buried her head in her lap.
Each of them wailed in pity for the other, and faint sounds of
women weeping in distress were heard throughout the
palace.

Medea was the first to speak. 'Sister,' she said, 'you left me
speechless when you talked of curses and avenging Furies.
How can I set your mind at rest? I only wish we could be sure
of rescuing your sons. However, I will do as you ask and take
the solemn oath of the Colchians, swearing by mighty Heaven
and by Earth below, the Mother of the Gods, that provided
your demands are not impossible I will help you as you wish,
with all the power that in me lies.'

When Medea had taken the oath, Chalciope said: 'Well
now, for the sake of my sons, could you not devise some
stratagem, some cunning ruse that the stranger could rely on
in his trial? He needs you just as much as they do. In fact he

has sent Argus here to urge me to enlist your help. I left him in the palace when I came to you just now.'

At this, Medea's heart leapt up. Her lovely cheeks were crimsoned and her eyes grew dim with tears of joy. 'Chalciope,' she cried, 'I will do anything to please you and your sons, anything to make you happy. May I never see the light of dawn again and may you see me in the world no more, if I put anything before your safety and the lives of your sons, who are my brothers, my dear kinsmen, with whom I was brought up. And you, am I not as much your daughter as your sister, you that took me to your breast as you did them, when I was a baby, as I often heard my mother say? But go now and tell no one of my promise, so that my parents may not know how I propose to keep it. And at dawn I will go to Hecate's temple with magic medicine for the bulls.'

Thus assured, Chalciope withdrew from her sister's room and brought her sons the news of her success. But Medea, left alone, fell a prey once more to shame and horror at the way in which she planned to help a man in defiance of her father's wishes.

Night threw her shadow on the world. Sailors out at sea looked up at the circling Bear and the stars of Orion. Travellers and watchmen longed for sleep, and oblivion came at last to mothers mourning for their children's death. In the town, dogs ceased to bark and men to call to one another; silence reigned over the deepening dark. But gentle sleep did not visit Medea. In her yearning for Jason, fretful cares kept her awake. She feared the great strength of the bulls; she saw him face them in the field of Ares; she saw him meet an ignominious end. Her heart fluttered within her, restless as a patch of sunlight dancing up and down on a wall as the swirling water poured into a pail reflects it.

Tears of pity ran down her cheeks and her whole body was possessed by agony, a searing pain which shot along her nerves and deep into the nape of her neck, that vulnerable spot where the relentless archery of Love causes the keenest pangs. At one moment she thought she would give him the magic drug for the bulls; at the next she thought no, she would rather die herself; and then that she would do neither, but patiently endure her fate. In the end she sat down and debated with herself in miserable indecision:

'Evil on this side, evil on that; and must I choose between them? In either case my plight is desperate and there is no escape; this torture will go on. Oh how I wish that Artemis with her swift darts had put an end to me before I had seen that man, before Chalciope's sons had gone to Achaea! Some god, some Fury rather, must have brought them back with grief and tears for us. Let him be killed in the struggle, if it is indeed his fate to perish in the unploughed field. For how could I prepare the drug without my parents' knowledge? What story shall I tell them? What trickery will serve? How can I help him, and fail to be found out? Are he and I to meet alone? Indeed I am ill-starred, for even if he dies I have no hope of happiness; with Jason dead, I should taste real misery. Away with modesty, farewell to my good name! Saved from all harm by me, let him go where he pleases, and let me die. On the very day of his success I could hang myself from a rafter or take a deadly poison. Yet even so my death would never save me from their wicked tongues. My fate would be the talk of every city in the world; and here the Colchian women would bandy my name about and drag it in mud – the girl who fancied a foreigner enough to die for him, disgraced her parents and her home, went off her head for love. What infamy would not be mine? Ah, how I grieve now for the folly of my passion! Better to die here in my room this very night, passing from life unnoticed, unreproached, than to carry through this horrible, this despicable scheme.'

With that she went and fetched the box in which she kept her many drugs, healing or deadly, and putting it on her knees she wept. Tears ran unchecked in torrents down her cheeks and drenched her lap as she bemoaned her own sad destiny. She was determined now to take a poison from the box and swallow it; and in a moment she was fumbling with the fastening of the lid in her unhappy eagerness to reach the fatal drug. But suddenly she was overcome by the hateful thought of death, and for a long time she stayed her hand in silent horror. Visions of life and all its fascinating cares rose up before her. She thought of the pleasures that the living can enjoy. She thought of her happy playmates, as a young girl will. And now, setting its true value on all this, it seemed to her a sweeter thing to see the sun than it had ever been before. So, prompted by Here, she changed her mind and put the box away. Irresolute no longer, she waited eagerly for Dawn to come, so that she could meet the stranger face to face and give him the magic drug as she had promised. Time after time she opened her door to catch the first glimmer of day; and she rejoiced when early Dawn lit up the sky and people in the town began to stir.

Argus left the palace and returned to the ship. But he told his brothers to wait before following him, in order to find out what Medea meant to do. She herself, as soon she saw the first light of day, gathered up the golden locks that were floating round her shoulders in disorder, washed the stains from her cheeks and cleansed her skin with an ointment clear as nectar; then she put on a beautiful robe equipped with cunning brooches, and threw a silvery veil over her lovely head. And as she moved about, there in her own home, she walked oblivious of all evils imminent, and worse to come.

She had twelve maids, young as herself and all unmarried, who slept in the ante-chamber of her own sweet-scented room. She called them now and told them to yoke the mules to her carriage at once, as she wished to drive to the splendid Temple of Hecate; and while they were getting the carriage ready she took a magic ointment from her box. This salve was named after Prometheus. A man had only to smear it on his body, after propitiating the only-begotten Maiden with a midnight offering, to become invulnerable by sword or fire and for that day to surpass himself in strength and daring. It first appeared in a plant that sprang from the blood-like ichor of Prometheus in his torment, which the flesh-eating eagle had dropped on the spurs of Caucasus. The flowers, which grew on twin stalks a cubit high, were of the colour of Corycian saffron, while the root looked like flesh that has just been cut, and the juice like the dark sap of a mountain oak. To make the ointment, Medea, clothed in black, in the gloom of night, had drawn off this juice in a Caspian shell after bathing in seven perennial streams and calling seven times on Brimo, nurse of youth, Brimo, night-wanderer of the underworld, Queen of the dead. The dark earth shook and rumbled underneath the Titan root when it was cut, and Prometheus himself groaned in the anguish of his soul.

Such was the salve that Medea chose. Placing it in the fragrant girdle that she wore beneath her bosom, she left the house and got into her carriage, with two maids on either side. They gave her the reins, and taking the well-made whip in her right hand, she drove off through the town, while the rest of the maids tucked up their skirts above their white knees and ran behind along the broad highway, holding on to the wicker body of the carriage.

I see her there like Artemis, standing in her golden chariot after she has bathed in the gentle waters of Parthenius or the streams of Amnisus, and driving off with her fast-trotting deer over the hills and far away to some rich-scented sacrifice. Attendant nymphs have gathered at the source of Amnisus or flocked in from the glens and upland springs to follow her; and fawning beasts whimper in homage and tremble as she passes by. Thus Medea and her maids sped through the town, and on either side people made way for her, avoiding the princess's eye.

Leaving the city and its well-paved streets, she drove across the plain and drew up at the shrine. There she got quickly down from her smooth-running carriage and addressed her maids. 'My friends,' she said, 'I have done wrong. I forgot that we were told not to go among these foreigners who are wandering about the place. Everybody in the town is terrified, and in consequence none of the women who every day foregather here have come. But since we are here and it looks as though we shall be left in peace, we need not deny ourselves a little pleasure. Let us sing to our heart's content, and then, when we have gathered some of the lovely flowers in the meadow there, go back to town at the usual time. And if you will only fall in with a scheme of mine, you shall have something better than flowers to take home with you today. I will explain. Argus and Chalciope herself have persuaded me against my better judgement – but not a word to anyone of what I say; my father must not hear about it. They wish me to protect that stranger, the one who took up the challenge, in his mortal combat with the bulls and take some presents from him in return. I told them I thought well of the idea; and I have in fact invited him to come and see me here without his followers. But if he brings his gifts and hands them over, I mean to share them out among ourselves; and what we give him in return will be a deadlier drug than he expects. All I ask of you when he arrives is to leave me by myself.'

With this ingenious figment Medea satisfied her maids. Meanwhile Argus, when his brothers had told him she was going to the Temple of Hecate at dawn, drew Jason apart and conducted him across the plain. Mopsus son of Ampycus went with them, an excellent adviser for travellers setting out, and able to interpret any omen that a bird might offer on the way. As for Jason, by the grace of Here Queen of Heaven, no hero of the past, no son of Zeus himself, no offspring of the other gods, could have outshone him on that day, he was so good to look at, so delightful to talk to. Even his companions, as they glanced at him, were fascinated by his radiant charm. For Mopsus, it was a pleasurable journey: he had a shrewd idea how it would end.

Near the shrine and beside the path they followed, there stood a poplar, flaunting its myriad leaves. It was much frequented as a roost by garrulous crows, one of which flapped its wings as they were passing by, and cawing from the treetop expressed the sentiments of Here:

'Who is this inglorious seer who has not had the sense to realize, what even children know, that a girl does not permit herself to say a single word of love to a young man who brings an escort with him? Off with you, foolish prophet and incompetent diviner! You certainly are not inspired by Cypris or the gentle Loves.'

Mopsus listened to the bird's remarks with a smile at the reprimand from Heaven. Turning to Jason, he said: 'Proceed, my lord, to the temple, where you will find Medea and be graciously received, thanks to Aphrodite, who will be your ally in the hour of trial, as was foretold to us by Phineus son of Agenor. We two, Argus and I, will not go any nearer, but will wait here till you come back. You must go to her alone and attach her to yourself by your own persuasive eloquence.' This was sound advice and they both accepted it at once.

Meanwhile Medea, though she was singing and dancing with her maids, could think of one thing only. There was no melody, however gay, that did not quickly cease to please. Time and again she faltered and came to a halt. To keep her eyes fixed on her choir was more than she could do. She was for ever turning them aside to search the distant paths, and more than once she well-nigh fainted when she mistook the noise of the wind for the footfall of a passer-by.

But it was not so very long before the sight of Jason rewarded her impatient watch. Like Sirius rising from Ocean, brilliant and beautiful but full of menace for the flocks, he sprang into view, splendid to look at but fraught with trouble for the lovesick girl. Her heart stood still, a mist descended on her eyes, and a warm flush spread across her cheeks. She could neither move towards him nor retreat; her feet were rooted to the ground. And now her servants disappeared, and the pair of them stood face to face without a word or sound, like oaks or tall pines that stand in the mountains side by side in silence when the air is still, but when the wind has stirred them chatter without end. So these two, stirred by the breath of Love, were soon to pour out all their tale.

Jason, seeing how distraught Medea was, tried to put her at her ease. 'Lady,' he said, 'I am alone. Why are you so fearful of me? I am not a profligate as some men are, and never was, even in my own country. So you have no need to be on your guard, but may ask or tell me anything you wish. We have come together here as friends, in a consecrated spot which must not be profaned. Speak to me, question me, without reserve; and since you have already promised your sister to give me the talisman I need so much, pray do not put me off with pleasant speeches. I plead to you by Hecate herself, by your parents, and by Zeus. His hand protects all suppliants and strangers, and I that now address my prayers to you in my necessity am both a stranger and a suppliant. Without you and your sister I shall never succeed in my appalling task. Grant me your aid and in the days to come I will reward you duly, repaying you as best I can from the distant land where I shall sing your praises. My comrades too when they are back in Hellas will immortalize your name. So will their wives and mothers, whom I think of now as sitting by the sea, shedding tears in their anxiety for us – bitter tears, which you could wipe away. Remember Ariadne, young Ariadne, daughter of Minos and Pasiphae, who was a daughter of the Sun. She did not scruple to befriend Theseus and save him in his hour of trial; and then, when Minos had relented, she left her home and sailed away with him. She was the darling of the gods and she has her emblem in the sky: all night a ring of stars called Ariadne's Crown rolls on its way among the heavenly constellations. You too will be thanked by the gods if you save me and all my noble friends. Indeed your loveliness assures me of a kind and tender heart within.'

Jason's homage melted Medea. Turning her eyes aside she smiled divinely and then, uplifted by his praise, she looked him in the face. How to begin, she did not know; she longed so much to tell him everything at once. But with the charm, she did not hesitate; she drew it out from her sweet-scented girdle and he took it in his hands with joy. She revelled in his need of her and would have poured out all her soul to him as well, so captivating was the light of love that streamed from Jason's golden head and held her gleaming eyes. Her heart was warmed and melted like the dew on roses under the morning sun.

At one moment both of them were staring at the ground in deep embarrassment; at the next they were smiling and glancing at each other with the love-light in their eyes. But at last Medea forced herself to speak to him. 'Hear me now,' she said. 'These are my plans for you. When you have met my father and he has given you the deadly teeth from the serpent's jaws, wait for the moment of midnight and after bathing in an ever-running river, go out alone in sombre clothes and dig a round pit in the earth. There, kill a ewe and after heaping up a pyre over the pit, sacrifice it whole, with a libation of honey from the hive and prayers to Hecate, Perses' only Daughter. Then, when you have invoked the goddess duly, withdraw from the pyre. And do not be tempted to look behind you as you go, either by footfalls or the baying of hounds, or you may ruin everything and never reach your friends alive.

'In the morning, melt this charm, strip, and using it like oil, anoint your body. It will endow you with tremendous strength and boundless confidence. You will feel yourself a match, not for mere men, but for the gods themselves. Sprinkle your spear and shield and sword with it as well; and neither the spear-points of the earthborn men nor the consuming flames that the savage bulls spew out will find you vulnerable. But you will not be immune for long – only for the day. Nevertheless, do not at any moment flinch from the encounter.

'And here is something else that will stand you in good stead. You have yoked the mighty bulls; you have ploughed the stubborn fallow (with those great hands and all that strength it will not take you long); you have sown the serpent's teeth in the dark earth; and now the giants are springing up along the furrows. Watch till you see a number of them rise from the soil, then, before they see you, throw a great boulder in among them; and they will fall on it like famished dogs and kill one another. That is your moment; plunge into the fray yourself.

'And so the task is done and you can carry off the fleece to Hellas – a long, long way from Aea, I believe. Go none the less, go where you will, go where the fancy takes you when you part from us.'

After this, Medea was silent for a while. She kept her eyes fixed on the ground, and the warm tears ran down her lovely cheeks as she saw him sailing off over the high seas far away from her. Then she looked up at him and sorrowfully spoke again, taking his right hand in hers and no longer attempting to conceal her love. She said:

'But do remember, if you ever reach your home. Remember the name of Medea, and I for my part will remember you when you are far away. But now, pray tell me where you live. Where are you bound for when you sail across the sea from here? Will your journey take you near the wealthy city of Orchomenus or the Isle of Aea? Tell me too about that girl you mentioned, who won such fame for herself, the daughter of Pasiphae my father's sister.'

As he listened to this and noted her tears, unconscionable Love stole into the heart of Jason too. He replied: 'Of one thing I am sure. If I escape and live to reach Achaea; if Aeetes does not set us a still more formidable task; never by night or day shall I forget you. But you asked about the country of my birth. If it pleases you to hear, I will describe it; indeed I should like nothing better. It is a land ringed by lofty mountains, rich in sheep and pasture, and the birthplace of Prometheus' son, the good Deucalion, who was the first man to found cities, build temples to the gods and rule mankind as king. Its neighbours call the land Haemonia, and in it stands Iolcus, my own town, and many others too where the very name of the Aeaean Island is unknown. Yet they do say that it was from these parts that the Aeolid Minyas migrated long ago to found Orchomenus, which borders on Cadmeian lands. But why do I trouble you with all this tiresome talk about my home and Minos' daughter, the far-famed Ariadne, that lovely lady with the glorious name who roused your curiosity? I can only hope that, as Minos came to terms with Theseus for her sake, your father will be reconciled with us.'

He had thought, by talking in this gentle way, to soothe Medea. But she was now obsessed by the gloomiest forebodings; embittered too. And she answered him with passion:

'No doubt in Hellas people think it right to honour their agreements. But Aeetes is not the kind of man that Minos was, if what you say of him is true; and as for Ariadne, I cannot claim to be a match for her. So do not talk of friendliness to strangers. But oh, at least remember me when you are back in Iolcus; and I, despite my parents, will remember you. And may there come to me some whisper from afar, some bird to tell the tale, when you forget me. Or may the Storm-Winds snatch me up and carry me across the sea to Iolcus, to denounce you to your face and remind you that I saved your life. That is the moment I would choose to pay an unexpected visit to your house.'

As she spoke, tears of misery ran down her cheeks. But Jason said: 'Dear lady, you may spare the wandering Winds that task, and your tell-tale bird as well, for you are talking nonsense. If you come to us in Hellas you will be honoured and revered by both the women and the men. Indeed they will treat you as a goddess, because it was through you that their sons came home alive, or their brothers, kinsmen, or beloved husbands were saved from hurt. And there shall be a bridal bed for you, which you and I will share. Nothing shall part us in our love till Death at his appointed hour removes us from the light of day.'

As she heard these words of his, her heart melted within her. And yet she shuddered as she thought of the disastrous step she was about to take. Poor girl! She was not going to refuse for long this offer of a home in Hellas. The goddess Here had arranged it all: Medea was to leave her native land for the sacred city of Iolcus, and there to bring his punishment to Pelias.

Her maids, who had been spying on them from afar, were now becoming restive, though they did not intervene. It was high time for the maiden to go home to her mother. But Medea had no thought of leaving yet; she was entranced both by his comeliness and his bewitching talk. At last however, Jason, who had kept his wits about him, said, 'Now we must part, or the sun will set before we know it. Besides, some passer-by might see us. But we will meet each other here again.'

By gentle steps they had advanced so far towards an understanding. And now they parted, he in a joyful mood to go back to his companions and the ship, she to rejoin her maids, who all ran up to meet her. But as they gathered round, she did not even notice them: her head was in the clouds. Without knowing what she did, she got into her carriage to drive the mules, taking the reins in one hand and the whip in the other. And off they trotted to the palace in the town.

She had no sooner arrived than Chalciope questioned her anxiously about her sons. But Medea had left her wits behind her. She neither heard a word her sister said nor showed the least desire to answer her inquiries. She sat down on a low stool at the foot of her bed, leant over and rested her cheek on her left hand, pondering with tears in her eyes on the infamous part she had played in a scene that she herself had staged.

Jason found his escort in the place where he had left them, and as they set out to rejoin the rest, he told them how he had fared. When the party reached the ship, he was received with open arms and in reply to the questions of his friends he told them of Medea's plans and showed them the powerful charm. Idas was the only member of the company who was not impressed. He sat aloof, nursing his resentment. The rest were overjoyed, and since the night permitted no immediate move, they settled down in peace and comfort. But at dawn they despatched two men to Aeetes to ask him for the seed, Telamon beloved of Ares, and Aethalides the famous son of Hermes. This pair set out on their errand, and they did not fail. When they reached the king, he handed them the deadly teeth that Jason was to sow.

The teeth were those of the Aonian serpent, the guardian of Ares' spring, which Cadmus killed in Ogygian Thebes. He had come there in his search for Europa, and there he settled, under the guidance of a heifer picked out for him by Apollo in an oracle. Athene, Lady of Trito, tore the teeth out of the serpent's jaws and divided them between Aeetes and Cadmus, the slayer of the beast. Cadmus sowed them in the Aonian plain and founded an earthborn clan with all that had escaped the spear of Ares when he did his harvesting. Such were the teeth that Aeetes let them take back to the ship. He gave them willingly, as he was satisfied that Jason, even if he yoked the bulls, would prove unable to finish off the task.

It was evening. Out in the west, beyond the farthest Ethiopian hills, the Sun was sinking under the darkening world; Night was harnessing her team; and the Argonauts were preparing their beds by the hawsers of the ship. But Jason waited for the bright constellation of the Bear to decline,* and then, when all the air from heaven to earth was still, he set out like a stealthy thief across the solitary plain. During the day he had prepared himself, and so had everything he needed with him; Argus had fetched him some milk and a ewe from a farm; the rest he had taken from the ship itself. When he had found an unfrequented spot in a clear meadow under the open sky, he began by bathing his naked body reverently in the sacred river, and then put on a dark mantle which Hypsipyle of Lemnos had given him to remind him of their passionate embraces. Then he dug a pit a cubit deep, piled up billets, and laid the sheep on top of them after cutting its throat. He kindled the wood from underneath and poured mingled libations on the sacrifice, calling on Hecate Brimo to help him in the coming test. This done, he withdrew; and the dread goddess, hearing his words from the abyss, came up to accept the offering of Aeson's son. She was garlanded by fearsome snakes that coiled themselves round twigs of oak; the twinkle of a thousand torches lit the scene; and hounds of the underworld barked shrilly all around her. The whole meadow trembled under her feet, and the nymphs of marsh and river who haunt the fens by Amarantian Phasis cried out in fear. Jason was terrified; but even so, as he retreated, he did not once turn round. And so he found himself among his friends once more, and Dawn arrived, showing herself betimes above the snows of Caucasus.

At daybreak too, Aeetes put on his breast the stiff cuirass which Ares had given him after slaying Mimas with his own

* See Introduction, p. 25.

hands in the field of Phlegra; and on his head he set his golden helmet with its four plates, bright as the Sun's round face when he rises fresh from Ocean Stream. And he took up his shield of many hides, and his unconquerable spear, a spear that none of the Argonauts could have withstood, now that they had deserted Heracles, who alone could have dealt with it in battle. Phaëthon was close at hand, holding his father's swift horses and well-built chariot in readiness. Aeetes mounted, took the reins in his hands, and drove out of the town along the broad highway to attend the contest, followed by hurrying crowds. Lord of the Colchians, he might have been Poseidon in his chariot driving to the Isthmian Games, to Taenarum, to the waters of Lerna, or through the grove of Onchestus, and on to Calaurea with his steeds, to the Haemonian Rock or the woods of Geraestus.

Meanwhile Jason, remembering Medea's instructions, melted the magic drug and sprinkled his shield with it and his sturdy spear and sword. His comrades watched him and put his weapons to the proof with all the force they had. But they could not bend the spear at all; even in their strong hands it proved itself unbreakable. Idas was furious with them. He hacked at the butt-end of the spear with his great sword, but the blade rebounded from it like a hammer from the anvil. And a great shout of joy went up; they felt that the battle was already won.

Next, Jason sprinkled his own body and was imbued with miraculous, indomitable might. As his hands increased in power, his very fingers twitched. Like a warhorse eager for battle, pawing the ground, neighing, pricking its ears and tossing up its head in pride, he exulted in the strength of his limbs. Time and again he leapt high in the air this way and that, brandishing his shield of bronze and ashen spear. The weapons flashed on the eye like intermittent lightning playing in a stormy sky from black clouds charged with rain.

After that there was no faltering; the Argonauts were ready

for the test. They took their places on the benches of the ship and rowed her swiftly upstream to the plain of Ares. This lay as far beyond the city as a chariot has to travel from start to turning-post when the kinsmen of a dead king are holding foot and chariot races in his honour. They found Aeetes there and a full gathering of the Colchians. The tribesmen were stationed on the rocky spurs of Caucasus, and the king was wheeling around in his chariot on the river-bank.

Jason, as soon as his men had made the hawsers fast, leapt from the ship and entered the lists with spear and shield. He also took with him a shining bronze helmet full of sharp teeth, and his sword was slung from his shoulder. But his body was bare, so that he looked like Apollo of the golden sword as much as Ares god of war. Glancing round the field, he saw the bronze yoke for the bulls and beside it the plough of indurated steel, all in one piece. He went up to them, planted his heavy spear in the ground by its butt and laid the helmet down, leaning it against the spear. Then he went forward with his shield alone to examine the countless tracks that the bulls had made. And now, from somewhere in the bowels of the earth, from the smoky stronghold where they slept, the pair of bulls appeared, breathing flames of fire. The Argonauts were terrified at the sight. But Jason planting his feet apart stood to receive them, as a reef in the sea confronts the tossing billows in a gale. He held his shield in front of him, and the two bulls, bellowing loudly, charged and butted it with their strong horns. But he was not shifted from his stance, not by so much as an inch. The bulls snorted and spurted from their mouths devouring flames, like a perforated crucible when the leather bellows of the smith, sometimes ceasing, sometimes blowing hard, have made a blaze and the fire leaps up from below with a terrific roar. The deadly heat assailed him on all sides with the force of lightning. But he was protected by Medea's magic. Seizing the right-hand bull by the tip of its horn, he dragged it with all his might towards the yoke, and then brought it down on its knees with a sudden kick on its bronze foot. The other charged, and was felled in the same way at a single blow; and Jason, who had cast his shield aside, stood with his feet apart, and though the flames at once enveloped him, held them both down on their fore-knees where they fell. Aeetes marvelled at the man's strength.

Castor and Polydeuces picked up the yoke and gave it to Jason – they had been detailed for the task and were close at hand. Jason bound it tight on the bulls' necks, lifted the bronze pole between them and fastened it to the yoke by its pointed end, while the Twins backed out of the heat and returned to the ship. Then, taking his shield from the ground he slung it on his back, picked up the heavy helmet full of teeth and grasped his unconquerable spear, with which, like some ploughman using his Pelasgian goad, he pricked the bulls under their flanks and with a firm grip on its well-made handle guided the adamantine plough.

At first the bulls in their high fury spurted flames of fire. Their breath came out with a roar like that of the blustering wind that causes frightened mariners to take in sail. But presently, admonished by the spear, they went ahead, and the rough fallow cleft by their own and the great ploughman's might lay broken up behind them. The huge clods as they were torn away along the furrow groaned aloud; and Jason came behind, planting his feet down firmly on the field.* As he ploughed he sowed the teeth, casting them far from himself with many a backward glance lest a deadly crop of earthborn men should catch him unawares. And the bulls, thrusting their bronze hoofs into the earth, toiled on till only a third of the passing day was left. Then, when weary labourers in other fields were hoping it would soon be time to free their oxen from the yoke, this indefatigable ploughman's work was done – the whole four-acre field was ploughed.

* See Notes on the Text, p. 197.

Jason freed his bulls from the plough and shooed them off. They fled across the plain; and he, seeing that no earthborn men had yet appeared in the furrows, seized the occasion to go back to the ship, where his comrades gathered round him with heartening words. He dipped his helmet in the flowing river and with its water quenched his thirst, then flexed his knees to keep them supple; and as fresh courage filled his heart, he lashed himself into a fury, like a wild boar when it whets its teeth to face the hunt and the foam drips to the ground from its savage mouth.

By now the earthborn men were shooting up like corn in all parts of the field. The deadly War-god's sacred plot bristled with stout shields, double-pointed spears, and glittering helmets. The splendour of it flashed through the air above and struck Olympus. Indeed this army springing from the earth shone out like the full congregation of the stars piercing the darkness of a murky night, when snow lies deep and the winds have chased the wintry clouds away. But Jason did not forget the counsel he had had from Medea of the many wiles. He picked up from the field a huge round boulder, a formidable quoit that Ares might have thrown, but four strong men together could not have budged from its place. Rushing forward with this in his hands he hurled it far away among the earthborn men, then crouched behind his shield, unseen and full of confidence. The Colchians gave a mighty shout like the roar of the sea beating on jagged rocks; and the king himself was astounded as he saw the great quoit hurtle through the air. But the earthborn men, like nimble hounds, leapt on one another and with loud yells began to slay. Beneath each other's spears they fell on their mother earth, as pines or oaks are blown down by a gale. And now, like a bright meteor that leaps from heaven and leaves a fiery trail behind it, portentous to all those who see it flash across the night, the son of Aeson hurled himself on them with his sword unsheathed and in promiscuous slaughter mowed them down, striking as he

145

could, for many of them had but half emerged and showed their flanks and bellies only, some had their shoulders clear, some had just stood up, and others were afoot already and rushing into battle. So might some farmer threatened by a frontier war snatch up a newly sharpened sickle and, lest the enemy should reap his fields before him, hasten to cut down the unripe corn, not waiting for the season and the sun to ripen it. Thus Jason cut his crop of earthborn men. Blood filled the furrows as water fills the conduits of a spring. And still they fell, some on their faces biting the rough clods, some on their backs, and others on their hands and sides, looking like monsters from the sea. Many were struck before they could lift up their feet, and rested there with the death-dew on their brows, each trailing on the earth so much of him as had come up into the light of day. They lay like saplings in an orchard bowed to the ground when Zeus has sent torrential rain and snapped them at the root, wasting the gardeners' toil and bringing heartbreak to the owner of the plot, the man who planted them.

Such was the scene that King Aeetes now surveyed, and such his bitterness. He went back to the city with his Colchians, pondering on the quickest way to bring the foreigners to book. And the sun sank and Jason's task was done.

BOOK FOUR

HOMEWARD BOUND

*Now tell us, Muse, in your own heavenly tongue how the Colchian
maiden schemed and suffered. Speak, Daughter of Zeus; for here
your poet falters and the words fail to come. What drove her to desert
her home? Was it the frenzy of a star-crossed love? Or must we
call it panic?*

ALL night Aeetes sat in his palace with his Colchian noblemen
planning a treacherous stroke against the Argonauts. He was
consumed with rage at the lamentable outcome of the test,
and by no means satisfied that his daughters had not had a hand
in the affair.

Meanwhile the goddess Here filled Medea's heart with
agonizing fears. She trembled like a slender fawn caught in
a woodland thicket and terrified by the baying of the hounds.
She realized at once that her father could not fail to know
what she had done for Jason, and that she would soon be
called on to pay the price in full. She also feared the maids
who had seen something of their secret meeting. Her eyes
burnt and there was a fearful roaring in her ears. Often in her
acute distress she groaned, she clutched her throat, she tore her
hair. Indeed she would have taken poison then and there and
died before her time, frustrating the designs of Here, had not
the goddess put it in her troubled mind that she might flee
with Phrixus' sons. This thought stilled her fluttering heart
and fortitude returned. She cleared her lap of deadly drugs
and poured them all back into their box. She kissed her bed;
she kissed the posts on either side of the folding doors; she
stroked the walls of her room. Then, tearing off one of her

long tresses, she left it there for her mother in memory of her girlhood and said her sad goodbye:

'Mother, I go, leaving this lock here in my stead. Farewell; for I am going far away. Farewell Chalciope; farewell my home and all it holds. Oh, Jason, you should never have come here! I wish the sea had been the end of you.'

With that and shedding many tears she went, much as a newly captured girl, torn from her own land by the fortune of war, makes off from some rich house before she is inured to work and schooled in the miseries of servitude under the cruel eye of a mistress. The slave-girl slinks away; but the beautiful Medea sped through the palace, and for her the very doors responding to her hasty incantations swung open of their own accord. She ran barefoot down narrow alleys, holding her mantle over her forehead with her left hand to hide her face, and with the other lifting up the hem of her skirt. Swiftly and fearfully she passed across the great city by a secret way, and so beyond the walls, unrecognized by any of the watch, who had not even seen her in her flight. From there she meant to reach the temple.* She knew the road well enough, having often roamed in that direction searching for corpses or for noxious roots, as witches do. But none the less she was afraid and trembled in her fear.

Rising from the distant east, the Lady Moon, Titanian goddess, saw the girl wandering distraught, and in wicked glee said to herself: 'So I am not the only one to go astray for love, I that burn for beautiful Endymion and seek him in the Latmian cave. How many times, when I was bent on love, have you disorbed me with your incantations, making the night moonless so that you might practise your beloved witchcraft undisturbed! And now you are as lovesick as myself. The little god of mischief has given you Jason, and many a heartache with him. Well, go your way; but clever as you are, steel yourself now to face a life of sighs and misery.'

* See Notes on the Text, p. 197.

So said the Moon. But Medea in her haste sped on and presently, to her relief, found herself on the high bank of the river, and looking across it caught the gleam of a bonfire which the Argonauts kept blazing all night in celebration of their triumph. She sent a clear call ringing through the dark to Phrontis, youngest son of Phrixus, on the other bank. He and his brothers, as well as Jason, recognized her voice and told the rest, who were speechless with amazement when they realized the truth. Medea called three times; three times at the bidding of the others Phrontis shouted back, and all the while they were rowing eagerly towards her.

Even before they had made fast to the opposite bank, Jason leapt lightly to the ground from *Argo*'s deck. He was followed by Phrontis and Argus, the sons of Phrixus, and at once Medea's arms were round their knees and she was making her appeal: 'My dear ones, save me from Aeetes, save yourselves! All is discovered, all; and there is nothing we can do. Let us sail away before that man can even mount his chariot; and I myself will give you the golden fleece, putting the guardian snake to sleep. But you, Jason, in the presence of your men must call the gods to witness the vows that you have made me. Do not expose me to insult and disgrace when I have left my country far away and have no kinsmen to protect me.'

She spoke in anguish and fell at Jason's feet; but what she said had warmed his heart. At once he raised her tenderly and embraced her. Then, to comfort her, he said: 'Dear lady, I swear, and may Olympian Zeus and his Consort Here, goddess of wedlock, be my witnesses, that when we are back in Hellas I will take you into my home as my own wedded wife.' And with that he took her right hand in his own.

Medea urged them to row with all speed to the sacred wood, so that while it was still dark they might seize and carry off the fleece in defiance of the king. This was no sooner said than done, and with alacrity. They took her on board at once, thrust *Argo* from the bank, and rowed off, waking the night as they struck the water with their pine-wood blades. It was then that Medea had a wild moment of regret. She started to go back, stretching her hands out to the shore. But Jason went to her with reassuring words and checked her desperate design.

He and Medea reached their goal at that late hour of night when the hunter, cutting short his sleep, sallies with his trusty hound before the glaring light of dawn can mar the quarry's trail and spoil the scent. They landed on a lawn called the Ram's Bed, as it was there that the ram that carried Minyan Phrixus on his back first flexed his weary knees. Near by, begrimed with smoke, was the base of the altar that Phrixus had set up to Zeus, the friend of fugitives, when he sacrificed the golden wonder, as Hermes had bidden him to do when he met him on the way. Here then, under Argus's direction, the crew set the pair ashore.

A path led them to the sacred wood, where they were making for the huge oak on which the fleece was hung, bright as a cloud incarnadined by the fiery beams of the rising sun. But the serpent with his sharp unsleeping eyes had seen them coming and now confronted them, stretching out his long neck and hissing terribly. The high banks of the river and the deep recesses of the wood threw back the sound, and far away from Titanian Aea it reached the ears of Colchians living by the outfall of Lycus, the river that parts from the loud waters of Araxes to unite his sacred stream with that of Phasis and flow in company with him till both debouch into the Caucasian Sea. Babies sleeping in their mothers' arms were startled by the hiss, and their anxious mothers waking in alarm hugged them closer to their breasts.

The monster in his sheath of horny scales rolled forward his interminable coils, like the eddies of black smoke that spring from smouldering logs and chase each other from below in endless convolutions. But as he writhed he saw the

maiden take her stand, and heard her in her sweet voice
invoking Sleep, the conqueror of the gods, to charm him.
She also called on the night-wandering Queen of the world
below to countenance her efforts. Jason from behind looked
on in terror. But the giant snake, enchanted by her song, was
soon relaxing the whole length of his serrated spine and
smoothing out his multitudinous undulations, like a dark and
silent swell rolling across a sluggish sea. Yet his grim head still
hovered over them and the cruel jaws threatened to snap
them up. But Medea, chanting a spell, dipped a fresh sprig of
juniper in her brew and sprinkled his eyes with her most
potent drug; and as the all-pervading magic scent spread
round his head, sleep fell on him. Stirring no more, he let his
jaw sink to the ground, and his innumerable coils lay stretched
out far behind, spanning the deep wood. Medea called to
Jason and he snatched the golden fleece from the oak. But she
herself stayed where she was, smearing the wild one's head
with a magic salve, till Jason urged her to come back to the
ship and she left the sombre grove of Ares.

Lord Jason held up the great fleece in his arms. The shimmer-
ing wool threw a fiery glow on his fair cheeks and forehead;
and he rejoiced in it, glad as a girl who catches on her silken
gown the lovely light of the full moon as it climbs the sky
and looks into her attic room. The ram's skin with its golden
covering was as large as the hide of a yearling heifer or a
brocket, as a young stag is called by hunting folk. The long
flocks weighed it down and the very ground before him as he
walked was bright with gold. When he slung it on his left
shoulder, as he did at times, it reached his feet. But now
and again he made a bundle of it in his arms. He was
mortally afraid that some god or man might rob him on the
way.

Dawn was spreading over the world when they rejoined
the rest. The young men marvelled when they saw the
mighty fleece, dazzling as the lightning of Zeus, and they all

leapt up in their eagerness to touch it and hold it in their hands. But Jason kept them off and threw a new mantle over the fleece. Then he led Medea aft, found her a seat, and addressed his men.

'My friends,' he said, 'let us start for home without delay. The prize for which we dared greatly and suffered misery on the cruel sea is ours. And the task proved easy, thanks to this lady, whom I intend, with her consent, to bring home with me and wed. You too must cherish her: she is the true saviour of Achaea and yourselves.

'I spoke of haste, for I am sure that Aeetes and his mob are on their way to bar our passage from the river to the sea. So man the ship, man every bench, two men on each, taking it in turns to row. That will leave half of you to hold aloft your ox-hide shields against the arrows of the enemy and protect us as we get away. Remember, we hold the future of our children, our dear country, and our aged parents in our hands. Hellas depends on us. We can plunge her in grief; we can bring her glory.'

With that he donned his arms. The eager crew responded with a great shout, and Jason drawing his sword cut through the hawsers at the stern. Then, in his battle gear, he took his stand beside Medea and the steersman Ancaeus; and *Argo* leapt forward to the oars as the crew strained every nerve to bring her clear of the river.

By now the haughty king and all his Colchians were well aware of Medea's love for Jason and the part she had played. In full armour they gathered in the market-place, countless as the waves of the sea whipped up by a winter storm, or the leaves that fall to earth in autumn from the myriad branches of the trees – and who can number them? So in their multitudes they streamed along the banks of the river in full cry. Aeetes in his fine chariot, with the wind-swift horses that Helios had given him, stood out above them all. In his left hand he held a round shield, in the other a long torch of pinewood, and his huge spear lay beside him pointing to the front. Apsyrtus held the reins.

But the ship, swept down the broad stream by the current and the strong men at the oars, was already standing out to sea. It was a bitter moment for Aeetes. In a frenzy, he lifted up his hands to Helios and Zeus calling on them to witness these outrageous deeds. And on the spot he threatened his whole people with dire pains if they should fail to lay their hands on his daughter. Whether they found her on land or caught the ship while still on the high seas, they must bring her to him, so that he might satisfy his lust for revenge, exacting payment for all that had been done. If not, they should experience in themselves the full force of his wrath and the weight of his avenging hand, paying with their own lives.

Thus the king thundered; and on the self-same day the Colchians launched their ships, equipped them, and put out. One might have taken their immense armada for an endless flight of birds, flock after flock, breaking the silence of the sea.

Meanwhile there was a fresh breeze for the Argonauts; Here had seen to it. She wished Medea to reach the Pelasgian land, bringing doom to the house of Pelias, as quickly as might be; and in the morning of the third day they made fast their stern cables on the Paphlagonian coast at the mouth of the River Halys. Medea had told them to land there and propitiate Hecate with a sacrifice. But with what ritual she prepared the offering, no one must hear. Nor must I let myself be tempted to describe it; my lips are sealed by awe. But the altar they built for the goddess on the beach is still there for men of a later age to see.

At this point it was natural for Jason and all his friends to think of Phineus and how he had told them they would return from Aea by a different route. But nobody knew exactly what the seer had meant, and they listened eagerly to all that Argus had to tell them. He said: 'We are going to Orchomenus. The prophet whom you met made that your destination and he never errs. There is indeed another route. Priests of the gods, who arose in Egyptian Thebes, have made this clear.

'Think of a time when the wheeling constellations did not yet exist; when one would have looked in vain for the sacred Danaan race, finding only the Apidanean Arcadians, who are said to have lived before the moon itself was there, feeding on acorns in the hills. These were the days before the noble scions of Deucalion ruled the Pelasgian land, when Egypt, mother of an earlier race, was known as the corn-rich country of the Dawn, and the Nile that waters all its length was called the Triton, a generous river flowing through a rainless land, yet by its floods producing crops in plenty. Now we are told that from this country a certain king set out, supported by a strong and loyal force, and made his way through the whole of Europe and Asia, founding many cities as he went. Some of these survive, though others have succumbed to the burden of the years. But to this day Aea stands, with people in it descended from the very men whom that king settled there. Moreover they have preserved tablets of stone which their ancestors engraved with maps giving the outlines of the land and sea and the routes in all directions. On these is shown a river, the farthest branch of Ocean Stream, broad and deep enough to carry merchantmen. They placed it at a great distance from Aea, giving it the name of Ister. Far away, beyond the North Wind, its headwaters come rushing down from the Rhipaean Mountains. Then it flows for a time through endless plains as a single stream. But when it reaches the borderlands of Thrace and Scythia it divides, one branch running down into the Ionian Sea,* the other flowing south into a deep gulf that stretches up from the Sicilian Sea – a sea that washes your own shores if I am right in thinking that the River Achelous flows into it from Hellas.'

* See Glossary, p. 205.

Argus finished, and the goddess gave her blessing to the route he had proposed by sending them a sign. With cries of joy they saw ahead of them a trail of heavenly light, showing them the way to go. So they left the son of Lycus there and with all their canvas spread sailed happily across the sea. They sighted the Paphlagonian mountains, but did not round Carambis, for the wind held and the celestial fire glowed in their van till they reached the mighty River Ister.

Now some of the Colchians, on a false trail, had passed out of the Black Sea between the Cyanean Rocks. The rest, with Apsyrtus in command, made for the Ister, and turned into the river by the Fair Mouth, gaining access to this, the farthest inlet of the Ionian Sea, by doubling a narrow neck of land. Thus they outstripped the Argonauts. For here the Ister embraces an island called Peuke, shaped like a triangle, the base presenting beaches to the sea, and the apex pointing up the river, which is thus divided into two channels, one known as the Narex and the other, at the lower end of the island, as the Fair Mouth. It was by the Fair Mouth that Apsyrtus and his Colchians sailed with all speed into the river, whereas the Argonauts went a long way up the coast to the upper end of the island.

The Colchian vessels spread panic as they went. Shepherds grazing flocks in the meadows by the river abandoned their sheep at the terrifying sight, taking the ships for live monsters that had come up from the sea, the mother of Leviathans. For none of the Istrian tribes, the Thracians and their Scythian friends, the Sigynni, the Graucenii, the Sindi, who had already occupied the great and empty plain of Laurium – none of these had ever set eyes on a sea-going vessel.

In due course the Colchian fleet reached Mount Angurus, and came at last, when they had left that mountain and the Laurian plain behind them, to the Rock of Cauliacus, where Ister is divided into two branches and so descends into widely separated seas. The Colchians sailed down the Illyrian branch into the Cronian Sea, and once there, blocked every exit to prevent the quarry from slipping through their hands. Meanwhile the Argonauts, who had followed them down the same river, reached the two Brygean Islands, which lie near the coast. These are sacred to Artemis, who had a temple on one of them, and they sought refuge from the forces of Apsyrtus on the other, knowing that their enemies, whatever they had done with the many other islands at the river mouth, had left these two strictly alone in deference to the Daughter of Zeus. But the rest were crowded with Colchians and barred every outlet to the open sea. In fact Apsyrtus had posted men on each of the neighbouring isles right up to the River Salangon and to the Nestian shore.

If the Minyae, outnumbered as they were, had fought it out at this point they would have met with disaster. But they evaded a pitched battle by coming to terms with the enemy. It was decided that the golden fleece, since Aeetes himself had said they should have it if they accomplished their allotted task, was theirs by right, and they could keep it, whether they had acquired it by clandestine means or openly defied the king and helped themselves. As for Medea – and here was the bone of contention – they would place her in chancery with the goddess Artemis and leave her alone, till one of the kings entitled to mete out justice should decide whether she was to go home to her father or follow the Argonauts to Hellas.

When Medea realized all that was involved in the terms of this treaty, she was appalled and could not rest till she had spoken to Jason in private. So she beckoned him to leave his friends, and when she had brought him far enough away, she faced him and broke into passionate protestations:

'My lord, what is this plan that you and my brother are making for my disposal? Has your splendid success destroyed your memory? Have you forgotten all you said to me when you were forced to seek my help? Where are the oaths you swore by Zeus, the suppliants' god? Where are the honied promises that I believed in when I defied convention and my own conscience, abandoning my country, the glories of my home, even my parents, everything I valued most? And now I am carried off, far away across the sea, with only the wistful halcyons for company. All this because I saw you through your troubles, saw that you won your battle with the bulls and giants and came out alive. And then the fleece, for which you crossed the sea. You got it through my own folly. I have disgraced my sex.

'And so I say that I am yours, your daughter, wife, and sister, and I follow you to Hellas. You should be ready to stand by me, come what may, instead of leaving me alone while you consult the kings. Why not run off with me, and no more said? You and I are in law and honour pledged to one another. Abide by that – or else draw your sword, slit my throat, and let me make amends to you for my infatuation.

'Think of my misery if the king to whom you both refer this infamous agreement hands me over to my brother. How am I to look my father in the face? As an honest woman? I can scarcely imagine the cruelty of his revenge, the tortures I should suffer for my crimes. And you, do you look forward to a happy home-coming? I hope that Here, Queen of Heaven, whose favourite you claim to be, will never let you have it. I hope that you will think of me some day when you yourself are suffering. I hope the fleece will vanish like an idle dream, down into Erebus. And may my avenging Furies chase you from your home and so repay me for all I have endured through your inhumanity. You have broken a most solemn oath. It is not in reason that my curses should miscarry.

'You are inflexible. But wait awhile. You and your friends think that this covenant has solved your problems, and I am nothing in your eyes. You will learn better soon.'

She boiled with rage. She longed to set the ship on fire, to break it up and hurl herself into the flames. But Jason calmed her. She had frightened him.

He said: 'Enough, my lady. I am no happier about this business than you. But we are seeking to stave off a fight, encircled as we are by a vast horde of enemies, and all on your account. Even the natives here are ready to take up arms for Apsyrtus, wishing to see you led back to your father like some captured girl. And if we faced them in the field, we should every one of us be slaughtered. Would it not mortify you even more if we were killed and left you to them as a prize?

'However, this truce will leave us free to plan a pitfall for Apsyrtus; and I cannot think that the natives would attack us for your sake to oblige the Colchians, if the Colchian commander, who is your brother and protector, were removed. As for his troops, I shall not hesitate to engage them if they refuse to let me through.'

He was trying to placate her: there was death in her reply. 'Plan now!' she said. 'Evil deeds commit us to expedients evil as the deeds themselves. It was I who took the first false step, blinded as I was and driven by the Powers that be to go my wicked way. If you will hold the Colchian spearmen off, I for my part will lure Apsyrtus into your hands. But you must keep him friendly. Offer him splendid gifts, and when his heralds are taking them away, I hope to persuade them to arrange a secret conference between myself and him. Then, if you have the stomach for the deed, kill him – I shall not blame you – and make war on the Colchians.'

So they agreed and set about the preparation of the fatal trap. Gifts for Apsyrtus were laid out in plenty, the kind of gifts that host and guest exchange. They even added to their number a sacred garment that had belonged to Hypsipyle. It was a purple robe which the divine Graces had made with their own hands for Dionysus in sea-girt Dia. Later, Dionysus gave it to his son Thoas, Thoas left it to Hypsipyle, and she, with many another piece of finery, gave it to Jason as a parting gift. It was a work of art, a joy for ever, as pleasing to the eye as to the sense of touch. And it still gave out the ambrosial perfume it received when the Lord Dionysus lay on it, tipsy with wine and nectar, embracing Minos' daughter, the fair young Ariadne, whom Theseus carried off from Cnossus and abandoned in the Isle of Dia.

Medea gave the heralds a message for Apsyrtus that would serve as bait. As soon as she had come to the temple of Artemis in accordance with the treaty, he was to meet her there under cover of night. She was planning to steal the golden fleece and return with him to the palace of Aeetes – they must confer. And as a pretext for her treachery she said that the sons of Phrixus had compelled her to go off with the Argonauts. Such was the lure; and she reinforced her words with magic, scattering to the four winds spells of such potency as would have drawn wild creatures far away to come down from their mountain fastnesses.

Unconscionable Love, bane and tormentor of mankind, parent of strife, fountain of tears, source of a thousand ills, rise, mighty Power, and fall on the sons of our enemies with all the force you used upon Medea when you filled her with insensate fury. For Apsyrtus did obey her call and she destroyed him foully. It rests with me to tell the sorry tale.

When the two parties in accordance with their pact left Medea on the Island of Artemis, they ran ashore at separate spots. Jason, going into ambush, waited for Apsyrtus and for his own men whom he expected later. Presently Apsyrtus himself, tempted by Medea's treacherous offer, came speeding over the sea in his own ship and landed on the sacred island at dead of night. Unescorted, he went straight up to his sister and began to sound her in the hope that she would have some plan for turning the tables on her foreign friends. He might have been a little boy trying to ford a winter torrent that a strong man could not cross. However, they agreed on every point. And now Jason leapt from his hiding-place with his naked sword uplifted. Medea quickly turned aside, covering her eyes with her veil so as not to see her brother's blood spilt; and Jason marked him down and struck him, as a butcher fells a mighty strong-horned bull. The deed was done at the temple of Artemis, which Brygi from the mainland coast had built. Apsyrtus sank to his knees in the porch and in his death throes cupped his hands over the wound to stanch the dark blood. Even so, as Medea shrank aside, he painted red her silvery veil and dress. With eyes askance the unforgiving and indomitable Fury took quick note of the heinous deed. But Jason, after lopping off the dead man's extremities, licked up some blood three times and three times spat the pollution out, as killers do in the attempt to expiate a treacherous murder. Then he hid the cold corpse in the earth. And there the bones still lie, among a people who have kept Apsyrtus' name alive.

By now the rest of the Argonauts were coming up. Medea signalled to them by raising a torch; and as soon as they saw the light they laid their own ship by the vessel that had brought Apsyrtus, and slaughtered the Colchian crew, falling on them like hawks on a flock of pigeons, or mountain lions leaping into a sheepfold and bringing havoc to the huddled flock. Not a man escaped death; they swept through the whole crew like a forest fire. Jason joined them, eager to lend a hand. But he came too late; they did not need his help and were already wondering whether he needed theirs.

They sat down to plot their future course. This needed careful thought, and they were still debating when Medea joined them. But Peleus was the first to come forward with a plan. 'We must embark,' he said, 'while it is still dark and row through the passage opposite to that commanded by the enemy. At dawn they will discover what has happened, and I am convinced that after that no consideration will induce them to prolong the chase. They will have lost their prince; there will be bitter quarrels that will break them up; and when their forces are dispersed, it should be easy for us to return here and resume our present course.' This, from the son of Aeacus, decided the young lords. They embarked at once and rowed with all their might, never pausing till they reached the sacred Isle of Amber, the innermost of all the Amber Islands at the mouth of the Eridanus.

Meanwhile the Colchians, when they heard of their prince's death, made ready to pursue the Minyae in *Argo* through all the length of the Cronian Sea. But Here damped their ardour by means of a terrific thunderstorm; and when, instead, they thought of going home, no goddess was needed to remind them of Aeetes' savage threats. In the end, deciding that Colchis was no place for them, they split up into several groups, which set out in different directions and established settlements. Some landed on the islands that the Argonauts had occupied, and these still live there; they call themselves Apsyrtians. Others settled down among the Encheleans, building a walled town by the deep and dark Illyrian river, where Harmonia and Cadmus were buried. Others again live in the mountains which are called the Thunderers, in memory of the day when the thunder of Zeus the son of Cronos deterred them from crossing to the island opposite.

When the Argonauts felt that they could safely do so, they left the Isle of Amber to resume their homeward voyage. But they found the sea ahead so cluttered with islets that a ship could scarcely thread her way between them. So they made for the Hyllean coast and anchored there. As before, the Hylleans * showed them no hostility and of their own accord helped them on their way; for which Jason rewarded them with a large tripod he had had from Apollo. This was one of a pair given him by Phoebus to serve him on his mission, when he went to holy Pytho to consult the god about that very voyage. Heaven had decreed that the land that held either of these tripods should never be laid waste by an invading force. Which is the reason why Jason's gift lies

* See Glossary, p. 205.

hidden to this day in Hyllean earth. Close to their own peaceful town they buried it deep, where nobody could ever find it.

Hyllus, their king, had died before the Argonauts' arrival. He was the son of the beautiful Melite by Heracles and was born in Phaeacian lands, for his father had come to King Nausithous and the Isle of Macris, nurse of Dionysus, to obtain absolution for the murder of his children. There Heracles fell in love with the water-nymph Melite, a daughter of the River Aegaeus, and she bore him the mighty Hyllus. But by the time Hyllus had reached man's estate he felt that he had lived long enough in the island of his birth under the stern eye of King Nausithous. So he collected a party of native Phaeacians and, assisted by the king himself, migrated with them to the Cronian Sea. And in those parts he settled, and was killed – by the Mentors, in the course of a cattle-raid.

Tell me now, Muses, how *Argo* travelled far beyond the Cronian Sea, leaving in Italy and the Ligurian Islands that are called the Stoechades innumerable traces which have been faithfully recorded. Whose was the hand, and what the need, that made them stray so far? And what winds carried them?

So signal was the downfall of Apsyrtus that Zeus himself, King of the gods, took umbrage at the horrid deed and ordained that they should wipe away the guilty stain of blood with the aid of Aeaean Circe and suffer endless hardships before they reached their homes. But none of them knew this. Standing out from the Hyllaean coast, they ran a long way south, leaving behind them the string of Liburnian islands that the Colchians had occupied, Issa, Dysceladus, and beautiful Pityeia. Next they approached Corcyra, where Poseidon found a home, far from her native land, for Asopus' daughter, Corcyra of the lovely locks, when in his passion he had made off with her from Phlius. The dark forests that cover the island give it a sombre look, and passing sailors call it Black Corcyra. After this, still favoured by a gentle breeze, they passed Melite, steep Cerossus, and out on the horizon, Nymphaea, the home of the powerful Calypso daughter of Atlas. Through the mist they even saw, or thought they saw, the Acroceraunian Mountains.

But now Here, remembering the wrath of Zeus and the plans he had for them, contrived to set them on their destined course. She raised a strong head wind which swept them straight back to the rugged Isle of Amber; and as they ran before the gale, there suddenly cried out to them in human speech the talking beam of Dodonian oak that Athene had fitted in the middle of *Argo*'s stem. The voice, announcing as it did the vengeful ire of Zeus, brought terror to the crew. It threatened them with endless wanderings across tempestuous seas till Circe should have purged them of the cruel murder of Apsyrtus; and it bade Polydeuces and Castor beg the immortal gods to grant them access to the Italian Sea, where they would find Circe, daughter of Perse and the Sun.

Out of the night *Argo* had spoken; and the Twins rose at once and lifted up their hands in prayer to Heaven for all its grace; but the rest were sunk in gloom. And *Argo* sped on under sail, up the Eridanus as far as ships can go.

They reached the outfall of that deep lake where Phaëthon, struck in the breast and half-consumed by a blazing thunderbolt, fell into the water from the chariot of the Sun. His wounded body smoulders to this day and sends up clouds of steam. Even the light-winged birds that try to fly across the water fail to reach the other side and with a helpless flutter plunge into the heat. All around, the Daughters of the Sun, encased in tall poplars, utter their sad and unavailing plaint. Shining drops of amber fall from their eyes on to the sands and are dried there by the sun. But when the wailing wind stirs the dark waters of the lake to rise above the beach, all the tears that have collected there are swept by the overflow into the river. The Celts, however, have another tale about these amber drops that are carried down the current. They say they are the many tears that Apollo shed for his son Asclepius when he visited the sacred people of the North. He was banished from the bright sky by his father Zeus, whom he blamed for having killed this son of his, who was borne by the Lady Coronis in splendid Lacereia at the mouth of the Amyrus. That is the tale according to the Celts.

It was not a place likely to delight the Argonauts. Indeed they could not even bring themselves to eat or drink. By day they were plagued to the point of exhaustion by the nauseating stench from Phaëthon's smouldering body, which the out-flow to the river emitted all the time. At night they had to listen to the loud lament of the shrill-voiced Daughters of the Sun, whose tears were borne along on the stream like drops of oil.

From this spot they made their way into the Rhone, a deep river which joins the Eridanus, raising a great commotion at the watersmeet. It rises at the world's end, by the gates and courts of Night, and flows on in three streams, one of which debouches on the shores of Ocean, another into the Ionian Sea, and the third, through seven mouths, into the great gulf of the Sardinian Sea. From the Rhone they passed into the storm-swept lakes that lie across the uncharted country of the Celts. And here they might have run into disaster. One outlet from the lakes led to a gulf of Ocean, which in their ignorance they were about to enter. Had they done so, they would never have got back alive. But they were saved by Here, who leapt down from heaven and called out to them from the Hercynian Rock. Terrified by the cry, which made the broad sky ring again, they turned back in obedience to the goddess and found the way that was to bring them home. Still guided by Here, they passed through countless Celtic and Ligurian tribes, coming to no harm, as the goddess spread a magic mist around them day by day; and so at last they reached the shore of the sounding sea. Leaving the Rhone by its central mouth, they crossed over to the Stoechades Islands, owing their safety on this occasion to Castor and Polydeuces. Which is why these sons of Zeus have ever since been honoured with altars and sacred rites, though this was not the only voyage where they played the part of saviours. Zeus put the ships of generations then unborn in the keeping of the Twins.

Leaving the Stoechades, they passed on to the island of Elba. They had toiled hard, and when they landed they scraped away the sweat with pebbles. Where they did this, skin-coloured pebbles strew the beach. Quoits and marvellous weapons that belonged to them are also found on the island, and it has a harbour which bears the name of Argo.

Passing swiftly over the Ausonian Sea, with the Tyrrhenian coast in sight, they came to the famous haven of Aea, took *Argo* close in, and tied up to the shore.

Here they found Circe bathing her head in the salt water. She had been terrified by a nightmare in which she saw all the rooms and walls of her house streaming with blood, and fire devouring all the magic drugs with which she used to bewitch her visitors. But she managed to put out the red flames with the blood of a murdered man, gathering it up in her hands; and so the horror passed. When morning came she rose from bed, and now she was washing her hair and clothes in the sea.

A number of creatures whose ill-assorted limbs declared them to be neither man nor beast had gathered round her like a great flock of sheep following their shepherd from the fold. Nondescript monsters such as these, fitted with miscellaneous limbs, were once produced spontaneously by Earth out of the primeval mud, when she had not yet solidified under a rainless sky and was deriving no moisture from the blazing sun. But Time, combining this with that, brought the animal creation into order. The Argonauts were dumbfounded by the scene. But a glance at Circe's form and eyes convinced them all that she was the sister of Aeetes.

As soon as she had dismissed the fears engendered by her

dream, Circe set out for home, but as she left she invited the young men to come with her, beckoning them on in her own seductive way. Jason told them to take no notice, and they all stayed where they were. But he himself, bringing Medea with him, followed in Circe's steps till they reached her house. Circe, at a loss to know why they had come, invited them to sit in polished chairs; but without a word they made for the hearth and sat down there after the manner of suppliants in distress. Medea hid her face in her hands, Jason fixed in the ground the great hilted sword with which he had killed Apsyrtus, and neither of them looked her in the face. So she knew at once that these were fugitives with murder on their hands and took the course laid down by Zeus, the god of suppliants, who heartily abhors the killing of a man, and yet as heartily befriends the killer. She set about the rites by which a ruthless slayer is absolved when he seeks asylum at the hearth. First, to atone for the unexpiated murder, she took a suckling pig from a sow with dugs still swollen after littering. Holding it over them, she cut its throat and let the blood fall on their hands. Next she propitiated Zeus with other libations, calling on him as the Cleanser, who listens to a murderer's prayer with friendly ears. Then the attendant Naiads who did her housework carried all the refuse out of doors. But she herself stayed by the hearth, burning cakes and other wineless offerings with prayers to Zeus, in the hope that she might cause the loathsome Furies to relent, and that he himself might once more smile upon this pair, whether the hands they lifted up to him were stained with a kinsman's or a stranger's blood.

When all was done she raised them up, seated them in polished chairs and taking a seat near by, where she could watch their faces, she began by asking them to tell her what had brought them overseas, from what port they had sailed to visit her and why they had sought asylum at her hearth. Horrible memories of her dream came back to her as she wondered what was coming; and she waited eagerly to hear a kinswoman's voice, as soon as the girl had looked up from the ground and she noticed her eyes. For all Children of the Sun were easy to recognize, even from a distance, by their flashing eyes, which shot out rays of golden light.

Medea, daughter of Aeetes the black-hearted king, answered all her aunt's questions, speaking quietly in the Colchian tongue. She told her of the quest and voyage of the Argonauts, of their stern ordeal, and how she herself had been induced to sin by her unhappy sister and had fled from her father's tyranny with Phrixus' sons; but she said nothing of the murder of Apsyrtus. Not that Circe was deceived. Nevertheless she felt some pity for her weeping niece.

'Poor girl,' she said, 'you have indeed contrived for yourself a shameful and unhappy home-coming; for I am sure you will not long be able to escape your father's wrath. The wrongs you have done him are intolerable, and he will soon be in Hellas itself to avenge his son's murder. However, since you are my suppliant and kinswoman, I will not add to your afflictions now that you are here. But I do demand that you should leave my house, you that have linked yourself to this foreigner, whoever he may be, this man of mystery whom you have chosen without your father's consent. And do not kneel to me at my hearth, for I never will approve your conduct and disgraceful flight.'

Medea's grief, when she heard this, was more than she could bear. She drew her robe across her eyes and wailed till Jason took her by the hand and led her out of doors shivering with fear. Thus they left Circe's house.

Nothing of this escaped Here, Wife of Zeus the son of Cronos. Iris pointed them out to her when she saw them leaving the hall. The goddess had asked her to watch for the moment when they set out for the ship; and now she urged her once again to help her: 'Dear Iris, if ever you have done my bidding, serve me now. Speed away on your light wings and ask Thetis to come here to me out of the salt sea depths. I need her. After that, go to the seacoast where the bronze anvils of Hephaestus are pounded by his mighty hammers, and tell him to let his bellows sleep till *Argo* has passed by. Next, go to Aeolus, king of the sky-born winds, and to him too convey my wishes, which are that he should order all the winds of heaven to cease. The sea must not be ruffled by a breeze. All I ask for is a soft air from the west, till the lords in *Argo* reach Alcinous' Phaeacian isle.'

Iris, spreading her light pinions, swooped down from Olympus and cleft the air. Plunging first into the Aegaean Sea where Nereus lives, she approached Thetis, delivered the message from Here, and urged her to go to the goddess. Then she went to Hephaestus and easily persuaded him to rest. The iron hammers ceased, the smoky bellows blew no more. Last of all, she went to Aeolus, the famous son of Hippotas, and when she had given him too her message, she rested her swift limbs, the errand done.

Meanwhile Thetis, leaving Nereus and her sisters in the sea, had reached Olympus and presented herself to Here. The goddess made her take a seat beside her and disclosed her mind. 'Listen, Lady Thetis,' she said. 'I was anxious to have a word with you. You know the strength of my regard for the noble son of Aeson and the others who supported him in his ordeal. Also that I brought them safely through the Wandering Rocks,* where fiery blasts rage and roar and the rollers break in foam on jagged reefs. But it still remains for for them to pass the great cliff of Scylla and the gurgling whirlpool of Charybdis.

'Now you will not have forgotten that I brought you up myself and loved you more than any other Lady of the Sea because you rejected the amorous advances of my consort Zeus. He, of course, has made a habit of such practices and sleeps with goddesses and girls alike. But you were frightened

* See Glossary, p. 209.

and out of your regard for me you would not let him have his will. In return for which he took a solemn oath that you should never be the bride of an immortal god. Yet in spite of your refusal he did not cease to keep his eye on you, till the day when the venerable Themis made him understand that you were destined to bear a son who would be greater than his father. When he heard this, Zeus gave you up though he still desired you. He wished to keep his power for ever and was terrified at the thought that he might meet his match and be supplanted as the King of Heaven. Then, in the hope of making you a happy bride and mother, I chose Peleus, the noblest man alive, to be your husband; I invited all the gods and goddesses to the wedding-feast; and I carried the bridal torch myself, in return for the good will and deference you had shown me. And there is something else that I must tell you, a prophecy concerning your son Achilles, who is now with Cheiron the Centaur and is fed by water-nymphs though he should be at your breast. When he comes to the Elysian Fields, it has been arranged that he shall marry Medea the daughter of Aeetes; so you, as her future mother-in-law, should be ready to help her now. Help Peleus too. Why are you still so angry with him? He was very foolish; but even the gods are sometimes visited by Ate.

'I have little doubt that Hephaestus and Aeolus will do what I have told them. Hephaestus will let his fires die down, and Aeolus will hold his gusty winds in check, letting none but a soft Zephyr blow till *Argo* reaches a Phaeacian port. It is for you to see that they come safely home. The only things I fear are the rocks and those tremendous waves. I count on you and your sisters to deal with these. And do not let my friends be so unwary as to fall into Charybdis, or at one gulp she will swallow them all. Nor let them go too near the hateful den of Ausonian Scylla, that wicked monster borne to Phorcys by night-wandering Hecate, whom men call Crataïs – or she may swoop down, take her pick and destroy them in her terrible jaws. What you must do is so to guide the ship that they escape disaster, if only by a hair's breadth.'

Thetis replied: 'If the fury of the flames and the storm-winds is indeed to be abated, I am confident. Given a fresh breeze from the west, I shall bring *Argo* safely through, whatever seas she may encounter. But time presses and I have a long way to go, first to my sisters to enlist their help, then to the place where the ship is moored to induce the men to sail at dawn if they wish to reach their homes.'

With that, Thetis dropped from the sky and plunged into the turmoil of the dark blue sea. There she called to all her sister Nereids to help her. They heard her call, and when they had assembled Thetis told them what Here wished and sent them speeding off to the Ausonian Sea. She herself, quick as the twinkle of an eye or the sun's rays when he springs from the world's rim, sped through the water to the beach of Aea on the Tyrrhenian coast. She found the young lords by their ship, passing the time with quoits and archery. Drawing near, she touched the hand of the lord Peleus, who was her husband. The rest saw nothing. She appeared to him only and to him she said:

'You and your friends have sat here long enough. In the morning you must cast off the hawsers of your gallant ship in obedience to Here. She is your friend and has arranged for the Daughters of Nereus to foregather quickly and bring *Argo* safely through the Wandering Rocks, as they are called, that being the way you must follow. But when you see me coming with the rest do not point me out to anyone. Keep my appearance to yourself, or you will make me even angrier than you did when you treated me in such a brutal fashion.' And with that she vanished into the depths of the sea.

Her husband felt a pang of remorse. He had never set eyes on her since the night when in a rage she had left her bridal bed. They had quarrelled about the illustrious Achilles. He was a baby then, and in the middle of the night she used to surround her mortal child with fire and every day anoint his tender flesh with ambrosia, to make him immortal and save him from the horrors of old age. One night Peleus, leaping out of bed, saw his boy gasping in the flames and gave a terrible cry. It was a foolish thing to do. Thetis heard, and snatching up the child threw him screaming on the floor. Then, passing quickly out of the house, light as a dream and insubstantial as the air, she plunged into the sea. She was mortally offended and she never returned.

Her appearance now left Peleus in a daze. Nevertheless he passed on all her orders to his comrades. They broke off at once in the middle of their games, prepared their supper and their beds, and after eating, slept through the night in their accustomed way. But when bright Dawn lit up the edge of heaven, a brisk wind sprang up from the west, and they left the shore and went on board. In high spirits they weighed anchor and put all their tackle in order. Then they raised the sail, making it taut with the yard-arm sheets. And the fresh breeze carried the ship on.

Before long they sighted the beautiful island of Anthemoessa, where the clear-voiced Sirens, Achelous' daughters, used to bewitch with their seductive melodies whatever sailors anchored there. Lovely Terpsichore, one of the Muses, had borne them to Achelous, and at one time they had been handmaids of Demeter's gallant Daughter, before she was married, and sung to her in chorus. But now, half human and half bird in form, they spent their time watching for ships from a height that overlooked their excellent harbour; and many a traveller, reduced by them to skin and bones, had forfeited the happiness of reaching home. The Sirens, hoping to add the Argonauts to these, made haste to greet them with a liquid melody; and the young men would soon have cast their hawsers on the beach if Thracian Orpheus had not intervened. Raising his Bistonian lyre, he drew from it the lively tune of a fast-moving song, so as to din their ears with a medley of competing sounds. The girlish voices were defeated by the lyre; and the west wind, aided by the sounding backwash from the shore, carried the ship off. The Sirens' song grew indistinct; yet even so there was one man, Butes the noble son of Teleon, who was so enchanted by their sweet voices that before he could be stopped he leapt into the sea from his polished bench. The poor man swam through the dark swell making for the shore, and had he landed, they would soon have robbed him of all hope of reaching home. But Aphrodite, Queen of Eryx, had pity on him. She snatched him up while he was still battling with the surf; and having saved his life, she took him to her heart and found a home for him on the heights of Lilybaeum.

The Argonauts sailed on in gloom. The Sirens were behind them, but worse perils lay ahead, at a place where two seas met and shipping came to grief. On one side the sheer cliff of Scylla hove in sight; on the other Charybdis seethed and roared incessantly; while beyond, great seas were booming on the Wandering Rocks, where but a little earlier flames from the glowing lava had shot up above the crags, and a pall of smoke had hidden the sun. By now Hephaestus had ceased to work; but even so hot vapour was still rising from the sea.

The Nereids, swimming in from all directions, met them here, and Lady Thetis coming up astern laid her hand on the blade of the steering-oar to guide them through the Wandering Rocks. While she played the steersman's part, nymph after nymph kept leaping from the sea and swimming round *Argo*, like a school of dolphins gambolling round a moving ship in sunny weather, much to the entertainment of the crew as they see them darting up, now aft, now ahead, and now abeam. But just as they were about to strike the Rocks, the Sea-nymphs, holding their skirts up over their white knees, began to run along on top of the reefs and breaking waves, following each other at intervals on either side of the ship. *Argo*, caught in the current, was tossed to right and left. Angry seas rose up all round her and crashed down on the Rocks, which at one moment soared into the air like peaks, and at the next, sticking fast at the bottom of the sea, were submerged by the raging waters. But the Nereids, passing the ship from hand to hand and side to side, kept her scudding through the air on top of the waves. It was like the game that young girls play beside a sandy beach, when they roll their skirts up to their waists on either side and toss a ball round to one another, throwing it high in the air so that it never touches the ground. Thus, though the water swirled and seethed around them, these sea-nymphs kept *Argo* from the Rocks. They were watched by the Lord Hephaestus himself, standing on the summit of a smooth rock and resting his great shoulder on the haft of his hammer. Here, Wife of Zeus, watched them too, taking her stand above the sunny sky, and in her terror at the sight she threw her arms round Athene.

The Nereids worked hard to heave *Argo* clear of the resounding rocks and it took them as long a time as daylight lingers in an evening of spring. But catching the wind at last, *Argo* ran ahead, and they were soon passing Thrinacie and the meadows where the cattle of the Sun are kept. Here the nymphs dived like sea mews into the depths, having carried out the orders of the Wife of Zeus. The Argonauts were close inshore, and through the mist the bleating of sheep and lowing of cattle came to their ears. Phaëthusa, the youngest daughter of Helios, was grazing the sheep in the dewy glades with a silver crook in her hand, while Lampetie looked after the cows and walked behind, swinging a staff of shining copper. They could see these cows feeding on the low ground and water-meadow by the river. Not one of them was dark; they were all milk-white and rejoiced in golden horns. When the Argonauts passed them, it was still daylight; by nightfall they were well out on the open sea. All was well; and in her own good time Dawn came once more to light them on their way.

In the Ceraunian Sea, fronting the Ionian Straits, there is a rich and spacious island, under the soil of which is said to lie (bear with me, Muses; it gives me little pleasure to recall the old tale) the sickle used by Cronos to castrate his father Uranus. Others call it the reaping-hook of Demeter of the underworld, who lived there once and taught the Titans to reap corn for food, in her affection for Macris. From this reaping-hook the island takes its name of Drepane, the sacred Nurse of the Phaeacians, who by the same token trace their origin to Uranus.

From the seas of Sicily, *Argo* with her load of trouble was wafted across to this Phaeacian isle. King Alcinous and his people received their visitors with open arms. Thank-offerings were made to the gods, and the whole town fêted them; they might have been welcoming their own sons. As for the Argonauts, they mingled freely with the crowds and could not have felt happier if they had found themselves in the heart of their own Haemonian land. Yet they were soon to arm for battle – a large force of Colchians had appeared in the offing.

This was the party that had passed out of the Black Sea through the Cyanean Rocks in pursuit of *Argo*. They now made insistent demands for the return of Medea to her father's house without parley. Failing which, they threatened savage reprisals on their own part at once, and more from Aeetes when he came. But set on fighting though they were, King Alcinous restrained them. It was his aim to bring the feud to an end without recourse to arms.

The prospect terrified Medea. She appealed to Jason's friends repeatedly, and to Alcinous' wife Arete, touching her knees with her hands. 'My queen,' she said, 'be gracious to your suppliant, and do not let the Colchians take me back to my father. You too are a woman and must know how easily a venial misdeed can lead us on to ruin. Such was my case: my wits forsook me. But I was not a wanton; and I swear by the Sun's sacred light and by the secret rites of Perses' night-wandering Daughter, that I never intended to run away from home with a set of foreigners. No; I had done wrong and it was fear of the consequences that turned my thoughts to flight – I had no other motive. Also, no one has touched me; I am still the virgin that I was at home. My lady, pity me, soften your husband's heart, and may the gods grant you honour, children, and a perfect life in a glorious city free from the ravages of war.'

Such was her tearful appeal to Arete. In approaching the Argonauts she used other pleas, saying to each of them in turn: 'You, my most illustrious lords, you and the help I gave you in your troubles are the sole cause of my affliction. Through me, the bulls were yoked and the deadly harvest of the earthborn men was reaped. Through me, you are homeward bound with the golden fleece on board. So here am I, who have lost my country and my parents and forfeited my home and all the joys of life, giving back your country and your homes to you. You can look forward to the joy of seeing your parents again. For me, no happiness remains, thanks to an unkind god. I am a thing despised, a wanderer in the hands of foreigners.

'Respect your covenants and oaths. Fear the suppliants' Fury. Fear Heaven's vengeance, if I fall into my father's hands and am foully done to death. I seek asylum in no temple of the gods, no fort, no other sanctuary. I look to you and you alone; and all I find is hearts of flint. Are you not put to shame when you see me in my desperation kneeling to a foreign queen? You were ready enough, when you wanted the fleece, to face all Colchis up in arms and the haughty king himself. Where is your bravery now, when the Colchians are cut off from their country and their king?'

Each of the men to whom she thus appealed did his utmost

to allay her fears and hearten her. They brandished their sharp spears, unsheathed their swords, and promised to stand by her to the end if justice were not done. In the midst of these alarms, Night with her gentle ban on man's activities descended on the company. She put the world to sleep; but not Medea. For her there was no rest; her heart was wrung with pain, and she let the tears run down her cheeks, like a patient working woman turning her spindle in the night, and as she hears her orphaned children cry, dropping a tear for her lost man and her own hard lot.

In their palace in the town, King Alcinous and Arete his admirable queen, had retired as usual to bed. As they lay there in the dark they discussed Medea's future and Arete, as became his wife, spoke to the king out of the fullness of her heart. 'My dear,' she said, 'I beg you, for my sake, to side with the Minyae and save this unhappy girl from the Colchians. Argos is close to our island and the Haemonians are our neighbours, whereas Aeetes lives far away and we do not even know him, we only know his name. She is a woman who has suffered much. She came to me with her troubles and she broke my heart. My lord, do not let the Colchians take her back to her father. She was out of her mind when she gave that man the magic charm for the bulls. Then, as we sinners often do, she tried to cover one fault with another by running away from her domineering father and his wrath. But I hear that Jason has given her his solemn oath that he will take her into his home as his wedded wife. That being so, my love, let no decision of your own cause Aeson's son to break his promise; nor, if you can help it, let the girl's angry father do her some frightful mischief. Fathers are much too jealous where their daughters are concerned. Remember how Nycteus treated the lovely Antiope. Think of Danae too and what she suffered on the high seas through her father's cruelty. Why, only recently and not so far from us, the brutal Echetus drove brazen spikes into his daughter's eyes, and now the miserable girl is wasting away in a gloomy cell, grinding grains of bronze.'

Alcinous was touched by his wife's prayers. 'Arete,' he said, 'I could certainly repel the Colchians by force of arms, siding with the young lords for Medea's sake. But I should think twice before defying a just sentence from Zeus. Nor would it be wise to make little of Aeetes, as you would have me do. There is no greater king; and far away as he is, he could bring war to Hellas if he wished. No; it is my duty to give a decision that the whole world will acknowledge as the best. I will tell you what I mean to do. If Medea is still a virgin, I shall direct them to take her back to her father. If she is a married woman, I will not separate her from her husband. Nor will I give a child of hers to the enemy if she has conceived.'

So said Alcinous and fell asleep at once. But Arete, taking to heart the wisdom of his words, rose from bed immediately and went through the house. Her waiting women all came up and fussed around their mistress. But she quietly beckoned to her herald and bade him convey her own shrewd counsel to the son of Aeson. He was to marry Medea and not to plead with Alcinous, as the king was going to tell the Colchians himself that he would restore Medea to her father if she were still a virgin, but would not separate the loving pair if she were a married woman.

Thus instructed the herald sped from the palace to convey Arete's opportune advice to Jason and tell him what the good king meant to do. He found the Argonauts keeping armed watch beside their ship in the harbour of Hyllus near the town. He gave them his message in full, and they were all delighted. It was happy news indeed that he had brought them.

They at once set about the customary rites. They mixed a bowl of wine for the blessed gods, led sheep to the altar with due ritual, and for that very night prepared a bridal bed for Medea in the sacred cave where Macris once had lived. Macris was the daughter of Aristaeus, the honey-loving shepherd who discovered the secret of the bees and the riches that the olive yields in payment for our toil. It was Macris who, in Abantian Euboea, took the infant Dionysus to her bosom and moistened his parched lips with honey, when Hermes had rescued him from the flames and brought him to her. But Here saw this and in her anger banished her from Euboea. So Macris came to the remote Phaeacian land, where she lived in the sacred cave and brought abundance to the people.

It was here then that they prepared a great bed, spreading the shining golden fleece on top of it, to grace the wedding and make it famous in story. Nymphs gathered flowers for them, and as they brought the many-coloured bunches into the cave in their white arms the fiery splendour of the fleece played on them all, so bright was the glitter of its golden wool. It kindled in their eyes a sweet desire. They longed to lay their hands on it, and yet they were afraid to touch it. Some of these nymphs were daughters of the River Aegaeus, others lived on the heights of the Meliteian Mount, others again were woodland sprites from the plains. All were sent to the wedding by Here, Wife of Zeus, who thus did honour to Jason. As for his bride, the place where the pair were brought together when the fragrant linen had been spread is still called the Sacred Cave of Medea.

The Argonauts, lest the Colchian foe should take them by surprise, picked up their battle-spears. Then, their temples wreathed with leafy twigs, they sang the hymeneal song in unison outside the bridal chamber to the clear notes of Orpheus' lyre. And so the pair were married in Alcinous' domain. Not that the lord Jason willed it so. He had meant their wedding to take place in his father's house when he returned to Iolcus, and so had Medea. It was Necessity that made them marry now. And since we men can never rest from care and tread securely in the path of happiness without some bitter thought for company, these two, though they loved and delighted in each other, were haunted by fear, fear that Alcinous' verdict might not be upheld.

Dawn's celestial beams chased black Night from the sky; the island beaches and the dewy paths across the distant fields laughed in the light; the streets were filled with noise and the whole town began to stir. On the far side of the island of Macris the Colchians also were afoot; and Alcinous went to them now, as he had promised, to give them his decision in Medea's case. He carried in his hand the judge's golden staff, equipped with which he meted out impartial justice to the people of the town. With him, company after company of Phaeacian nobles marched in procession, fully armed. Crowds of women poured out from the city to see the lordly Argonauts, and countrymen flocked in to meet them when they heard the news, which had passed from mouth to mouth, sponsored by Here. One man led in the best ram of his flock; another brought a heifer that had never toiled; others set down two-handled jars of wine ready for the mixing-bowls; and far and wide the smoke of burnt-offerings rose into the air. The women brought their own appropriate gifts, embroidered robes, golden trinkets, and all the other finery that goes to deck a bride. They saw the famous Argonauts and marvelled at their comeliness; they saw Orpheus in among them beating the ground with his gleaming sandal to the time of his song and his ringing lyre. When he sang of the wedding, all the nymphs joined in the lovely marriage song; and then again, as they circled in the dance they sang alone, tendering their thanks to Here, who had put it in Arete's mind to reveal the wise decision of the king.

From the moment when he delivered judgement and it was known that the pair were now man and wife, Alcinous remained inflexible. He was shaken by no deadly fears, no dread of Aeetes' enmity. He had taken oaths that were not to be broken and he would not break them. So when the Colchians perceived that their protestations were in vain, and were told that if they did not accept his ruling he would close his harbours to their ships, they recalled their own king's threats and besought Alcinous to receive them as friends. And there on the island they lived for a long time with the Phaeacians. Later on, the Bacchiadae, whose native place was Ephyra, settled there too, and the Colchians crossed to an island opposite, only to leave it at a later date and pass over to the Ceraunian Mountains where the Abantes lived, to join the Nestaeans, and so reach Oricum. But all this was the work of ages. And still the altars which Medea built on the island at the shrine of Shepherd Apollo are laden year by year with offerings to the Fates and the Nymphs.

When the Argonauts left, Alcinous gave them many parting gifts, and so did Arete, who also presented Medea with twelve Phaeacian maids from the palace to attend her. They sailed from Drepane on the seventh day with a fresh breeze that Zeus had sent at dawn; and *Argo* sped before the wind. But they were not destined yet to set foot in Achaea. Before that could be, fresh trials awaited them on the confines of Libya.

The Ambracian Gulf, the land of the Curetes, the narrow islands that include the Echinades – all these they passed in turn with their canvas spread; and they had just sighted the land of Pelops when they were caught by a northerly gale which swept them south for nine days and nights over the Libyan Sea and drove them deep into Syrtis. This is a gulf from which no shipping can escape, once it has been carried in. There are shoals everywhere, with tangled masses of seaweed from the depths, over which the spindrift blows; and beyond, sand stretching to the dim horizon; no living creature on the ground or in the air. The tides often run high, retreating from the coast only to come racing back and roar across the outer beach. It was one of these flood tides that caught *Argo* and incontinently swept her up to the inner shore, leaving her there with her keel for the most part high and dry. The crew leapt down and were dismayed by what they saw – mist, and a landscape insubstantial as the mist itself, stretching away, unbroken and immense. They could descry no watering place, no path, no distant farmstead. Silence reigned over a lifeless world.

In their misery they asked one another on what unknown shore the gale had thrown them up. They wished that they had cast all fear away and dared to sail once more through the Clashing Rocks, even against the will of Zeus. They might have perished, but they would at least have aimed at glory. As it was, how could they survive, even for a few days, here where the winds had boxed them in? They looked with horror at the desert spreading out before them from the margin of an empty continent.

Their helmsman Ancaeus, himself unmanned by the disaster, could not conceal his grief. 'This is indeed catastrophe,' he said, 'and there is no way out. We are bound to suffer frightful hardships, here in this desolate spot, even if we get an offshore wind. I have looked all round and as far as I can see there are shoals everywhere, with great breakers rolling in over the white sand. Our good ship here would have been smashed to pieces long before she reached the land, if a flood tide had not floated her in from the deep sea. But now the tide is ebbing and there is nothing left but light surf scarcely deep enough to cover the ground. No ship could ride in it. And so, if you ask me, we might as well give up all hope of sailing home. Let someone else, who feels the urge to get us out, sit down at the helm and show what he can do. For I myself do not believe that Zeus designs to end our sufferings with the sight of home.'

Ancaeus wept, and those who knew anything of navigation joined in his despair. The hearts of all were chilled, their cheeks grew pale, and they began to stray, dragging their feet along the endless beach. So, in some doomed city, when the gods' statues are sweating blood and bellowing is heard in the temples, or the midday sun has been eclipsed and stars shine out in the darkened sky, men wander ghostlike in the streets, expecting war, or pestilence, or the flooding of their fields by torrential rain.

When night approached they tearfully embraced one another, took loving leave and separated, each seeking a spot where he could fall on the sand and die alone. By spreading out and passing one another, all were able to find places for themselves, and once there they wrapped their heads in their cloaks and lay without food or drink, all night and into the day, waiting for a miserable death. Elsewhere, Medea's maids had gathered round their mistress. They laid their golden tresses in the dust and all night long made piteous lament, shrill as the twittering of unfledged birds fallen from a cleft in the rock and crying for their mother, and sad as the music that is echoed by dewy meadows and the river's lovely stream when swans begin to sing on the banks of Pactolus.

And now it seemed that all these gallant men would die there with their task unfinished, passing from life unnoticed and unsung by humankind. But as they wasted there in misery, they were observed with pity by the highborn nymphs that guard the Libyan shore. These were the nymphs who found Athene when she issued in her gleaming panoply from her Father's head and bathed her in the water of Trito. Now, at high noon, when Libya lay scorched under a burning sun, they came to Jason and gently removed the cloak from his head. Jason looked up, but in awe of their divinity he turned his eyes aside. Then the nymphs, seeing that he was alone, spoke out and reproved him in friendly tones for lying there in such abandonment.

'Why this despair?' they said. 'Are you not the men who fetched the golden fleece? We know how you have roamed the world. We know of each heroic deed that you have done on land or sea. For we who speak to you as mortals do are goddesses, the highborn solitary Spirits of the land, wardens and daughters of Libya. Up then! Banish your own despondency and rouse your men, remembering this. When Amphitrite has unyoked the horses from Poseidon's rolling chariot, you must repay your mother for what she suffered all the long time she bore you in her womb. Thus. you may yet return to the sacred land of Achaea.'

They spoke, and the next moment their place was empty, they were neither to be seen nor heard. Jason looked around him and sat up. 'Glorious Spirits of the wilderness,' he cried, 'be gracious to me! I do not fully understand your prophecy of our return, but I will assemble all my friends and tell them, in the hope that we may find the clue and so be saved. Many heads are wiser than one.'

With that he leapt up and shouted to his men, standing there with the dust on him like a tawny lion calling across the jungle for his mate with a great roar that terrifies the cattle and their herdsmen in the fields and shakes the wooded glens of mountains far away. But to them there was no menace in his voice: they heard a comrade calling to his friends, and they came trooping in with downcast looks. Jason made them sit down by the ship, together with the women, and told them everything:

'Listen, my friends, I have been visited in my distress by three goddesses. They wore goat-skin capes reaching from neck to waist, and looked to me like young girls. Standing over me they removed the mantle from my head with gentle hands and told me to get up and rouse you also. They said that when Amphitrite had unyoked the horses from Poseidon's rolling chariot we were to recompense our mother amply for what she had suffered all the long time she bore us in her womb. Now I admit that the meaning of this oracle eludes me. At the same time they told me they were divine Spirits, wardens and daughters of Libya, and they professed to know all about us and our adventures on the sea and land. Then, in a moment, they were there no more; a kind of mist or cloud had come between us.'

The Minyae listened with amazement to his tale. It was followed by the most astounding prodigy. A great horse came bounding out of the sea, a monstrous animal, with his golden mane waving in the air. He shook himself, tossing off the spray in showers. Then, fast as the wind, he galloped away.

Peleus was overjoyed and at once explained the portent to the others. 'It is clear to me,' he said, 'that Poseidon's loving wife has just unyoked his team. As for our mother, I take her to be none but the ship herself. *Argo* carried us in her womb; we have often heard her groaning in her pain. Now, we will carry *her*. We will hoist her on our shoulders, and never resting, never tiring, carry her across the sandy waste in the track of the galloping horse. He will not disappear inland. I am sure that his hoofprints will lead us to some bay that overlooks the sea.' Peleus finished, and they all felt that he could not have interpreted the portent better.

I am the mouthpiece of the Muses. What follows is their tale; and a voice from Heaven, a voice that cannot lie, tells me that these, the noblest of all sons of kings, by their own might and hardihood carried their ship and all it held, shoulder-high, nine days and nights, across the desert dunes of Libya. But who can tell the pain and misery that the work entailed? They surely were scions of the gods to take on such a task. True, they had no choice. And yet they carried her, all the long way, as cheerfully as when they waded in with her and set her down from their sturdy shoulders in the Tritonian lagoon.

Once there, it was their first concern to slake the burning thirst that was added to their other aches and pains. They dashed off, like mad dogs, in search of fresh water; and they were fortunate. They found the sacred plot where, till the day before, the serpent Ladon, a son of the Libyan soil, had kept watch over the golden apples in the Garden of Atlas, while close at hand and busy at their tasks the Hesperides sang their lovely song. But now the snake, struck down by Heracles, lay by the trunk of the apple-tree. Only the tip of his tail was still twitching; from the head down, his dark spine showed not a sign of life. His blood had been poisoned by arrows steeped in the gall of the Lernaean Hydra, and flies perished in the festering wounds.

Close by, with their white arms flung over their golden heads, the Hesperides were wailing as the Argonauts approached. The whole company came on them suddenly, and in a trice the nymphs turned to dust and earth on the spot where they had stood. Orpheus, seeing the hand of Heaven in this, addressed a prayer to them on behalf of his comrades: 'Beautiful and beatific Powers, Queens indeed, be kind to us, whether Olympus or the underworld counts you among its goddesses, or whether you prefer the name of Solitary Nymphs. Come, blessed Spirits, Daughters of Ocean, make yourselves manifest to our expectant eyes and lead us to a place where we can quench this burning, never-ending thirst with fresh water springing from a rock or gushing from the ground. And if ever we bring home our ship into an Achaean port, we will treat you as we treat the greatest goddesses, showing our gratitude with innumerable gifts of wine and offerings at the festal board.'

Orpheus sobbed as he prayed. But the nymphs were still at hand, and they took pity on the suffering men. They wrought a miracle. First, grass sprang up from the ground; then long shoots appeared above the grass; and in a moment three saplings, tall, straight and in full leaf, were growing there. Hespere became a poplar; Erytheis an elm; Aegle a sacred willow. Yet they were still themselves; the trees could not conceal their former shapes – that was the greatest wonder of all. And now the Argonauts heard Aegle in her gentle voice tell them what they wished to know.

'You have indeed been fortunate,' she said. 'There was a man here yesterday, an evil man, who killed the watching snake, stole our golden apples, and is gone. To us he brought unspeakable sorrow; to you release from suffering.

'He was a savage brute, hideous to look at; a cruel man, with glaring eyes and scowling face. He wore the untanned skin of an enormous lion and carried a great club of olive-wood and the bow and arrows with which he shot our monster here. It appeared that he, like you, had come on foot and was parched with thirst. For he rushed about the place in search of water; but with no success, till he found the rock that you see over there near the Tritonian lagoon. Then it occurred to him, or he was prompted by a god, to tap the base of the rock. He struck it with his foot, water gushed out, and he fell on his hands and chest and drank greedily from the cleft till, with his head down like a beast in the fields, he had filled his mighty paunch.'

The Minyae were delighted. They ran off in happy haste towards the place where Aegle had pointed out the spring, and once there the whole crowd milled round the cranny in the rock, like a swarm of burrowing ants busy round a little hole, or flies alighting by a drop of honey and struggling fiercely with one another for access to the delicious stuff.

Refreshed at last, with water dripping from their lips, they began to talk of Heracles and the strange chance that had enabled him, though far away, to save his friends when they were parched with thirst. And when someone suggested that a party should set out in the hope of finding him as he trudged across the mainland sands, those who were specially fitted for the task responded. But they did not go together. As the night wind had effaced the tracks with shifting sand, they began their search in different directions. The two sons of the North Wind relied on their wings, Euphemus on his nimble feet, Lynceus on his long sight, while Canthus, the fifth man to join in the quest, was impelled to go, not only by the hand of Fate, but by his own chivalry. He wished to learn from Heracles where he had left Polyphemus son of Eilatus, a friend of his. He was anxious to have the whole story. But he never heard it. Polyphemus, after founding a splendid city in

Mysia, had become homesick and tramped through the Asian mainland in search of *Argo*. He reached the country of the Chalybes, who live near the coast, and there he met his doom. He is commemorated by a monument that stands under a tall poplar close to the sea. As for Heracles, Lynceus thought he saw a lonely figure on the verge of that vast land, as a man, when the month begins, sees or thinks he sees the new moon through the clouds. He went back and told his comrades that there was now no chance of overtaking Heracles. Euphemus of the swift feet and the two sons of Thracian Boreas also returned. They too had failed.

But alas for Canthus, struck down in Libya by the hand of Death. He had found a grazing flock and was driving them off for his famished comrades when the shepherd who followed them came up to defend his property, threw a stone at him, and killed him. Caphaurus, the man who did this, was no weakling, but a grandson of Phoebus and the virtuous lady, Acacallis, whom her own father, Minos, banished to Libya when she was carrying the god's offspring in her womb. In due course the noble child was born – they call him Amphithemis or Garamas. He married a Tritonian nymph and she gave him two sons, Nasamon and the powerful Caphaurus, who, as we have seen, killed Canthus in defence of his sheep. But he did not escape the avenging hands of the Minyae when they heard of the outrage. They dealt with him, found Canthus' body, and brought it back to their camp, where they bewailed and buried him. They also took the sheep.

On the very same day Mopsus son of Ampycus met a cruel fate. He was a prophet, but that did not save him from the final bitterness, for no one can turn Death aside. A fearsome snake lay in the sand, sheltering from the midday sun. It was too sluggish to attack a man who showed no wish to harm it, or to fly at anyone who shrank away. And yet, for any creature living on the face of Mother Earth, one drop of its black poison in his veins was a short cut to the world below.

Paeëon himself (if I may tell the truth without offence) could not have saved the victim's life, even if the fangs had only grazed the skin. For when the godlike Perseus, whom his mother called Eurymedon, flew over Libya bringing the Gorgon's newly severed head to the king, every drop of dark blood that fell from it to the ground produced a brood of these serpents. Mopsus, stepping forward with his left foot, brought the sole down on the tip of the creature's tail, and in its pain the snake coiled round his shin and calf and bit him halfway up the leg, tearing the flesh. Medea and her women-servants shrank back in horror. But Mopsus bravely put his hand on the bleeding wound, for the pain was not intense. Yet the poor man was doomed. A paralysing numbness was already creeping through him, and a dark mist began to dim his sight. Unable to control his heavy limbs, he sank to the ground and soon was cold. Jason and his friends gathered round him, dumbfounded by the sudden tragedy. Mopsus was dead; and they could not leave him in the sunshine even for a short time, for the poison at once began to rot his flesh and mouldering hair fell from his scalp. So they set to work with bronze mattocks and quickly dug him a deep grave. In their sorrow for the pitiable dead, the women and the men alike tore their hair. They gave him solemn burial, marched in full armour three times round the grave, and raised a mound above it.

A south wind blew across the sea, and they embarked, meaning to find a way out of the Tritonian lagoon. But as they had no definite aim they drifted helplessly the whole day long. *Argo*'s course as she kept nosing round for a navigable outlet was as tortuous as the path of a snake wriggling along in search of shelter from the scorching sun, and peering about him with an angry hiss and scintillating eyes, till he slips into his lair through a cleft in the rock. In the end Orpheus suggested that they should bring out the great tripod that Apollo had given Jason and offer it to the gods of the land, who might thus be induced to help them on their way. So they went ashore; and no sooner had they set up the tripod than the great god Triton appeared before them, taking the form of a young man. He picked up a clod of earth and held it out to them by way of welcome, saying:

'Accept this gift, my friends. Here and now, I have no better one with which to welcome strangers such as you. But if you have lost your bearings, like many a traveller in foreign parts, and wish to cross the Libyan Sea, I will be your guide. My father Poseidon has taught me all its secrets, and I am the king of this seaboard. You may have heard of me though you live so far away – Eurypylus, born in Libya, the country of wild beasts.'

Euphemus gladly held his hand out for the clod and said: 'My lord, if you know anything of the Minoan Sea and the Peloponnesus, we beg you to tell us. Far from meaning to come here, we were driven ashore on the borders of your land by a heavy gale. Then we hoisted our ship, and for all her weight, carried her across country till we came to this lagoon. And now we have no idea how to get out of it and reach the land of Pelops.'

Triton, stretching out his hand, pointed to the distant sea and the deep mouth of the lagoon. At the same time he explained: 'That is the outlet to the sea; the smooth, dark water marks the deepest spot. But on either side of it are beaches where the rollers break – you can see the foam from here – and the fairway in between them is a narrow one. The misty sea beyond it stretches from here to the sacred land of Pelops, on the other side of Crete. Once you are out in the open, keep the land on your right and hug the coast as long as it runs north. But when it trends towards you and then falls away, you may safely leave it at the point where it projects and sail straight on. A happy voyage then! And if the work is heavy, do not let that distress you. Young limbs should not object to toil.'

Thus encouraged by the friendly god the Argonauts embarked at once. They were determined to escape from the lagoon by rowing and the ship forged ahead under their eager hands. Meanwhile Triton picked up the heavy tripod and walked into the water. They saw him stepping in; yet in a moment he had disappeared, quite close to them, tripod and all. But their hearts were warmed. They felt that one of the blessed ones had come to them and brought good luck. They urged Jason to kill the best of their sheep and hold it out to the god with words of praise. Jason hastily selected one, lifted it up, and killed it over the stern, praying in these words: 'God of the sea, you that appeared to us on the shore of these waters, whether the Ladies of the Brine know you as that sea-wonder Triton, or as Phorcys, or as Nereus, be gracious and grant us the happy return that we desire.'

As he prayed he slit the victim's throat and threw it into the water from the stern. Whereupon the god emerged from the depths, no longer in disguise but in his own true form, and grasping the stem of their hollow ship drew her on towards the open sea. So does a man trot along beside a fast horse gripping his bushy mane, as he brings him in to race in the great arena; and nothing loath, the horse goes with him, tossing up his head in pride and making the foam-flecked bit ring out as he champs it in his jaws to this side and that.

The body of the god, front and back, from the crown of his head to his waist and belly, was exactly like that of the other immortals; but from the hips down he was a monster of the deep, with two long tails, each ending in a pair of curved flukes shaped like the crescent moon. With the spines of these two tails he lashed the surface of the water, and so brought *Argo* to the open sea, where he launched her on her way. Then he sank into the abyss, and the Argonauts cried out in wonder at the awe-inspiring sight.

They spent that day on shore. The harbour there bears *Argo*'s name and there are signs of her stay, including altars to

Poseidon and Triton. At dawn they spread the sail and ran before the west wind, always keeping the desert on their right. The next morning they sighted the headland, and at the same time could see a corner of the sea that lay beyond the jutting cape. Here the west wind dropped and a breeze sprang up from the south, driving white clouds before it; they rejoiced to hear it whistle in the rigging. But when the sun sank and the evening star appeared, the star that tells the shepherd to bring in his sheep and the weary ploughman to plough no more, the wind failed them. In the darkness of the night they furled the sail, lowered the tall mast, and sat down to their polished pinewood oars. They rowed hard for the rest of that night, all through the day and through the night that followed it; and they were still far from land when the high rocks of Carpathus saluted them. From that point they were to cross to Crete, the greatest island in the sea.

But when they sought shelter in the haven of Dicte they were prevented from making fast to the shore by Talos, a bronze giant, who broke off lumps of rock from the cliff to hurl at them. A descendant of the brazen race that sprang from ash-trees, he had survived into the days of the demigods, and Zeus had given him to Europa to keep watch over Crete by running round the island on his bronze feet three times a day. His body and his limbs were brazen and invulnerable, except at one point: under a sinew by his ankle there was a blood-red vein protected only by a thin skin which to him meant life or death.

He terrified the Argonauts, and exhausted though they were they hastily backed water. Indeed, what with thirst and other pains, they would have been driven away from Crete in a sorry frame of mind, but for Medea, who stopped them as they turned the ship about.

'Listen to me,' she said. 'I think that I and I alone can get the better of that man, whoever he may be, unless there is immortal life in that bronze body. All I ask of you is to stay here, keeping the ship out of range of his rocks till I have brought him down.'

They took the ship out of range, as Medea had asked, and rested on their oars waiting to see what marvellous device she would employ. Medea went up on the deck. She covered both her cheeks with a fold of her purple mantle, and Jason led her by the hand as she passed across the benches. Then, with incantations, she invoked the Spirits of Death, the swift hounds of Hades who feed on souls and haunt the lower air to pounce on living men. She sank to her knees and called upon them, three times in song, three times with spoken prayers. She steeled herself with their malignity and bewitched the eyes of Talos with the evil in her own. She flung at him the full force of her malevolence, and in an ecstasy of rage she plied him with images of death.

Is it true then, Father Zeus, that people are not killed only by disease or wounds, but can be struck down by a distant enemy? The thought appals me. Yet it was thus that Talos, for all his brazen frame, was brought down by the force of Medea's magic. He was hoisting up some heavy stones with which to keep them from the anchorage, when he grazed his ankle on a sharp rock and the ichor ran out of him like molten lead. He stood there for a short time, high on the jutting cliff. But even his strong legs could not support him long; he began to sway, all power went out of him, and he came down with a resounding crash. Thus a tall pine up in the hills is left half-felled by the woodman's sharp axe when he goes home from the woods, but in the night is shaken by the wind, till at last it snaps off at the stump and crashes down.

That night they spent on shore in Crete. But in the first light of dawn they built a shrine for Minoan Athene. Then, after drawing water, they embarked and sat down to the oars, meaning to start by rounding Cape Salmonium.

The next night caught them well out in the wide Cretan Sea, and they were frightened, for they had run into that sort

of night that people call the Pall of Doom. No star, no moon-
light, pierced the funereal dark. Black chaos had descended on
them from the sky, or had this darkness risen from the
nethermost abyss? They could not tell whether they were
drifting through Hades or still on the water. All they could do
was to commit their course to the sea, with no idea where it
would take them. But Jason lifted up his hands to Phoebus and
in a loud voice called on him to save them, weeping as he
prayed. He promised the god innumerable offerings, gifts in
Pytho, gifts in Amyclae, gifts in Ortygia; and Leto's Son was
quick to hear him. He came down swiftly from Olympus to
the two Melantian Rocks which lie there in the sea, and alighting on one of them held up his golden bow in his right hand.
The bow shot beams of dazzling light into the dark all round;
and now they could see an islet, one of the Sporades, opposite
the small island of Hippuris. They anchored there.

Dawn came soon after and showed them the low island on
which they had landed. They called it Anaphe, or Revelation,
because Apollo had revealed it to them when they were be-
nighted. In the shelter of some trees they consecrated ground
and built him an altar in the shade, calling him the Lord of
Light, whose beacon fire had lit them from afar. On that
lonely coast they had little to offer him, but they offered what
they could, with the result that when Medea's Phaeacian
maids, who were accustomed to the rich sacrifices made in
Alcinous' palace, saw them using water for libations on the
burning logs they could no longer refrain from laughing. The
men, seeing the joke themselves, retaliated with some
ribaldry, which was the signal for a light-hearted exchange of
insult and repartee. This frolic of the Argonauts is commemorated by the island women, who chaff the men whenever they are sacrificing to Apollo, Lord of Light and protector
of the Isle of Revelation.

As the next morning was fair, they cast their hawsers off
and sailed. Euphemus then remembered that he had had a

dream in the night, and in deference to Hermes, god of dreams, he took pains to recall it. He had dreamt that he was holding to his breast the lump of earth which the god had given him and was suckling it with streams of white milk. The clod, small as it was, turned into a woman of virginal appearance; and in an access of passion he lay with her. When the deed was done, he felt remorse – she had been a virgin and he had suckled her himself. But she consoled him, saying in a gentle voice: 'My friend, I am of Triton's stock and the Nurse of your children; no mortal maid, but a Daughter of Triton and Libya. Give me a home with Nereus' Daughters in the sea near Anaphe, and I will reappear in the light of day in time to welcome your descendants.'

Euphemus, after committing his dream to memory, told it to Jason. The dream reminded Jason of an oracle of Apollo's, and putting the two things together, he made a prophecy himself, exclaiming: 'My noble friend, you are marked out for great renown! When you have thrown this clod of earth into the sea, the gods will make an island of it, and there your children's children are to live. Triton received you as a friend with this little piece of Libyan soil. It was Triton and no other god that met us and gave you this.'

Euphemus heard Jason's prophecy with joy and did not make it void. He threw the clod into the depths of the sea, and there grew up from it an island called Calliste, the sacred Nurse of his descendants. These lived at first in Sintian Lemnos, till they were driven out by the Tyrrhenians and found a new home in Sparta. Later they left Sparta and settled in Calliste under the leadership of Autesion's son, the noble Theras, who named the island Thera, after himself. But long before this happened Euphemus' days were over.

Sailing swiftly on, they left great stretches of the rolling sea behind them and put in at Aegina. They were short of water but wished to waste no time, as the wind still held. So they turned the business of watering into a game, racing one another to the spring, and back again with water to the ship. To this day the young Myrmidons of Aegina, carrying big jars full of water on their shoulders, race one another on the track with nimble feet.

Farewell, heroic, happy breed of men! Your blessing on this lay of mine. And as the years go by, may people find it a sweeter and yet sweeter song to sing. Farewell; for I have come to the glorious finish of your labours. After Aegina you suffered no mishap, no gale opposed your voyage home. The coast of Attica slipped quietly by; you sailed at ease inside Euboea, past Aulis, past the cities of Opuntian Locris; and with joyful hearts you stepped ashore at Pagasae.

NOTES ON THE TEXT

I have in the main, but not at every point, followed the Oxford Text (R. C. Seaton, 1900), making no emendations of my own, though I feel that one is called for in Book IV, 50. Here we are told that Medea was making for the *temple*. But at this juncture she had no good reason for doing so; and as she went there every day, why should the poet tell us that she knew the way? Everything indicates that she meant to reach the *ship*, as she eventually did.

It is difficult to accept the *Loeb* translation of a sentence in Book III, 1334 ff.: 'And Jason followed, pressing down the ploughshare with firm foot.' This suggests that he hopped along on the other; and in addition, it is by no means established that the word translated 'ploughshare' really meant 'ploughshare'. I believe that Apollonius is here using a Doric word meaning 'field', as used by his contemporary, Theocritus – it is not the only Doric word that occurs in the poem. However, one of my correspondents has stressed the fact that the participle 'pressing' is, in the Greek, not present but aorist, so that we might translate, 'Jason followed, *after* pressing down the ploughshare . . .,' i.e. at the beginning of the furrow. This might do, but for the whole context, which definitely places Jason in the *middle* of his operations. I may add that this is not the only place where Apollonius uses an aorist for a present participle.

SELECT BIBLIOGRAPHY

GENERAL:

Oxford Classical Dictionary (New edition, Oxford University Press, 1970).
Oxford Companion to Classical Literature, ed. Sir Paul Harvey (corrected edition, Oxford University Press, 1940).
Dictionary of Ancient Greek Civilization (Methuen, 1966).
Everyman's Classical Dictionary, ed John Warrington (1961).
The Civilization of Greece, François Chamoux (George Allen & Unwin, 1965).
The Greeks, M. I. Finley (Chatto & Windus, 1963).
The Greeks, H. D. F. Kitto (Penguin Books, 1951).

GEOGRAPHY AND HISTORY:

Murray's Classical Atlas for Schools, G. B. Grundy (2nd edition, 1917).
Everyman's Classical Atlas, J. O. Thomson (1961).
A History of Greece, J. B. Bury (3rd edition revised by Russell Meiggs; Macmillan, 1956).
A History of Greece, N. G. L. Hammond (2nd edition; Oxford University Press, 1967).
The Greeks Overseas, John Boardman (Penguin Books, 1964).
The Ancient Explorers, M. Cary & E. H. Warmington (Methuen, 1929).
The Ancient Mariners, Lionel Casson (Gollancz, 1960).
A History of Ancient Geography, J. O. Thomson (Cambridge University Press, 1948).
A History of Ancient Geography, H. F. Tozer (2nd edition with additional notes by M. Cary; Biblo & Tannen, New York, 1964).

MYTHOLOGY AND RELIGION:

A Handbook of Greek Mythology, H. J. Rose (6th edition; Methuen, 1958).
Dictionnaire de la Mythologie Grècque et Romaine, Pierre Grimal (3rd edition corrected; Presses Universitaires de France, 1963).
The Myths of the Greeks and Romans, Michael Grant (Weidenfeld & Nicolson, 1962).
The Greeks and their Gods, W. K. C. Guthrie (Methuen, 1954).
The Gods of the Greeks, C. Kerenyi (Thames & Hudson, 1951).
The Heroes of the Greeks, C. Kerenyi (Thames & Hudson, 1959).
Greek Oracles, H. W. Parke (Hutchinson. 1967).

SELECT BIBLIOGRAPHY

LITERATURE AND ART:

A History of Greek Literature, Albin Lesky (Methuen, 1966).
A Handbook of Greek Literature, H. J. Rose (4th edition corrected; Methuen, 1961).
Hellenistic Poetry and Art, T. B. L. Webster (Methuen, 1964).
Greek Art, John Boardman (Thames & Hudson, 1964).
Myth and Legend in Early Greek Art, K. Schefold (Thames & Hudson, 1966).

EDITIONS OF APOLLONIUS RHODIUS:

Apollonii Rhodii Argonautica: Hermann Fränkel (Oxford Classical Texts, 1961). (Text with apparatus criticus)
Apollonius Rhodius Argonautica: G. W. Mooney (University of Dublin Press, 1912; reissued by Adolf M.Hakkert, Amsterdam, 1964). (Text, introduction & commentary)
Apollonius Rhodius Argonautica: R. C. Seaton (Loeb Classical Library, Heinemann, 1912). (Text and translation)
Apollonius Rhodius Argonautica, Book III: M. M. Gillies (Cambridge, 1928). (Text, commentary, etc.)

BOOKS AND ARTICLES ABOUT APOLLONIUS RHODIUS:

The Voyage of the Argonauts, J. R. Bacon (Methuen, 1925).
La Géographie dans les Argonautiques d'Apollonios de Rhodes, Emile Delage (Bibliothèque des Universités du Midi, Fasc. XIX, 1930).
Biographie d'Apollonios de Rhodes, Emile Delage (Bibliothèque des Universités du Midi, Fasc. XIX *bis*).
Beobachtungen zur epischen Technik des Apollonios Rhodios, P. Händel (Munich, 1954).
Odyssee und Argonautika, K. Meuli (Berlin, 1921).
Le Problème des Argonautes, Recherches sur les aspects religieux de la legende, R. Roux (E. de Boccard, Paris, 1949).
'Apollonius Rhodius and the Homeric epic', J. Carspecken in *Yale Classical Studies*, Volume 13, 1952.
'Apollonius' Argonautica: Jason as Anti-Hero', Gilbert Lawall in *Yale Classical Studies*, Volume 19, 1966.
'Le retour des Argonautes d'après les Argonautiques d'Apollonios de Rhodes', R. Senac in *Bulletin de l'Association Guillaume Budé*, Supplément Lettres d'Humanité, tome XXIV, Quatrième Série, Numéro 4, December 1965.

GLOSSARY

The names of only the more important characters, human and divine, are included. The geographical entries (also limited in number) are designed as a help to those who wish to follow the voyages of *Argo* with the aid of a modern atlas.

ACHERUSIAS. A promontory on the Bithynian coast near the ancient town of Heracleia; the modern Cape Baba.

ACHILLĒS. Son of Peleus and Thetis. Appears in the poem only as an infant, though Here promises Thetis that he shall be married to Medea in the Elysian Fields. The poets Ibycus and Simonides preceded Apollonius in making this curious arrangement for his after-life.

ĀEA. The capital city of Colchis and home of King Aeetes. The name Aea or Aeaea was also given to the home of Circe, sister of Aeetes, on the west coast of Italy.

ĀEĒTĒS. Son of Helios the Sun and Perse; king of the Colchians; brother of Circe; father of Apsyrtus, Chalciope, and Medea.

ĀEOLUS. Son of Hellen; father of Athamas; grandfather of Phrixus. His sons and descendants were called Aeolids.

ĀEOLUS. Son of Hippotas; the mythical King of the Winds.

ĀESON. Father of Jason; excluded from the throne of Iolcus by his half-brother Pelias, but allowed (according to Apollonius) to remain in the city.

ĀETHALIDĒS. Son of Hermes and Eupolemeia; the herald of the Argonauts.

ALCIMĔDĒ. Daughter of Phylacus; wife of Aeson; mother of Jason.

ALCINŎUS. Son of Nausithous; king of the Phaeacians; husband of Arete.

AMPHITRĪTĒ. Wife of the Sea-god Poseidon.

AMYCUS. King of the Bebryces, a tribe whom the Argonauts encounter on the Bithynian coast.

ANĀURUS. A river of Thessaly flowing into the Gulf of Pagasae.

ANCĀEUS. Son of Lycurgus of Tegea; the Argonaut who is allotted the seat in *Argo* next to Heracles.

ANCĀEUS. Son of Poseidon and Astypalae; the Argonaut who takes the helm after the death of Tiphys.

APHRODĪTĒ. Daughter of Zeus; goddess of love; wife of Hephaestus; mother of Eros; also called Cytherea, Cypris, and Queen of Eryx in Sicily.

APOLLO. Son of Zeus and Leto; god of prophecy, of the arts, of healing, and of embarkation and happy landings; also called Phoebus and Phoebus Apollo.

APSYRTUS. Son of Aeetes and Asterodeia; half-brother of Medea; also called Phaëthon, the Shining One.

ARĒS. Son of Zeus and Here; god of war.

ARĒTĒ. Wife of Alcinous the Phaeacian king.

ARGUS. Son of Arestor; the builder of *Argo*; does not figure in the tale after his namesake has appeared on the scene.

ARGUS. Son of Phrixus and Chalciope. *See under* PHRIXUS.

ARIADNĒ. Daughter of Minos and Pasiphae. *See under* THESEUS.

ARTEMIS. Daughter of Zeus and Leto; goddess of the chase and protectress of wild animals. It was one of her functions to kill women with her darts, i.e. she administered sudden death by disease.

ASSYRIA. A district of Asia Minor lying on the north coast in the neighbourhood of the Rivers Halys and Iris. It was inhabited by the Leucosyri or White Syrians.

ATĒ. Daughter of Zeus; a personification of blind folly or infatuation.

ATHAMAS. Father of Helle and Phrixus (*q.v.*); king of Orchomenus.

ATHĒNĒ. Daughter of Zeus; goddess of wisdom and patroness of the arts and crafts; also called Pallas Athene, and the Lady of Trito in reference to her birth, from the head of Zeus, at the Tritonian lagoon in Libya.

AUGEĪAS. Son of Helios (?); the Argonaut who is introduced to King Aeetes as his half-brother but not recognized by him as such.

AUSONIA. A Greek name for Italy.

BITHYNIA. A district of Asia Minor lying on the north coast, and bounded on the west by Mysia, on the east by Paphlagonia.

BORĔAS. The North Wind; father of Zetes and Calaïs and of Cleopatra wife of Phineus.

BRĪMO. A somewhat obscure goddess of the underworld whom Apollonius identifies with Hecate.

BRYGEAN ISLANDS. Presumably off the Illyrian coast, near the modern Rijeka. *See also under* LIBURNIAN ISLANDS.

CALAÏS. Son of Boreas and Oreithyia; brother of Zetes.

CANTHUS. Son of Canethus; an Argonaut who is killed in Libya.

CARAMBIS. A promontory on the Paphlagonian coast; the modern Cape Kerempeh.

CASTOR. Son of Tyndareus (or Zeus?) and Lede; twin brother of Polydeuces (*q.v.*).

CAULIACUS. *See under* ISTER.

CERAUNIAN SEA. An ancient name for the Ionian Sea (*q.v.*).

CHALCIŎPĒ. Daughter of King Aeetes and Eidyia; elder sister of Medea; widow of Phrixus; mother of Argus and his three brothers.

CHEĪRON. Son of Cronos and Philyra; the Centaur who looked after Achilles and Aristaeus in their infancy.

CIRCĒ. Daughter of Helios the Sun and Perse; sister of Aeetes; aunt of Medea.

COLCHIS. A land lying at the eastern end of the Black Sea and including part of the Caucasus; the kingdom of Aeetes; also called Cytaïs.

CORCYRA. *See under* PHAEACIA.

CRONIAN SEA. An ancient name for the Adriatic.

CRONOS. Son of Uranus and Earth; father, by Rhea, of Zeus, Poseidon, Hades, Here and Demeter; the ex-King of Heaven who was deposed by Zeus.

CYANEAN ROCKS. The legendary Symplegades or Clashing Rocks, situated at the northern end of the Bosporus.

CYPRIS. *See under* APHRODITE.

CYTHERĒA. *See under* APHRODITE.

CYZICUS. King of the Doliones. The city of Cyzicus stood on an island close to the southern or Phrygian shore of the Propontis. Here was Mt Dindymum or Bear Mountain, one of the seats of the goddess Rhea (*q.v.*), the 'Dindymian Mother'.

DĒMĒTĒR. Daughter of Cronos and Rhea; mother of Persephone (IV, 897).

GLOSSARY

DINDYMUM. *See under* CYZICUS.

DIONȳSUS. Son of Zeus and Semele; god of the vine; worshipped with orgiastic rites.

DODONIAN OAK. The famous oracle of Zeus. For its connexion with the Argonauts, see H. W. Parke, *Oracles of Zeus: Olympia, Dodona, Ammon* (Blackell, 1967).

ĒIDȳIA. Daughter of Tethys and Ocean; consort of King Aeetes, and mother of Chalciope and Medea.

ĔRĂTŌ. The Muse of love-songs and wedding festivities.

ĒRĬDĂNUS. Presumably the River Po in northern Italy. See Introduction.

EROS. Son of Aphrodite; the little god of love; known to the Romans as Cupido, and sometimes multiplied.

EUPHĒMUS. Son of Poseidon and Europa; a leading Argonaut.

GLAUCUS. A minor marine divinity.

HĀDĒS. Son of Cronos and Rhea; god of the dead, who received the underworld as his portion when he and his brothers Zeus and Poseidon divided the world between them. Apollonius also uses Hades as a place name, just as we do.

HAEMONIA. An ancient name of Thessaly in northern Greece.

HALYS. A river of Asia Minor flowing into the Black Sea east of Sinope; the modern Kizil Irmak.

HECĂTĒ. Daughter of Perses and Asteria; a goddess of the underworld and of witchcraft who is not mentioned by Homer. When Apollonius (III, 847) writes of 'the only-begotten Maiden' he means Hecate, not Persephone daughter of Demeter.

HĒLIOS. The Sun-god; father, by Perse, of Aeetes, Circe, and Pasiphae; and, by Clymene, of Phaëthon; also of Augeias (*q.v.*).

HELLĒ. Daughter of Athamas; sister of Phrixus (*q.v.*).

HĒPHAESTUS. Son of Zeus and Here; husband of Aphrodite; the lame Master-Smith and Artificer of Olympus.

HĒRACLĒS. Son of Zeus and Alcmene; hero of the Twelve Labours.

HERCYNIAN ROCK. *See under* RHINE.

HĒRĒ. Daughter of Cronos and Rhea; sister and wife of Zeus; queen of Olympus.

HERMĒS. Son of Zeus and Maia; ambassador of the Olympians; god of dreams.

HYLAS. Son of Theiodamas; squire of Heracles.

HYLLĒANS. Ancient geographers are vague about this people and their land. I take it to be the peninsula of Istria, where Pula now stands. *See under* ISTER.

Book IV, 522–7 is one of those passages which suggest that Apollonius abridged the first version of his poem. In our version there is no mention of a previous visit of Jason's to the Hylleans.

HYPSĬPŸLĒ. Daughter of Thoas king of Lemnos.

IDAS. Son of Aphareus; a quarrelsome and insubordinate Argonaut.

IDMON. Son of Abas (or Apollo?); a seer who sailed in Argo but perished in Bithynia.

IOLCUS. A town in Thessaly not far from the northern shore of the Gulf of Pagasae; the capital city of Pelias' kingdom and the home town of Jason. Recent excavations show that it was an important city as far back as the fifteenth century B.C.

IONIAN SEA. A part of the Mediterranean lying between Greece and Italy, and separated from the Adriatic by the Ionian Straits.

The same name is given twice (Book IV, 289 and 308) to that part of the Black Sea into which the Danube flows. This mistake (if it is one) has given rise to several emendations, none of them convincing. In defence of the MS reading, it is worth noting that the Ionians of Miletus founded colonies on the west, as well as the north and south coasts of the Black Sea.

IRIS. A Messenger of the Olympian gods.

IRIS. A river of Asia Minor flowing into the Black Sea east of the River Halys; the modern Yeshil Irmak.

ISTER. The River Danube. To follow the Colchian fleet and Argo from its mouth into the Adriatic, we must place the Rock of Cauliacus near its confluence with the River Save, and imagine that the Save, instead of running into it there, ran out of it and eventually fell into the northern Adriatic near the modern Rijeka.

JASON. Son of Alcimede and Aeson the rightful king of Iolcus; leader of the Argonautic expedition.

LEMNOS. A large island in the northern part of the Aegean Sea.

LĒTŌ. Mother, by Zeus, of Apollo and Artemis.

LIBURNIAN ISLANDS. A string of islands lying along the Illyrian coast of the Adriatic, southward from the modern Rijeka.

LȲCUS. Son of Dascylus; king of the Mariandyni, a people visited by the Argonauts on the Bithynian coast.

LYNCĒUS. Son of Aphareus; an Argonaut famous for his keen sight.

MACRIS. Daughter of Aristaeus; Nurse of Dionysus. She gave her name to the island of Drepane or Corcyra. *See under* PHAEACIA.

MĒDĒA. Daughter of King Aeetes and Eidyia; sister of Chalciope.

MELEĀGER. Son of Oeneus and Althaea. In his youth, sails in *Argo*. His later exploits are described by Homer (*Iliad* IX).

MINYAE. A Greek race whose ancestral hero was Minyas. Apollonius uses the name for the Argonauts in general.

MOPSUS. Son of Ampycus; soothsayer of the Argonauts up to the time of his death in Libya.

MYSIA. A district of Asia Minor lying on the south coast of the Propontis.

NĒRĒUS. A sea-god; father of Thetis and the other Nereids or Sea-nymphs.

ORCHOMENUS. Son of Minyas; king of the Minyan city of Orchomenus in Boeotia.

PĀĒĒON. The Physician of the gods, as in the *Iliad*; not Apollo.

PAGASAE. The port of Iolcus (*q.v.*); the launching place of *Argo*.

PAPHLAGONIA. A district of northern Asia Minor extending from Bithynia on the west to the River Halys on the east.

PELASGIAN. A name given by the Greeks to their country and its earliest inhabitants.

PĒLEŪS. Son of Aeacus; husband of Thetis; father of Achilles; one of the leading Argonauts.

PĔLIAS. Son of Poseidon and Tyro; the unrightful king of Iolcus who sent Jason out in quest of the golden fleece; father of Acastus, an Argonaut.

PELOPONNĒSUS. The 'Island of Pelops'; the southern peninsula of Greece.

PERSĒ. Daughter of Ocean, wife of Helios; mother of Aeetes and Circe.

PERSĔPHŎNĒ. Daughter of Demeter; wife of Hades; queen of the dead.

PERSĒS. Son of the Titan Crius; father of the goddess Hecate.

PHAEĀCIA. Apollonius identifies the Phaeacia of the *Odyssey* with Corcyra (Corfu) under the names of Drepane or Macris. He gives the name of Black Corcyra to an island lying off the Dalmatian coast north-west from Corfu.

PHAËTHON. Nickname of King Aeetes' son Apsyrtus (*q.v.*).

PHAËTHON. Son of Helios and Clymene.

PHĀSIS. A river flowing through Colchis and debouching into the eastern part of the Black Sea.

PHĪNEŪS. Son of Agenor; husband of Cleopatra (daughter of Boreas and sister of Zetes and Calaïs); a blind prophet visited by the Argonauts in his home on the coast of Thynia (*q.v.*).

PHOEBUS. *See under* APOLLO.

PHRIXUS. Phrixus and Helle were children of Athamas (son of Aeolus and king of Orchomenus) by his first wife Nephele. Ino, the second wife of Athamas, was jealous of her step-children. Distorting an oracle concerning a pest that was afflicting the country, she suggested to Athamas that Phrixus should be sacrificed. Phrixus escaped, together with Helle, on the back of a flying ram with a golden fleece provided for them by the god Hermes. Helle fell off the ram's back and was drowned in the Hellespont (Dardanelles). But the golden ram encouraged Phrixus to proceed and eventually landed him in Colchis, where it was sacrificed to Zeus. Phrixus gave its fleece to Aeetes, king of Colchis, and in return the king gave him his daughter Chalciope in marriage. They had four sons, Argus, Cytissorus, Melas and Phrontis. On his deathbed, Phrixus told these sons of his to travel to Orchomenus in the hope of recovering the estate of their grandfather Athamas, who, in the interval, had been banished from his kingdom. On their way they were shipwrecked and picked up by Jason, as Apollonius relates in Book II.

PHRYGIA. *See under* CYZICUS.

POLYDEŪCĒS. Son of Lede and Tyndareus (or Zeus? Apollonius impartially calls him son of Tyndareus and son of Zeus); the patron of boxers, known also as Pollux. He and his twin brother Castor were worshipped as the protectors of travellers by sea.

POLYPHĒMUS. Son of Eilatus; an elderly Argonaut and friend of Heracles, with whom he was left on shore in Mysia.

POSEIDON. Son of Cronos and Rhea; younger brother of Zeus; chief god of the sea and also god of horses; husband of Amphitrite.

PROMETHEUS. Son of the Titan Iapetus; punished by Zeus for having given fire to man.

PROPONTIS. The Sea of Marmora.

RHEA. Wife of Cronos; Mother of the chief gods of the last Olympian régime. She was identified with a Phrygian nature-goddess 'the Great Mother', and called Cybele and Dindymene. *See also under* CYZICUS.

RHINE. Apollonius does not mention this river by name, but is presumably thinking of it when he takes *Argo*, by a wrong turning, down a northward running river that would have brought her to Ocean. The name Hercynian (IV, 640) was applied by the Romans to a large area of southern and central Germany.

SINOPE. The name of this ingenious virgin was given to the city of Sinope (a colony of Miletus) on the Paphlagonian coast, west of the mouth of the River Halys; modern name, Sinub.

SPORADES. A scattered group of islands in the Aegean Sea, north of Crete. They include Thera (later known as Santorin) and Anaphe.

STOECHADES. The Îles d'Hyères, lying off the Mediterranean coast east of Toulon.

SYRTIS. There were two Syrtes. Apollonius is probably describing the eastern Syrtis, now known as the Gulf of Sydra, on the coast of Tripoli.

TELAMON. Son of Aeacus; father of Aias; one of the leading Argonauts.

THEBES. The chief city of Boeotia in Greece.

THEBES. An ancient capital city of Egypt.

THEMIS. Daughter of Uranus and Earth; divine exponent of law and order.

THERMODON. A small river flowing into the Black Sea, east of the River Iris, near Themiscyra; the modern Termeh.

THESEUS. Son of Aegeus king of Athens; failed to join the Argonauts, but is mentioned as the hero who slew the Minotaur in the Cretan labyrinth with the help of Ariadne daughter of Minos, and later deserted her in the Isle of Dia or Naxos.

THĒTIS. A Sea-nymph; daughter of Nereus and Doris; wife of Peleus; mother of Achilles.

THRINACIĒ. Sicily.

THȲNIA. There is some doubt concerning the location of this land where Phineus lived, but Apollonius clearly places Phineus' home on the west or European coast of the Bosporus, facing Bithynia on the east, and some way south of the Clashing Rocks.

TIPHYS. Son of Hagnias; steersman of *Argo* till his death in Bithynia.

TRĪTON. Son of Poseidon and Amphitrite; a sea-god.

TRĪTONIAN LAGOON. A great salt lake on the coast of Libya.

TYNDARĔUS. Husband of Lede. *See under* POLYDEUCES.

TYRRHĒNIA. The Greek name for Etruria or Tuscany. The Etruscans are thought to have come to Italy from Asia Minor, a view which Apollonius seems to endorse by recording their occupation of Lemnos (IV, 1760).

URĂNUS. Husband of Earth, and Father of Cronos, who supplanted him in Olympus, only to be supplanted himself by Zeus.

WANDERING ROCKS. Apollonius confounds our attempts to locate these legendary rocks by causing Here to boast that she has seen *Argo* safely through, before the ship has reached them. Allowing this to be a slip, and noting the course that Homer gives Odysseus, we may assume that Apollonius places them south of Scylla and Charybdis (Straits of Messina), off the east coast of Sicily, not far from Etna and its volcanic fires. But some ancient writers placed them north of the Straits, and the whole question is further confused by the fact that they were often identified with the Clashing Rocks (*q.v.*).

ZĒTĒS. Brother of Calaïs (*q.v.*).

ZEUS. Son of Cronos and Rhea; the supreme Olympian god. Apollonius makes several references to his infancy, which was spent in a cavern on Mt Dicte in Crete.

NOTES TO MAP

1) This map is intended to be a simplified diagram to help the reader follow the Argonauts' route. It does not pretend to be an exact geographical representation of the countries concerned. Neither does the map include the many places referred to by Apollonius which are not connected with the actual voyage. R. R. Graves, *The Greek Myths* (Penguin, 1955), has an excellent map of places connected with Greek Mythology.

2) Some of Apollonius' geography is incorrect and in other places he appears to be being deliberately vague. As is appropriate to the tale, some of his geography is unashamedly 'mythological' and was recognized by his contemporaries as such. It is difficult to decide which, if any, of Apollonius' errors are due to ignorance and which are deliberately introduced for artistic reasons.

3) The most important geographical errors are in Apollonius' descriptions of the rivers of Europe.

No branch of the Danube flows into the Adriatic though the source of a tributary, the Sava, is not far inland.

When Apollonius describes the three branches of the Rhodanus he would appear to be referring to the Rhine (which he at no point mentions by name), the Po, which is traditionally identified with the Eridanus, and the Rhône. Although these three rivers do not meet, they or their tributaries rise close together and trade routes passed from one to another.

The location of Lake Tritonis and the credibility of the portage have been much disputed. Two alternative routes in Libya are given.

KEY TO NUMBERS ON MAP

1. Pagasae
2. Iolchus
3. Mt Olympus
4. Mt Ossa
5. Mt Pelion
6. Sciathus
7. Pallene
8. Mt Athos
9. Imbros
10. Samothrace
11. Gulf of Melas

12. Hellespont
13. Cyzicus
14. Istria
15. Islands including Issa, Black Corcyra and Melite
16. Drepane/Macris (Corcyra)
17. Echinades
18. Attica
19. Aulis
20. Locris

N.B. Synonyms for Greece: Achaea, Hellas, Pelasgian Land, Dardania
Synonyms for Italy: Ausonia, Tyrrhenian Land

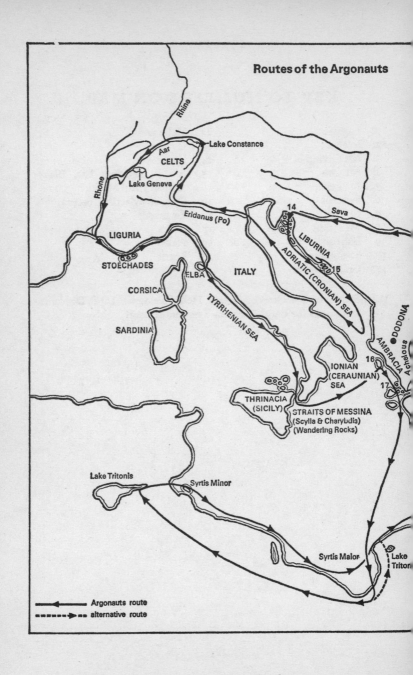

Routes of the Argonauts

Rhine

Aar

CELTS

Lake Constance

Rhone

Lake Geneva

Sava

Eridanus (Po)

14

LIBURNIA

LIGURIA

15

STOECHADES

ADRIATIC (CRONIAN) SEA

ELBA

ITALY

CORSICA

TYRRHENIAN SEA

SARDINIA

DODONA

AMBRACIA

Acheloüs

16

IONIAN (CERAUNIAN) SEA

17

THRINACIA (SICILY)

STRAITS OF MESSINA (Scylla & Charybdis) (Wandering Rocks)

Lake Tritonis

Syrtis Minor

Syrtis Major

Lake Tritonis

Argonauts route

alternative route

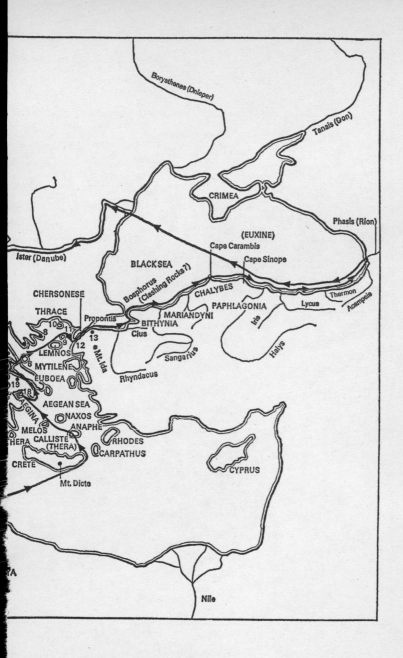

Borysthenes (Dnieper)

Tanais (Don)

CRIMEA

Phasis (Rion)

(EUXINE)

Cape Carambis

Ister (Danube)

Cape Sinope

BLACK SEA

Thermon

CHERSONESE

Bosphorus (Clashing Rocks?)

CHALYBES

Lycus

Acampsis

THRACE

PAPHLAGONIA

Propontis

MARIANDYNI

Iris

10 11

BITHYNIA

8   9

Cius

Mt. Ida

Halys

12

13

LEMNOS

Sangarius

6 MYTILENE

Rhyndacus

EUBOEA

19

18

AEGEAN SEA

EGINA

NAXOS

ANAPHE

MELOS

RHODES

HERA

CALLISTE (THERA)

CARPATHUS

CRETE

CYPRUS

Mt. Dicte

YA

Nile

Visit Penguin on the Internet
and browse at your leisure

◆ preview sample extracts of our forthcoming books
◆ read about your favourite authors
◆ investigate over 10,000 titles
◆ enter one of our literary quizzes
◆ win some fantastic prizes in our competitions
◆ e-mail us with your comments and book reviews
◆ instantly order any Penguin book

and masses more!

'To be recommended without reservation ... a rich and rewarding on-line experience' – Internet Magazine

www.penguin.co.uk

READ MORE IN PENGUIN

In every corner of the world, on every subject under the sun, Penguin represents quality and variety – the very best in publishing today.

For complete information about books available from Penguin – including Puffins, Penguin Classics and Arkana – and how to order them, write to us at the appropriate address below. Please note that for copyright reasons the selection of books varies from country to country.

In the United Kingdom: Please write to *Dept. EP, Penguin Books Ltd, Bath Road, Harmondsworth, West Drayton, Middlesex UB7 ODA*

In the United States: Please write to *Consumer Sales, Penguin Putnam Inc., P.O. Box 12289 Dept. B, Newark, New Jersey 07101-5289*. VISA and MasterCard holders call 1-800-788-6262 to order Penguin titles

In Canada: Please write to *Penguin Books Canada Ltd, 10 Alcorn Avenue, Suite 300, Toronto, Ontario M4V 3B2*

In Australia: Please write to *Penguin Books Australia Ltd, P.O. Box 257, Ringwood, Victoria 3134*

In New Zealand: Please write to *Penguin Books (NZ) Ltd, Private Bag 102902, North Shore Mail Centre, Auckland 10*

In India: Please write to *Penguin Books India Pvt Ltd, 11 Community Centre, Panchsheel Park, New Delhi 110017*

In the Netherlands: Please write to *Penguin Books Netherlands hv, Postbus 3507, NL-1001 AH Amsterdam*

In Germany: Please write to *Penguin Books Deutschland GmbH, Metzlerstrasse 26, 60594 Frankfurt am Main*

In Spain: Please write to *Penguin Books S. A., Bravo Murillo 19, 1° B, 28015 Madrid*

In Italy: Please write to *Penguin Italia s.r.l., Via Benedetto Croce 2, 20094 Corsico, Milano*

In France: Please write to *Penguin France, Le Carré Wilson, 62 rue Benjamin Baillaud, 31500 Toulouse*

In Japan: Please write to *Penguin Books Japan Ltd, Kaneko Building, 2-3-25 Koraku, Bunkyo-Ku, Tokyo 112*

In South Africa: Please write to *Penguin Books South Africa (Pty) Ltd, Private Bag X14, Parkview, 2122 Johannesburg*

PENGUIN AUDIOBOOKS

A Quality of Writing That Speaks for Itself

Penguin Books has always led the field in quality publishing. Now you can listen at leisure to your favourite books, read to you by familiar voices from radio, stage and screen. Penguin Audiobooks are produced to an excellent standard, and abridgements are always faithful to the original texts. From thrillers to classic literature, biography to humour, with a wealth of titles in between, Penguin Audiobooks offer you quality, entertainment and the chance to rediscover the pleasure of listening.

You can order Penguin Audiobooks through Penguin Direct by telephoning (0181) 899 4036. The lines are open 24 hours every day. Ask for Penguin Direct, quoting your credit card details.

A selection of Penguin Audiobooks, published or forthcoming:

Little Women by Louisa May Alcott, read by Kate Harper

Emma by Jane Austen, read by Fiona Shaw

Pride and Prejudice by Jane Austen, read by Geraldine McEwan

Beowulf translated by Michael Alexander, read by David Rintoul

Agnes Grey by Anne Brontë, read by Juliet Stevenson

Jane Eyre by Charlotte Brontë, read by Juliet Stevenson

The Professor by Charlotte Brontë, read by Juliet Stevenson

Wuthering Heights by Emily Brontë, read by Juliet Stevenson

The Woman in White by Wilkie Collins, read by Nigel Anthony and Susan Jameson

Nostromo by Joseph Conrad, read by Michael Pennington

Tales from the Thousand and One Nights, read by Souad Faress and Raad Rawi

Robinson Crusoe by Daniel Defoe, read by Tom Baker

David Copperfield by Charles Dickens, read by Nathaniel Parker

The Pickwick Papers by Charles Dickens, read by Dinsdale Landen

Bleak House by Charles Dickens, read by Beatie Edney and Ronald Pickup

PENGUIN AUDIOBOOKS

READ MORE IN PENGUIN

A CHOICE OF CLASSICS

Aeschylus	The Oresteian Trilogy
	Prometheus Bound/The Suppliants/Seven against Thebes/The Persians
Aesop	Fables
Ammianus Marcellinus	The Later Roman Empire (AD 354–378)
Apollonius of Rhodes	The Voyage of Argo
Apuleius	The Golden Ass
Aristophanes	The Knights/Peace/The Birds/The Assemblywomen/Wealth
	Lysistrata/The Acharnians/The Clouds
	The Wasps/The Poet and the Women/The Frogs
Aristotle	The Art of Rhetoric
	The Athenian Constitution
	De Anima
	Ethics
	Poetics
Arrian	The Campaigns of Alexander
Marcus Aurelius	Meditations
Boethius	The Consolation of Philosophy
Caesar	The Civil War
	The Conquest of Gaul
Catullus	Poems
Cicero	Murder Trials
	The Nature of the Gods
	On the Good Life
	Selected Letters
	Selected Political Speeches
	Selected Works
Euripides	Alcestis/Iphigenia in Tauris/Hippolytus
	The Bacchae/Ion/The Women of Troy/Helen
	Medea/Hecabe/Electra/Heracles
	Orestes and Other Plays

READ MORE IN PENGUIN

A CHOICE OF CLASSICS

Hesiod/Theognis	**Theogony** and **Works and Days/ Elegies**
Hippocrates	**Hippocratic Writings**
Homer	**The Iliad**
	The Odyssey
Horace	**Complete Odes and Epodes**
Horace/Persius	**Satires** and **Epistles**
Juvenal	**Sixteen Satires**
Livy	**The Early History of Rome**
	Rome and Italy
	Rome and the Mediterranean
	The War with Hannibal
Lucretius	**On the Nature of the Universe**
Marcus Aurelius	**Meditations**
Martial	**Epigrams**
Ovid	**The Erotic Poems**
	Heroides
	Metamorphoses
Pausanias	**Guide to Greece** (in two volumes)
Petronius/Seneca	**The Satyricon/The Apocolocyntosis**
Pindar	**The Odes**
Plato	**Early Socratic Dialogues**
	Gorgias
	The Last Days of Socrates (Euthyphro/ The Apology/Crito/Phaedo)
	The Laws
	Phaedrus and **Letters VII and VIII**
	Philebus
	Protagoras and **Meno**
	The Republic
	The Symposium
	Theaetetus
	Timaeus and **Critias**

READ MORE IN PENGUIN

A CHOICE OF CLASSICS

Plautus	**The Pot of Gold/The Prisoners/The Brothers Menaechmus/The Swaggering Soldier/Pseudolus**
	The Rope/Amphitryo/The Ghost/A Three-Dollar Day
Pliny	**The Letters of the Younger Pliny**
Pliny the Elder	**Natural History**
Plotinus	**The Enneads**
Plutarch	**The Age of Alexander** (Nine Greek Lives)
	The Fall of the Roman Republic (Six Lives)
	The Makers of Rome (Nine Lives)
	The Rise and Fall of Athens (Nine Greek Lives)
	Plutarch on Sparta
Polybius	**The Rise of the Roman Empire**
Procopius	**The Secret History**
Propertius	**The Poems**
Quintus Curtius Rufus	**The History of Alexander**
Sallust	**The Jugurthine War** and **The Conspiracy of Cataline**
Seneca	**Four Tragedies** and **Octavia**
	Letters from a Stoic
Sophocles	**Electra/Women of Trachis/Philoctetes/Ajax**
	The Theban Plays
Suetonius	**The Twelve Caesars**
Tacitus	**The Agricola** and **The Germania**
	The Annals of Imperial Rome
	The Histories
Terence	**The Comedies (The Girl from Andros/The Self-Tormentor/TheEunuch/Phormio/The Mother-in-Law/The Brothers)**
Thucydides	**The History of the Peloponnesian War**
Virgil	**The Aeneid**
	The Eclogues
	The Georgics
Xenophon	**Conversations of Socrates**
	A History of My Times
	The Persian Expedition